PRAISE FOR THE AU
CLOSURE: BASED ON A TRUE STORY

"Readers will be pulled in by the intensity of emotions and the drama that is featured in the writing. It's a beautiful story, beautifully told." *—Readers' Favorite*

"A writer to watch. Author Tasche Laine . . . splashes onto the novel front with much aplomb. She is a natural, taking us through the twists and turns of first love with much self-reflection and humor. Laine's clever writing style—real-life sprinkled with emails and letters—keep us on the edge of our seats wanting more. Tara and Trey caused me to quickly turn each page, excited about where they would take me next. Laine has the innate ability to know exactly where to end each chapter and keep us engrossed as we dive into the next one. This will not be the last we hear of Tasche Laine. Only the first in a long career of novels . . . if we are so lucky."
—Tamara Anne Fowler, *Edit Kitten*

"Get ready for your heart to go on an emotionally drowned roller coaster ride while reading *Closure*! . . . with many incredible lessons, her personal story has a little bit of everything you could want in a book. Tasche Laine is officially one of my new favorite authors!"
—Heidi Lynn's Book Reviews

"I was instantly attracted to this story . . . ordered the book as soon as it was available and soaked it all up in two days! I couldn't put it down because I just had to know where they ended up!" —Pam K.

"Profound . . . makes you rethink life choices." —Alma

"*Closure,* by author Tasche Laine, really made an impact within the first few chapters. . . . the journey of two people discovering love, not just within each other but within themselves, . . . grounded in spirituality as much as a love story . . . profound and deeply connected to the relationship two people have as they go through life connected but never able to be together. At times sad, emotional, heartwarming, heartbreaking, but a darn good story I'd definitely recommend!"
—Scott B. Allan, *Book Reviewer*

"I love that it was a real life love story . . . it wasn't all about a happy ending, more about Real life. Real love. It showed the struggle and the raw emotion of being in love. . . . so relatable and believable I could not put it down."
—Renna Best

"Heartbreakingly relatable . . . the author does an amazing job at drawing you in. I could feel exactly what she felt, and that is definitely talent when it comes to writing. Well done!"
—H. Schaefer

"I loved this story. It's the kind where you can identify with the characters and immerse yourself in it. Very well written and with characters to win the heart, make *Closure* a must read."
—Kathleen Bulfon

"An emotional read, *Closure* is tumultuous and tender, naive and dark, maddening and revealing as it transcends decades."
—Cheryl E. Rodriguez, *Readers' Favorite*

"A thorough and heartfelt examination of love and the human spirit that may very well leave you in tears. Bring some tissues, because I can't recommend this enough!"
—Andrew Wood

CLOSURE

CLOSURE

based on a true story

TASCHE LAINE

The following is based on a true story and is considered a fictional memoir (a hybrid of autobiographical facts and fictionalized aspects). Names, dates, characters, some places and locales, and several incidents have been changed or are used fictitiously to protect the privacy of the individuals depicted. The opinions expressed are those of the characters and should not be confused with the author's. Dialogues have been recreated for literary effect.

ISBN-13: 978-1-7321261-0-7 (eBook)
ISBN-13: 978-1-7321261-1-4 (pbk.)

Skye Blue Press
Vancouver, WA

For Tiana

1 a boy and a girl

"I NEED TO CATCH MY COURAGE SO I CAN KISS YOU," Trey declared. The ten-year-old boy raced around the basement, grasping at the air with his outstretched hands, then cupping them as if about to catch a butterfly. "Got it!" he exclaimed, and put his hands up to his mouth, making a gulping sound.

With big brown eyes, and the longest eyelashes I had ever seen, he gazed at me and said, "I'm ready to kiss you now."

I felt the butterflies in my stomach as we walked toward each other and met at the center of the room. I closed my eyes, clenched my fists, and held my breath in anticipation. Then I felt his warm breath on my face as his soft lips caressed mine.

That was my first kiss—and the last time I was to see Trey Thompson, my childhood sweetheart, for five years.

Our moms were close friends so Trey and I got to see each other often and we soon became inseparable. He was two months older than me and we did everything together. Sometimes he would announce to his mom,

"When I grow up, I'm going to marry Tara!" Our moms just smiled and laughed. Call it fate, destiny, kismet, soul mates—or being in the right place at the right time—even at that young age we seemed to read each other's minds, one always knew what the other wanted to do.

There we were, two kids having to say goodbye to each other at his parents' home in Seattle because Trey, his mom and his little brother, were moving to Arizona. They were leaving as his parents had divorced, and his mom wanted to start over somewhere new. But Arizona was so far away. It might as well have been on the other side of the world as far as we were concerned. We didn't think we'd ever see each other again.

Saying goodbye was difficult. I was losing my best friend, whom I also had a huge crush on. While our moms were upstairs saying their own goodbyes, Trey asked me to go downstairs to the basement with him so we could have some privacy. When we got downstairs he told me he wanted to kiss me. But we were just kids and super nervous, so he decided to make a game out of it to lighten the mood. Thus, the "catching courage game" was born.

It was now Christmas–time, five years later, and I, Tara Carter, was fifteen. My family and I had moved to the tiny town of Stonewood, Oregon, just outside Portland. We moved shortly after Trey's family moved to Phoenix five years earlier. Trey's family drove up through Oregon on their way to visit relatives in Seattle for the holidays. His mom, Jill, called and asked if they could stay with us for a night. I was a nervous wreck.

I hadn't seen Trey since we were ten. A lot happens between ten and fifteen—we weren't little kids anymore—we'd gone through puberty. I kept going through the scenario in my mind over and over of what it would be like to see him again. *Would he still be cute? Would he think I was cute? Would I still like him? What would we talk about? How tall would he be now?* You know, all those crucially, ever-so-important questions teenage girls ponder over teenage boys.

The phone rang. According to my mom they were about an hour away and she gave them directions to our house. I changed my outfit about five times—and then ended up wearing the first one I'd had on—a light purple sweater and jeans. My brown hair was feathered "Farrah Fawcett" style, and I had blue eyes. People often told me I looked like Brooke Shields, so I plucked my thick eyebrows until the resemblance was gone.

I was so excited and nervous that I couldn't sit still. The minutes dragged on for an eternity. My head hurt from the frenzy I had worked myself into. My thoughts were chaotic: *Uh–oh, I see headlights; a car is pulling into the driveway. No, I'm not ready! What do I say? Should I sit here and look nonchalant or greet him at the door?* T minus five seconds … *Oh, they're walking up the sidewalk. Ok be calm. No, I can't sit here. Ok I'll stand up. Somebody's ringing the doorbell. Oh God I can't stand it!*

"MOM!" I yelled. *Oh good, she's answering the door. Ok, be cool.* The door opens and—*Hey, wait a minute! Trey doesn't have blond hair—who the hell is that?*

"Hi, Chad, come on in. How was your trip?" asked my mother.

"Fine. Can I use your bathroom?" replied Chad, Trey's ten-year-old brother.

"Sure. It's down the hall on the left." *Why is this taking so long? Where is he? I can't just stand here. Oh! Here he comes now . . . Nope, that's his mom. Oh no! What if he didn't come with them? No!*

As our moms hugged each other in the doorway, I walked up to Trey's mom and blurted, "Hi. Where's Trey?" All patience and politeness out the window.

"Hi Tara! My, how you've grown! Such a pretty girl. You look just like your mother," Jill said.

"Thanks," I managed. "Where's Trey?"

"He's getting our bags out of the car," she replied.

"I'll go help him."

As I rushed past our moms still chatting at the door I ran right into, you guessed it— "Trey!" I exclaimed, my face flushed, heart racing and neck straining from looking up so high.

"Hey Tara," he said, all cool and casual. "How's it goin'?"

I thought I was going to die of embarrassment from running into him like that and not being able to speak, but he didn't seem to notice. In fact, he seemed a little nervous himself. Now that I had stepped back and really looked at him, he didn't look like the same skinny kid I remembered.

Actually, he was very tall—five eleven to my five three. He had broad shoulders and I could see his muscles through his light blue t–shirt *(been working out, no doubt)*. His light brown hair from childhood was now thicker and dark brown, and yes, he still had those killer brown eyes and long eyelashes—even his eyebrows were perfectly sculpted with a little arch to them. He was now ruggedly handsome instead of boyishly cute, and his skin was flawless; not one trace of acne. *Geesh, how is that even possible?*

I picked up his bag and we walked into the house together, unaware of anyone else in the world, staring into each other's eyes.

"Two little lovebirds sittin' in a tree—"

"Chad, cut that out or else!" warned Trey.

"Or else what?" Chad retorted. "What ya gonna do big guy? Huh? Beat me up in front of your girrrlfriend?"

"Chad! You little—"

"Boys! That's enough," Jill scolded. "Is that any way to act in front of Tara and her mother?"

"Sorry," Trey mumbled, as he kicked Chad in the leg.

"Ow!" yelped Chad.

"That's a warning," Trey whispered. "You behave or I'll really kick you hard."

The next few hours went excruciatingly slow as we ate dinner. Then we sat in the living room and watched TV.

Our parents didn't make things any easier. They made us pose together for pictures and said, "What a cute couple," as they cooed and talked about us like we weren't there. We spoke little and sat on opposite ends of the couch, with his brother between us, for over an hour. I tried to watch what was on TV but couldn't concentrate because all I wanted to do was talk to Trey, to be with him without our families around watching our every move. This night was turning into a disaster.

But then something wonderful happened. It was time for Chad to go to bed and my mom suggested that Trey and I go into the den to watch TV. *Thank you Mom!* I turned on the TV and sat down on the futon next to Trey.

Alone at last but we were still shy around each other. I felt like I had enough butterflies in my stomach to supply a zoo. We made small talk for a while and he told me what life was like in Arizona. We talked about school and sports and interests.

Finally, I boldly asked him, "Do you need to find your courage again?"

"What are you talking about?"

"Don't you remember? In the basement the last time we saw each other, you needed to catch your courage before you could kiss me."

"Oh yeah," he grinned. "I think I see my courage right here." His hand reached behind my head and closed on the air. "Got it," he smiled victoriously. And then he kissed me.

We stayed in the den talking and kissing and laughing until sunrise. The old familiarity came back, and we were completely at ease with each other again. It was magical—but then he had to go.

"I better get back to my bed before my mom notices I'm not there," Trey said, as he stood up.

"I don't want you to go," I pouted.

"Don't worry, I'll see you in a few hours, later this morning. We don't have to say goodbye yet." He gave me a quick kiss and hug then turned and walked out to the living room and his waiting foldout hide-a-bed, hoping to sneak into it before his mom woke up. I dreamily walked down the hall in the opposite direction, crawled into my own bed, and blissfully dozed off with thoughts of seeing him again as soon as I woke up.

When I woke up three hours later, I rushed out to the living room and found nothing but folded blankets and a note on the dining room table from his mom. She thanked us for our hospitality and explained that they wanted to hit the road early. The note said they didn't want to wake us, so they left quietly.

"No! He can't leave without saying goodbye!" I shouted into the quiet living room.

I was devastated. My wailing woke up my mom. I was beside myself with sudden grief and longing and there was nothing she could do for me. I knew then that my life would never be the same. I didn't know what was going to happen, but I knew I would never forget him. If there were a way, I would see him again.

2   the birthday party

MY EARLIEST MEMORY of Trey goes back to the day of my 4th birthday party even though we had already been friends for about a year.

It was a rare warm sunny afternoon in May in Seattle, Washington. Typically, this area of the Pacific Northwest would be overcast and drizzling so this proved to be a good start to a great day. My friends sat around a little table on the grass, in my front yard, and watched as my mom brought over a homemade chocolate cake with four lit candles on top.

"Okay, Tara, it's time to close your eyes and make a wish so you can blow out your birthday candles," declared my mom.

I took in a deep breath and closed my eyes tight, chest puffing out. *What to wish for?* "Mmm...got it!" I opened my eyes, blew out the candles, and beamed at my friends.

"What a big girl! Good job, sweetie!" my mom beamed back. Then, "Who wants cake?" Everyone giggled and raised their hands. My mom took out the candles, whisked the cake away, and came back with cake and vanilla ice cream on paper plates for all.

Trey sat next to me, the only boy at the party. He wore a white button–down dress shirt with black corduroy pants. I wore a pink turtleneck sweater, pink crocheted vest and purple tie–dyed pants. His gift to me was a Barbie doll with brown hair like mine and, when I opened it, the smile he gave me was magnetic. Even then.

I found my soul mate before I knew what a soul mate was, before I even started looking. But life has a funny way of working out and things are not always as they seem. Our journey is about love—the purest kind in existence; the kind that, if you're lucky, you get to experience once in a lifetime—innocent, trusting, selfless, unconditional . . . first love.

First love stays with some people and changes them forever. It is the love we compare everyone else to. We don't quite get over it because it is so profound, so all consuming, intoxicating, forgiving; the term "lovesick" comes to mind. This is my story, about a couple of kids who fell in love, while life happened nonetheless.

3   pen pals

OVER THE NEXT few months after that fateful visit, I began to think of Trey less and less. That summer I met someone new, older and exciting. He was a twenty-one-year-old college student with a summer job at 7-Eleven. I met him at 7-Eleven as I also had my first summer job there. I had just turned sixteen, received my driver's license, and thought I was pretty cool. Everything was going great and I almost never thought about Trey.

But one unusually foggy, windy and rainy day in the middle of July, something life–altering happened; something that shook me to my core with an intense fear I had never known. Yet my fear quickly dissolved into peace and the only way I can describe it is as a "religious experience." I put this in quotes because my family was not religious. We did not go to church, and I had never read the bible.

I was on my way to work in my mother's baby blue 1975 Volkswagen Rabbit. I had been a licensed driver for all of one month.

The pavement on the freeway was slippery and the rain came down in sheets. I was in the right–hand lane of a three–lane freeway, traveling north on I-5, driving under fifty miles per hour, and following a slow–moving pick–up truck. I signaled to pass him and was proceeding into the center lane when a giant black truck pulled out from behind me and sped up, deciding he wanted to be in the center lane at the same time I did. Only he was driving over seventy. If I had continued to veer into the middle lane, I would have hit his passenger door. To avoid a major collision, I swerved.

In my inexperience as a new driver, coupled with the heavy rain, I over–steered and ran into the embankment on the right side of the freeway. Bouncing off the concrete edge, my car then spun around as it hydroplaned and careened sideways across all three lanes of traffic. The front end of my car crashed into the median barrier and crumpled like an accordion. The sudden impact caused the car to move with rapid force across the freeway again—this time backwards. I felt like a pinball in a pinball machine ricocheting from side to side.

I landed on a steep grassy hill and began to roll forward. I snapped out of my reverie, stomped on the brake, yanked up the emergency brake and turned off the ignition. Then I took out the keys and threw them on the floor just to make sure the car wasn't going anywhere.

While the accident was happening, time seemed to stand still. I went from feeling fear and complete helplessness to feeling calm and observing myself going through the motions. I became a witness in my own car crash. I remember vivid details. I could see the looks of terror on the other drivers' faces as I passed them by; I could see sheer disbelief in their eyes. It's as if it was all playing out in slow motion on a TV screen in front of me. I felt like I could even see myself. I consider what happened to me to be an out–of–body experience—I left my body and watched the whole thing from outside, from above the car.

My mom's car was declared totaled and I walked away with minor whiplash and a faint red seatbelt burn—otherwise unscathed.

Miraculously, there were no other cars involved. Let me say that again—*NO ONE* hit me while I was bounding across the freeway—not once, but twice, in traffic and heavy rain. They said I was lucky to be alive. Was it luck? Divine intervention? A guardian angel? What about the out–of–body part? I didn't know and I couldn't explain it, but I felt like I'd been given a second chance.

And what did I do with my chance? I'd love to tell you I invented the cure for cancer or some other amazing, wondrous achievement, but no, I was sixteen. I did what kids my age did: I put it out of my mind and went back to my self–absorbed, angst–filled teenage life.

Two weeks after the accident, my ultra–cool older boyfriend pressured me to have sex with him, knowing I was a virgin, and knowing I was very naïve and innocent. He took my innocence against my will. When it was over, he threw his bathrobe at me and told me to cover up. He said he couldn't stand the sight of me cold and shaking.

I stopped believing I had a guardian angel looking out for me. Whatever seed of faith I had was crushed that night. I broke up with him the next day and never saw him again.

I heard he dropped out of college and joined the army. I remember secretly hoping that wherever they'd sent him, he'd been shot.

Summer had ended and it was time for my junior year of high school—*yay, not*. I got the mail after school, like I always did. Two weeks into the school year there was a letter addressed to me with handwriting I didn't recognize. The return address was from New Mexico. Who did I know in New Mexico? No one I could think of.

I stared at the envelope for a while before opening it. Then it dawned on me . . . it was from Trey.

I was almost afraid to open it, feeling nervous all over again. My stomach felt queasy and my fingers were shaking by the time I decided to open it, making it difficult to get the letter out of the envelope. I read it slowly, savoring it. Then I read it over and over again before I was able to write back.

That letter changed my life, as well as the months that followed upon receiving his initial correspondence. Over the course of that year we became pen pals and best friends. We told each other everything—our secrets, fears, and dreams. We became closer than I thought two people could—especially long distance. Here's that first letter:

Dear Tara,

Howdy! I'm not really sure why I'm writing you, but I've been thinking about you a lot lately, so I decided to drop a line and see how you're doing. It's been almost a year since we stopped by. There sure have been a lot of changes in my life since then. Right now I'm away at school in New Mexico, a military high school. Can you believe that? Life is a whole lot different here. We get up at 5:30 each morning and don't stop working until 10:00 at night. It was hard to adjust to the schedule at first. But the place kind of grows on you. Either the place grows on you or your first–sergeant does.

While I'm here, my only contact with the civilian world is through the mail. There are a lot of things I miss, but the thing I miss most is girls. I haven't seen a civilian girl since I got here seven weeks ago. I must admit that's one of the reasons I'm writing you. I'd do anything to get a girl to write me. Most of my buddies had girlfriends when they left, so they get letters regularly. It's starting to get depressing.

It's a challenge to stay here because I have no rank. I'm an official R.A.T. (Recruit–at–Training). I won't get a rank until the end of my first year. Until then, I take orders from anyone, from private on up. I must get permission to rest, eat, walk, talk, sit down, stand up...etc. The only privacy I have is during my two-and-a-half hours of forced study time. Some nights I use all my time doing homework. Sometimes though I find time to write letters, like this one.

I'm sending a picture of myself, as you would recognize me, with long hair. When I got here, they chopped most of it off. It's grown back a bit now but not nearly as much as I had in this picture. I'll send you a better picture when I get one, whether you write me back or not.

This letter is only me saying 'Hi.' Don't feel like you should have to write back. You probably have a boyfriend who might object to it. You would if I lived there. Tell your folks I said 'hi' to them too please.

Love,
Trey

Well, what do you think I did? After receiving a letter like that of course I wrote back—the same day, complete with pictures. I received his second letter a week later. We continued to write to each other for months. Sometimes I'd get a letter every day. As the weeks went by our letters grew more and more serious and we declared our love for one another. We began planning when we'd be able to see each other again.

His letters were descriptive, detailed and well–written. I would read them over and over until I had them memorized. I could picture him at his military school. I visualized myself sitting in the stands at his football games, cheering him on—his number was 38 (his buddies called him 38 Special). He played linebacker.

The letters soon became more personal, complimentary and romantic. Occasionally he would even write to me in French, since we were both taking high school French at the time, *"Tu es tres belle et tu as les plus belles zeux. Je t'adore! Nous avons été fait pour chaque autre."* (You are very beautiful and you have the most beautiful eyes. I adore you! We were made for each other). Not bad for a first-year student, eh?

Actually, the French writing impressed me—Trey knew I was planning to go on a trip to France and England that summer. I was saving all my money, taking French in high school, and excited to go. His writing French in his letters just showed me how thoughtful he was and how well he knew me.

It was uncanny how he could read me, and he always said just the right things. He was quite the flatterer too, *"As soon as I got your letter it felt like the sun came out from behind the clouds. Now I'm having a great day and I won't let anyone or anything get me down."*

In another letter he took a more serious tone:

> *I love you! I've loved you all along. I would have said so earlier but I didn't want to scare you. All I've done since last December is think about you. I am so glad I got up enough nerve to write you. If you really love me like I love you, then nothing can keep us apart too long. I can't stop thinking about you and how much I want to be with you.*

Then another:

> *I want you so bad. Well, I really want you*
> *good, but I'll take you anyway I can. You are very*
> *special to me and I feel more for you than any*
> *other girl that ever existed. I use you for my*
> *motivation when I do something that takes effort,*
> *like weightlifting. I love you. If not for you I would*
> *feel empty. Like you said, I don't have any*
> *patience, but I would wait for you forever if I had*
> *to. Thank God I don't! We will be together before*
> *long, I promise. T–N–T is perfect. You light my*
> *fuse! I'll write you again tomorrow just to show*
> *you that I would do anything to make you happy.*
> *Until then,*
> *Love,*
> *Trey*

He would often recite lyrics from songs he knew, *"I'm listening to the stereo thinking about you. Again. I love to put the thought of you to music (quoting 'Stay with Me' by Foghat.)*

And then there was the dream he had repeatedly about being late for our wedding because he couldn't find the church. Or the one where his best friend picks him up in a tux and takes him to the church. He sees me in my wedding dress and is too speechless to say, "I do."

The fact that he had dreams of us getting married showed me how real our relationship was to him. We were much more than just pen pals, more than a couple of teenagers writing thoughts and feelings on paper. We really loved each other, and I could tell him anything. He told me over and over how special and beautiful I was. I was certain that he was the only person in the world who understood me.

Our parents didn't understand how serious we were. No one did. He signed many of his letters, *"T–N–T you light my fuse"* or *"I love you forever."* I believed him.

And then—the letters stopped. He stopped calling me too. I sent a Christmas card to his home address, but when I didn't hear anything, I got worried. I knew he went home during Christmas break, but I didn't understand why he broke off contact so abruptly. I called and left a message on his answering machine Christmas Day, but he never called back.

When school started again in January, I called his military academy. The cadet who answered the phone told me Trey never came back from Christmas furlough. He didn't know the situation but was pretty sure Trey had dropped out.

What? I was sure there must be a mistake. I wrote to one of his good buddies there, but he didn't write back. I tried to reach him at home, but no luck there either.

I had no idea what was going on and couldn't believe—no, wouldn't believe—that he would stop writing without an explanation, just like that. I was sure something was wrong. I even thought it might be some kind of conspiracy at the military school. Perhaps I'd seen too many movies.

Two more weeks went by and still nothing. Finally, I tracked him down in Phoenix, at his mom's. When he answered the phone, he was withdrawn and distant, uncommunicative. The pregnant pauses on the other end of the phone were unbearable. This was not the same person who had written me those beautiful love letters— couldn't be. *Maybe the body snatchers took him?*

He admitted on the phone that he had stopped writing. He said his life was complicated and busy. He did drop out of military school and was back at his old public high school. He'd let his parents down.

He'd hated it at that school and had been miserable there. His mom didn't make life a picnic for him back home either. He said he'd disappointed her. He was down on himself, too, and said he didn't feel like writing anymore for a while. He had to get his life back in order and figure out what he was going to do next. I told him I understood and felt sorry for him. I gave him space and I stopped writing for a while, too.

But I kept the faith. I was sure he was going through a phase, a momentary slump. Once he snapped out of it, we'd start making plans to see each other again and everything would be fine.

I called him two months later, on his birthday. A girl answered the phone. When he got on, he said he couldn't talk and was cold toward me. He finally admitted that the girl was his new girlfriend and said it wouldn't be a good idea for me to call him anymore. He said it wouldn't be fair to his new girlfriend or to me for us to continue a long–distance relationship. I refused to believe he'd used me just to get letters because he was lonely and isolated in New Mexico. I fell for all his romantic ramblings. He couldn't possibly have written that stuff without meaning it. All I knew now was that he had a new girlfriend and I had wasted seven months being faithful to some long–distance pen pal.

I had been a sixteen-year-old high school junior who had faithfully stayed home every weekend. I had avoided parties, dating, and the local social scene—wasting my time on him. I was deeply hurt—and also deeply a "teenager."

I decided to fight fire with fire. I started dating again. It didn't take me long to get a new boyfriend. I found one just in time for prom. Long–distance relationships weren't worth it. He was smart to have ended it. Besides, we were too young to be so serious and committed like that—right?

4 vive la france

SUMMER HAD ARRIVED and I was about to embark on a six-week bicycle tour through France and England. I went with a tour company in Portland called "Riding High Bicycle Touring Co" that specialized in taking teens to Europe. We had been training every Saturday for months, and I was ready! Besides, it was a welcome distraction from thinking about Trey.

I was deemed the group interpreter, even though I'd only taken two years of high school French. I wanted to be fluent in the language someday, but I was nowhere near that at the time of the trip. Needless to say, I did a lot of pantomiming and had to look up words in my French–English dictionary often.

One morning when I woke up, the first words out of my mouth were in French, so I decided to challenge myself to speak only French the entire day. Breakfast consisted of 'pain et confiture de fraise avec café au lait,' and it was 'très délicieux' (bread and strawberry jam with coffee & milk; very delicious). After breakfast, we biked to Chartres, where we visited the medieval Cathédrale

Notre–Dame de Chartres, built circa 1145. It was the most beautiful cathedral I had ever seen.

We were two weeks in and had already seen several museums, churches, and cathedrals; so, when I say the Chartres Cathedral was the most beautiful of them all, please believe me.

At seventeen years old I had never seen anything like it and completely lost myself in the beautiful architecture and exquisite stained-glass windows. There were endless lit candles, as well as organ music, and even chanting nuns. It was a strange day to decide to speak only French, but at the moment, I was so awe struck that I was rendered speechless anyway.

My friend Lisa soon caught on to what I was doing, "Hey Tara, if you can go the whole day without speaking or writing in English, I'll buy you an Orangina. But if you screw up and say even one word in English—you owe me one!"

"C'est un pari!" (It's a bet!)

Word about the bet spread quickly, so everyone had their ears open and tried to make me speak "their language." John Lemming, the group's leader, bought us all a pâtisserie and took a group photo; he said our final destination for the day was Versailles.

The first mistake of the day was when our fearless leader took us down a one–way street—the wrong way! A car sped toward us and he crashed into it, dented it, and somehow remained completely uninjured.

Once we finally got out of town—we headed for Rambouillet. What a nightmare. There were tons of bugs on the narrow, two–lane road and it was the hottest biking day we'd had so far. I wore a Snoopy tank top and blue shorts and was soon covered with bugs. Every few minutes I had to stop and wipe off my sunglasses—it was so gross. There were also many semis on the steep and curvy road. I choked on their exhaust fumes as they passed me.

A trucker in the oncoming lane was driving slowly so the trucker behind him decided to overtake him. But he didn't see me and pulled ahead into my lane—heading straight for me. He was going downhill, and I was going up on a steep incline. There was no shoulder on the side of the road—it just sloped down the hill—but there were a few trees jutting out along the hillside. I had milliseconds to get out of the way, so I aimed for a tree, plowed into it, then quickly hugged it as the truck driver barreled past me, a mere centimeter from my bike and body.

I thought for sure I was going to be flattened like a Bugs Bunny cartoon and quivered with trepidation at my impending death. Once I realized he was gone, and I was still in one piece, I summoned all my false bravery and yelled the only two French curse words I knew—over and over while shaking my fist. Unfortunately, there was no one around to witness my stunning display of courage and I couldn't tell the group when we all met up because of my stupid bet with Lisa. I didn't know how to say, "I almost got run over by a semi" in French and they wouldn't have understood me anyway.

When I finally reached Rambouillet and the outside café where everyone was waiting, I kept my cool and said, "Je ne sais pas" (I don't know) when anyone asked me a question I couldn't answer. I loaded up on some energizing *chocolat* and we were off.

We had to take a busy highway all the way to Versailles, thirty-one kilometers. With eight kilometers left, and the others way ahead of me, I fell and skinned my knee. But then I realized John was behind me because his daughter, Mindy, got a flat tire. We tried to hitchhike but to no avail. No one wanted to stop for three people with bicycles.

We stopped in a small town to fill up our water bottles and use the bathroom, but we had to catch up to the group. John patched Mindy's tire and we rode as fast as we could to Versailles. He complained that I was too slow, but my knee was killing me. Still, I managed to bike through the pain and we soon reached the Château de Versailles. We locked up our bikes and looked for our group. We walked all over and didn't see them anywhere.

We got back on our bikes and rode to the center of town and then to the other side of the Palace—which was enormous. At last we found Doug, one of the kids from our group, riding on the other side of the Palace. He was sent as a scout to look for us. We followed Doug to the rest of the gang, who were waiting for us at a nearby café. I was never happier to see them! And yet, I couldn't even tell them about my ordeal.

I sat in silence as we ate our usual delicious dinner of yogurt, bread, cheese, pâté and ham. I was eager to get to the campsite, so I could take care of my knee and put this day behind me. But when we arrived at the campsite, they were full. Fortunately, John sweet–talked them into letting us camp there anyway. We set up our tents at the top of a steep hill, far into the wooded area, separated by the crowded trailers.

I rinsed my knee off in the sink at the campsite restroom. I had to pick out little pebbles and debris and it stung. Without thinking, I cursed, "Shit!" Guess who walked in right then? Yep, Lisa.

"Ha! You said shit! You lost the bet!" she pointed at me and cried out with glee.

"Oh, come on! That was the first non–French word I've said all day, I swear. You wouldn't believe what happened to me today. I should have won that bet!"

"Nope, the day's not over. Fair is fair, and I heard you," she smiled triumphantly. She was right, what could

I say? The next day I bought her the Orangina, otherwise I never would have heard the end of it.

Overall, my Europe trip was amazing, and I have wonderful memories to cherish, but I remember being particularly sad in Paris. As I walked up the steps inside the Eiffel Tower (the elevators were out) in the most romantic city in the world, I missed Trey and wondered what he was doing at that moment, half way around the world.

5   the visit

THERE WAS A LETTER waiting for me when I got home from Europe. Trey had broken up with what's–her–name and missed me again, naturally.

Dear Tara,

Hi. Today is June 6th and it's 109 degrees outside. I'm just sitting here sweating. When it gets this hot, I don't have the energy for anything. While I was opening this notebook I passed a letter I wrote to you, but never sent. It didn't seem 'right.' I promise I will send this one.

I've grown. I am now scant millimeters from six feet. I weigh about 180 lbs. Summer school is on the agenda for me. I also might be going to basic training for the Reserves this summer. I doubt it though. I think I'll wait and see about a spot in a Special Forces unit next fall. That leaves me here doing nothing all summer. I lift weights twice a day, but that doesn't pay (at least not in money). My dad and I are in a fight and we haven't spoken to each other since March. So my chances for a visit to the Northwest are minimal.

I'm reminded now of a song (everything reminds me of a song) but this one is perfect (quoting 'Possible Pasts' by Pink Floyd).

You are very special to me, Tara. You are the only thing that kept me going when I was at military school. No matter what happens, I will always remember that. But I get the feeling that someone has something planned for us. Otherwise, how could we be far apart for so long and yet be so close to each other? We haven't seen each other for a year and a half. I would like to see you in person. Maybe if we stay in touch long enough we'll end up nearer to each other and you wouldn't have to wonder what would happen if we weren't so far apart.

This is a hopeful letter and I promise it was not written because of guilt (it should be). I promise that I will make every effort to write you back. It's summer now so that will be easier. I have been irresponsible these last few months and feel shamed that your friend said I seem mature for my age. It was such a nice compliment, and it was so undeserved.

My hair is almost to my shoulders now. It's harder to take care of but it looks better. Another big difference is that I smile again now. It feels so good to write this letter. I hope you enjoy it. It's long overdue. You really are tolerant to put up with all my bullshit. As I finish this letter I'm looking forward to taking a shower, relaxing in bed and thinking about you. You are such a nice thought. (T-N-T You light my fuse, still)

Love,
   Trey

Being the forgiving, hopeless romantic that I was, I called him right then. We made plans to see each other, I booked a ticket to Phoenix, and two weeks later Trey was picking me up at the airport. Luckily, I'd been thrifty on my Europe trip, and still had money left over. I asked my mom if I could go almost as an afterthought. I was asking to visit the guy I'd been head–over–heels over for a year and a half—she didn't dare say no. Besides, she trusted Trey's mom completely and knew I'd be well taken care of.

I must have imagined what it would be like to see him again a thousand different times. Of course, there was always music. And we were always running toward each other in slow motion—but then again, I already told you I'd seen too many movies.

We were both seventeen now and a lot changes between fifteen and seventeen. Maybe not quite as much as between ten and fifteen, but a lot.

My flight was pleasant enough. I flew out of Portland, changed planes in San Francisco, then flew non–stop to Phoenix. It was a sunny day in July and a great day for a plane ride. Of course, when my plane landed, and I walked to the gate—it was nothing like in the movies. But you already knew it wouldn't be, didn't you? Well, you were right.

The gate terminal was under construction, so passengers had to walk through an obstacle course and meet their parties in the main terminal. I was so excited to see him I thought I was about to explode. *I have so much built–up anticipation and now I have to maneuver through this construction? Another delay?*

The walk to the main terminal seemed to take days. It was a Friday. I remember humming the tune, "Friday Night," from the syndicated TV series, "Fame," along the way.

As I walked into the main terminal, I spotted him instantly—he definitely stood out from the crowd. "Hi Tara, how was your flight?" he asked as he reached out and hugged me.

"Hi! It was great! I mean—um, it went faster than I thought it would. I actually got a little sleep." I managed to say while smiling so wide my jaw was already hurting.

He took my hand and led me toward baggage claim. It was so good to see him. He looked great—even better than I remembered; his pictures didn't do him justice. He seemed happy to see me, yet there was an underlying melancholy about him I couldn't figure out. He was polite, and somewhat reserved.

He asked me about my trip and how my parents were. He even asked me about the weather—small talk. Not at all what I expected but it was nice. Still, I was a little skeptical and made a mental note of his peculiar behavior.

When we arrived at his house his family made me feel welcome. Even his little brother was nice to me. But Trey was acting strange—being quiet and sullen, very odd.

There was a thunder and lightning storm my first night there. Trey and I sat on the covered porch and watched the storm together, but not together. He was clearly in his own world. I didn't understand it. He knew I had just flown sixteen hundred miles to see him, yet he was completely withdrawn. He hardly said a word to me. We talked about 'safe' topics like rain and thunder. Then he started getting philosophical but wasn't making sense. I couldn't follow what he was saying. We'd never had trouble communicating before. It was my first night there and I didn't have a clue what I'd done wrong.

He finally said he was tired and went to bed. I stayed in the room down the hall. I went to my room completely baffled. He was acting like he didn't want me to be there. After all we'd written in our letters to each other—all the innuendos and flirtatious remarks about what he was going to do to me when he saw me. He certainly wasn't shy the last time I saw him.

No. He wasn't shy. That wasn't it. Something was wrong, very wrong. I just didn't know what. Come to think of it, he didn't even kiss me hello at the airport. He hadn't kissed me at all. I was determined to get to the bottom of it, whatever it was. *I didn't fly out here to be ignored for ten days.*

The next day, his mom made him take me to see the local sights. He did the obligatory host thing, but again, I could tell his mind was somewhere else. Why wouldn't he talk to me? What was going on in his head? I couldn't reach him. I couldn't get him to open up to me.

His mom made excuses for his moodiness and tried to smooth everything over by lavishing attention on me. She planned activities for us to do to keep me entertained during the week. I felt like I was hanging out with a barely breathing corpse. His heart just wasn't in it. I didn't pry right away. I knew something was troubling him and I sensed by the way he was acting that it was big. I wanted to let him tell me naturally in his own way; but he wasn't talking.

After five days of putting up with his distant moodiness I couldn't take it anymore, so I confronted him. I almost did it the night before, but I was so angry I thought I'd better cool off first.

Trey had a few friends over and we played cards. They were nice and included me in their conversations. However, Trey made no effort to include me in anything. In fact, he deliberately ignored me to the point of it being unbearably awkward for everyone. So I left.

To vent some of my anger I wrote him a scathing letter but had no intention of giving it to him. Well, the next day, he found the letter in my room while looking for a book. He said I was being cruel and that I didn't understand.

"Then make me understand," I demanded. "Trey, I can't help you if you won't even talk to me. Please, tell me what's been bugging you. I want to help you—"

"You can't help me! No one can!" he suddenly blurted out. "You don't even know what you're talking about so just leave it alone, okay?" He turned and walked out the sliding back door. He began pacing around the back yard and I followed him.

"No, I won't leave it alone. I didn't fly all the way down here to be ignored! If you didn't want me to come you should have told me before I wasted all this time and money. I don't understand why you're treating me like this. I thought you loved me. I thought you wanted to be with me . . . I love you! Why are you acting like this?"

"I can't tell you."

"What? What do you mean, you can't tell me? Trey, I know everything about you. We've been through so much—"

"Not everything. There are some things you don't know which makes it very difficult for me to tell you what's wrong now."

"Whatever it is, you can trust me. I won't tell anyone if you don't want me to. I just hate to see you hurting like this. Why can't you tell me?"

"You can't tell anyone! Swear to it—especially my mom. If you tell my mom I swear I'll kill you!"

"Okay! Okay. I won't tell anybody. Trey, are you in some kind of trouble?"

"You could say that."

"What? Did you do something illegal? Are you wanted by the poli—"

"No, it's nothing like that."

"Then tell me damn it! Please, I beg you! I can't keep playing these guessing games. What—"

"Lucy's pregnant!" he vehemently shouted. I felt like I'd just been hit in the stomach. Yet, I managed to stay calm and simply asked, "The girl who answered the phone when I called you on your birthday?"

"Yeah."

"What are you going to do?"

"I don't know!"

"Then why did you let me visit you?"

"I just found out the day you flew in. It was too late to stop you. Don't you see what's happened? My whole life is ruined!"

He took a deep breath and looked at me hard. Then continued, "It's not what you think. I broke up with her months ago, but she kept it from me. She waited 'til she was four months pregnant to tell me. She waited 'til it was too late to have an abortion—she tricked me. I didn't even love her. She told me she was on the pill and she wasn't. We only went out a few months. We only fooled around a few times. I guess it only takes once though, huh?"

I didn't know what to say. I was in shock. I wanted to comfort him and tell him everything would be okay, but I didn't know if it would. He was only seventeen. She was two years older than him and already had another child. In his eyes, his life was ruined. I felt sorry for him, but I was mad at him too. How could he sleep with her and write to me at the same time?

As if he could read my thoughts he said, "I stopped writing you when I started dating her. I never—I was faithful to you the whole time I was writing you. When I went back home and saw her, I couldn't write you. I couldn't make you wait for me like that. I could never do that to you. I figured once I was with her I didn't deserve you. But I didn't have the guts to tell you about her either. It was easier for me just to stop writing. I'm sorry. I know I hurt you. I never meant to hurt you. I never stopped loving you . . ."

I was surprised how well I held my composure. I didn't cry. I didn't falter. In an even, steady voice I simply said, "What are you going to do, Trey?"

"Well, I won't deny that it's my child. I suppose I'll have to tell my mom sooner or later, but I gotta get use to the idea first. I mean—I'm going to be a father. Whoa. I haven't even finished high school yet. I don't know, Tar. I really don't know. I've got a lot more thinking to do. Right now I hate her. I hate her because she lied to me, and I hate her for not telling me sooner, for not trusting me—"

"Would you have made her get an abortion?"

"Hell yes! I mean—that's no way to get a guy. We broke up! How do I know she's not lying to me still—and it's not someone else's?"

"Did you ask her that?"

"Yeah I asked her. She insists it's mine. She swears she hasn't been with anyone else since we broke up, but I don't know if I believe her. I mean, she lied about everything else, why not lie about this too?"

"Were you with her four months ago? Is it possible that it's your child?"

"Yes."

"Then she probably isn't lying about the paternity, Trey. There are ways to test it, but I don't see how she could lie about something like thi—"

"That's just it! How could she lie about any of it? The pill? Not telling me for four goddamn months! I don't know what I'm going to do, I just don't know . . ." his voice trailed off into quiet sobs. Once he started crying, he couldn't stop. I held him in my arms as he cried. My own tears soon began to flow freely as well.

"Oh Trey," I whispered. "Trey, I'm so sorry."

We sat together in silence for a long time. I just held him and stroked his head. I wanted to make the pain go away. I wanted to make the whole mistake just go away. I couldn't believe this was happening.

Now that I knew what the problem was, it didn't make things easier between us, except that I could leave him alone to ponder his dilemma. I certainly couldn't give him answers or advice on what to do. I made the best of the time I had left.

Trey's friends and family were more than willing to show me around and keep me entertained for the remainder of my stay. They thought Trey and I were having trouble getting along and that accounted for his depressed and uncooperative attitude. I let them think what they wanted. I made a vow to Trey that I wouldn't tell anyone, and I didn't.

I enjoyed the dry heat of the Arizona summer perhaps a little too much. I got so sunburned one day that I just wanted to be shot and put out of my misery. Trey's brother, Chad, just smiled and shook his head when he saw me lying on the couch, writhing in agony. He went to the kitchen, got a butcher knife and went out to the back yard with it.

When he came back in, he was carrying two Aloe Vera stocks. He gave me one and told me to peel back the skin from it, while he rubbed the other one on my legs. It was a miracle plant. I couldn't believe how quickly the soothing relief came. Aloe Vera plants grew everywhere down there. That plant saved my life. Okay, perhaps not, but it was the best sunburn remedy I'd ever tried.

By the next day I felt a lot better and Trey's mom arranged for me to go to the border town of Nogales, Mexico with their cousins. I think she was embarrassed that her son was ignoring me, and she felt sorry for me. The cousins were friendly and made me feel welcome right away, so thankfully it wasn't awkward as we navigated through the various flea markets and street vendors.

"Cheaper than K-Mart, Amigo. No charge for lookin'," were the shopkeepers' laments as they pushed their wares. It was fun to barter with them; they seemed to encourage it. I guess that way both merchant and patron felt like they got a good deal. It worked—I felt like I got lots of good deals—silly trinkets and souvenirs. Who knows how much the stuff I bought was actually worth. They probably had a good laugh after the silly naïve American girl spent all her money in their stores. Oh well, for a moment I forgot about Trey and his problem and thoroughly enjoyed myself. It was a good day.

My last night there, I reassured Trey that his secret was safe with me. I told him he could call and talk to me any time (especially since I was one of the only people who knew). I told him I still cared for him and would always be there as a friend, no matter what. He said he appreciated it and tried to apologize for everything turning out the way it did. I cut him off, told him it didn't matter now and wished him well. I told him that whatever he decided I just wanted him to be happy. We said goodbye, gave each other a quick hug and I went to bed.

The next morning, I woke up at six and went out to the living room just as Trey was leaving for his summer school class. Our eyes met and locked as we mouthed the word "bye" to each other. He turned, was out the door and gone. I think he said more in that one look than he had said to me the entire ten days I was there. Of course, I went back to bed and cried until my eyes were swollen and red.

Trey's mom drove me to the airport and was all smiles as though nothing unusual had happened. She gave me a warm hug and invited me to come back again the next summer. I thanked her for her hospitality and was on my way.

During my flight back to Portland all I thought about was Trey, and I wondered what he would do about his dilemma. I told myself I had to forget about him, forget about us, and the way things were. I expected I'd probably never hear from him again . . . but I hoped that I would.

MY MOM AND STEP–DAD, Jack, greeted me at the airport. They were all smiles and questions. "How was your trip, sweetheart?" my mom inquired.

"Tell us all about it!" Jack chimed in.

"You look great!" said Mom. "You're so tan. How are Jill and Trey?"

"The trip was fun, I even got to go to Mexico. It was really neat. Jill is doing well. She was super nice to me. She worried that I wasn't having a good time. She didn't want me to be bored so she kept planning activities for me. It was kind of funny, actually," I managed, with a smile and false–bravado.

But Mom saw right through my act (I was afraid she would). She knows me too well, and I've never been able to lie to her. Usually, I wouldn't want to because we're so close, but I promised Trey I wouldn't reveal his secret— and it was killing me.

"So, what happened? What's wrong?" she inquired knowingly.

"Trey and I didn't hit it off after all. No big deal, it just wasn't meant to be, I guess. Oh, we're still friends but nothing happened." *She's not buying it.* "He has some personal problems that are in the way of having a relationship right now. Besides, we decided we both live too far away from each other and it just wouldn't work anyway."

Mom nodded thoughtfully. Jack said, "Well, kiddo, it's probably for the best."

It worked! They fell for it. Now, how long can I keep this up? "Yeah, you're probably right. It just hurts a little that's all. I mean, I thought he was 'the one' and now it turns out that he isn't, ya know?"

"You've got lots of time to meet the right person, Tara," Jack said. "Get out there and have some fun first!"

"Yeah, okay."

We got my suitcase and headed home. I was so glad the questions had finally stopped; I didn't know how much more I could take. As soon as we got home I went straight to my room and cried.

Then I had to put on the same act for my friends when they wanted to hear all about it too. It was awful. I let everybody think Trey didn't like me and there was nothing I could do about it. I treated it casually and soon it blew over. No one knew my inner turmoil. No one knew how I secretly pined for him and hoped that we'd see each other again, and that everything would work out—somehow.

I got a job bussing tables at the food court in the mall for the remainder of the summer. I kept myself busy and slowly began to heal inside. When school started up again, I got back together with my old boyfriend and prom date from last spring, Scott Benson.

I began to put Trey out of my head so I could enjoy my senior year of high school—so I could enjoy my life.

We got a Christmas card and letter from Jill. Enclosed was a wallet–sized family portrait. Trey looked better than ever. She wrote about the birth of his baby girl and what a proud grandmother she was, making the best of it like she always did. She put in parentheses, "You knew, didn't you?" I guess she suspected Trey told me everything and that I had known all along. She finally realized what had been depressing her son during my visit. I'm sure it explained a lot of things for her.

Well, it was out in the open now. Mom saw the look on my face when I read the card. Blinking back the tears I told her the story right then, about the whole miserable trip. I assured her that I'd wanted to tell her so many times, but I'd given my word, it wasn't my news to tell. She understood and nothing more needed to be said. She was my mom and she comforted me and held me until my crying subsided.

The letter also said that Trey was going to try to make it work with Lucy and be a responsible father. He moved in with her and took care of the baby while she worked nights, so he could go to school during the day. *Wow, what a way to spend your senior year of high school.* I still felt sorry for him, even though I got mad at myself for feeling anything at all.

But time marches on. I managed to fill my time with drama (as if I didn't have enough of it already). I was in school plays and developed a fondness for theatre. Escape from reality at its finest. Whatever it was, it got me through high school. I also grew very fond of Scott, my on and off boyfriend and co–lead in two plays, which made high school endurable.

Scott and I had a lot in common and got along well. We both loved theatre and performing, and were also active in the Ski Club at school—which comprised of going up to Mt. Hood Meadows, via school bus, every Saturday during ski season. However, there was one particular Saturday I'll never forget—the day he nearly died.

It was a balmy forty-five degrees in January, with light winds; for skiing, that's not good because the snow starts to melt and turns icy. Everyone complained about the icy conditions and warning signs were posted, but that didn't stop Scott from wanting to ski the most difficult runs anyway. He was a fearless, advanced skier who wasn't going to let a little ice slow him down. Scott had brown hair and eyes, dark complexion, perfect teeth and a dazzling smile. With his athletic build he looked like a born skier, especially that day.

As we put our lunches away, we discussed where to ski that afternoon, "Hey Tar, how 'bout we ski the Jump Run?" Scott asked.

"You mean Dead Man's Run? That's what they call it you know. I don't like that one; the trails are too narrow and there are too many trees," I complained.

"Oh, come on, you baby! Where's your sense of adventure?"

"Oh fine, but I'm not going over all the jumps. I'll save those for you! Just, try not to get too far ahead and leave me alone in the woods, okay?"

"Sure, whatever. Come on, last one to the chairlift is a rotten egg!"

The run was in a secluded, heavily forested area off to the right of the chairlift and was covered with moguls and jumps. For Scott, the more difficult the runs the better, and he skied over every jump with gusto shouting, "woo-hoo" or "yee-haw" every time he caught air. Lacking his bravado and confidence, I skied behind him at a much slower, more cautious pace, and skied around as many jumps as possible.

When he got too far ahead of me, which was often, he stopped and waited for me to catch up, sometimes shouting, "Come on ya ol' ninny!"

I could see him most of the time and skied as fast as I felt I could without losing control. But then he took a hairpin turn and disappeared in a forest. When I got to that spot, it intersected with another path and I couldn't tell which way he had gone.

Something shiny and metal caught my eye further down—a pair of skis stuck out of the snow in front of an enormous tree. My legs grew wobbly and a terrible knot formed in my stomach as I skied closer to the disembodied skis. When I arrived, I realized they were attached to legs and, to my horror, I realized they were Scott's legs.

He was lying face down in a tree well and his legs and skis were all that was visible. I immediately removed my own skis, then dug snow out from around him so I could get him out of the ditch, while asking him questions.

"Scott? Are you hurt? Are you in any pain?"

"No," he answered in a far away, monotone voice.

"Are you okay?"

"No."

"Do you want me to take off your skis?"

Scott moaned and moved slightly, so I unfastened his skis and partly lifted, partly drug him out of the ditch as carefully as I could. I rolled him over onto his back and began treating him for shock, checking the ABC's (Airway, Breathing, Circulation) covering him with my coat, and examining him for broken bones.

"Tell me when it hurts, okay?" I felt his right leg, "Does this hurt?"

Again, all he could muster was, "No."

I touched his left leg and he flinched. "Scott, tell me where it hurts! Are you okay? Will you answer me? Can you talk? Are you in any pain at all?" I was getting exasperated.

"No."

I didn't understand why he wouldn't or couldn't talk; the only first aid training I'd had was part of our Health unit at school. I was overwhelmed with fear and concern for Scott, and not knowing what to do next. As I was trying to get a grip and assess the situation, he lost consciousness. I began looking for help and noticed trees all around us—and not a soul in sight. Except for my short, panicked breaths, all was eerily silent.

I became preoccupied with getting help and was unaware that Scott had struggled to his hands and knees. I turned and gaped at him in astonishment and disbelief as he began to crawl away. Bewildered, I ran over, grabbed him and rolled him over again; he appeared to be delirious. Then he began to tremble with minor convulsions. I pinned him down as he struggled against my grip. I tried to calm him down by speaking soothingly but couldn't penetrate his delirium. I covered him with my coat again and used my ski hat and scarf to prop up his head. I held him until his seizures subsided.

At last, a lone skier stopped by. "What happened?"

"Get the Ski Patrol up here as fast as you can! Hurry!" I shouted. As he began to ski away, I uttered a meek, "Please?"

As I waited for the Ski Patrol to arrive my mind swam in a sea of chaos and fear. *What is taking so long? How much time has passed? What is wrong with Scott? Did that guy even get the Ski Patrol? Maybe I should try to flag down someone else?*

Scott had another seizure and snapped me out of my chaotic thoughts. I bent over him and held him down as he convulsed. I tried to keep a cool head and control my emotions.

All at once his seizure stopped and he went limp in my arms. I quickly checked his pulse, inundated with renewed terror. *Is he breathing?* I felt his chest and abdomen—*Yes! Thank God!*

I couldn't help but think how vulnerable he looked, just lying there. He began to moan softly. "It's okay," I soothed. "It's gonna be okay. You'll be okay. Everything will be okay!" I repeated these words over and over. He began to tremble again, and I couldn't stop the tears from rolling down my cheeks. *Will they ever get here?* Time stood still as all I could do was sit there, hold his gloved hand, and wait for help to arrive.

A man in a red jacket with a white armband and red cross on his sleeve skied toward us. Two more men in red coats appeared, dragging an empty sled with bundles of blankets heaped upon it. The first man asked what happened and then shot a series of questions at me. Scott roused to consciousness and opened his eyes. He was also asked several questions. Hope began to stir in me as I realized he actually answered some questions. He knew his name and what high school he attended. Then he passed out again.

They laid him in the sled while I watched, riveted to the spot as they strapped him in. I felt queasy and hoped it was just a bad dream; but it was all too real. I tried to choke back the tears that were stinging my face as I watched two men in red coats ski down the mountain with their precious cargo being carried stretcher–style in a sled between them.

Scott was treated at the First–Aid room on Mt. Hood and then taken via ambulance to Gresham Community Hospital, fifty miles away. He had a minor concussion and a bruised knee, but they couldn't explain the seizures. Miraculously, he sustained no major injuries and made a full recovery. However, he broke up with me a couple weeks later when a new girl at school caught his eye.

I went to a small school, in a small town, where everybody knew everybody, and everybody else's business. I wasn't into that because I valued my privacy and tended to be shy and introverted. Therefore, by the time I turned eighteen and graduated, I was ready to "get out of Dodge!"

My high school guidance counselor, Mrs. Tank, advised me not to go to college. She said college wasn't for everyone and that she didn't think I should waste my parents' money on something I probably wouldn't get anything out of, and probably wouldn't finish anyway. *By the way, where the hell did she get her degree and has she been fired yet?* What kind of 'guidance' is that crap? Despite the fact that I made nearly straight A's all four years, was in National Honor Society, took AP and Honors classes, and was salutatorian, I decided to take her advice—I planned to skip college.

This decision, naturally, didn't thrill my parents. What was I going to do if I wasn't going to college? I had to do *something!* Partly to get everyone off my back and mostly because I wanted to travel, I enrolled in a correspondence course for the travel industry, to train for a flight attendant position. The course was designed with thirty lessons, each with its own test, and allowed me to work at my own pace.

Once I completed the lessons, there was a six–week resident training in Florida. The courses, training and airfare cost twenty-five hundred dollars. Sounded like a good deal to me. I knew I had to come up with the tuition myself, so, like I said, when I graduated high school, I got out of that small town and moved in with my father and step–mother in Seattle.

7   the green river killer

MY PARENTS DIVORCED when I was two years old. Although I visited my dad summers and school vacations, I didn't feel I actually knew him. He had been a busy and emotionally distant man. When I turned eighteen I wanted to get to know my dad. We agreed that once I moved in with him, he'd help me get a job at Boeing and that would pay my tuition to the travel school—so that's what I did.

I worked as a Records Clerk, making six dollars an hour. It was 1984 and the prevailing minimum wage in Washington State was two dollars and thirty cents an hour. I felt proud and lucky to have my job at Boeing.

Things were going well with Dad and his wife, Carolyn, who was pregnant with their first child, and I was excited to be getting a new baby sister. The job was okay, and even though I was the youngest employee there by at least twelve years, I managed to make a few work friends who helped pass the time at a tedious job of typing and filing.

Speaking of friends, the strangest thing happened. I was flipping through the Sunday paper one morning when I saw an advertisement for the Seattle Pacific Northwest

Ballet's production of *The Nutcracker*. The ad included a photograph of a beautiful ballerina who looked familiar. I quickly scanned the photo credits and saw her name jump out at me from the page, Belinda Barrows. I couldn't believe it. Remember that small town I mentioned? The one I couldn't wait to get out of? She was from there and now she was a professional ballerina for the Pacific Northwest Ballet and she had the lead role in *The Nutcracker*. I was so excited to see her that I called the box office right then and bought a ticket. I also tried to look her up to get her number, but it was unlisted.

Belinda had three sisters and was two years older than me. I was best friends with her younger sister, Ava, all through grade school. Ava was my age.

The whole family was gorgeous; they all looked like models who had just walked out of a magazine photo shoot. They had lived in a big house with lots of land and owned horses. I always thought they were rich, but being a kid, I had no idea how rich they were or even what their dad did for a living.

I used to pretend I was part of their family and I loved sleepovers at Ava's house. Being raised as an only child, I was enamored with Ava's sisters, and they were always nice to me. I never knew their heritage, other than being part Italian; they were sort of exotic looking. They all had thick, long dark brown hair, big brown eyes, dark eyelashes, and perfect, olive skin. I thought Ava was easily the prettiest girl in school, and she was kind and sweet to everyone.

Unfortunately, Ava's family moved about twenty miles away after fifth grade. At the time, twenty miles may just as well have been the other side of the world, considering Ava and I didn't drive and were dependent on our parents to keep in touch. We did manage to visit each other a few times over the years, a weekend here, a weekend there.

The last time I recall seeing her was when we were fifteen and sophomores in high school. She stayed with me over the weekend and we went to a high school party together. She borrowed my good jeans and somehow busted the zipper.

Then she just vanished. I heard she moved again, but no one seemed to know where and I didn't have a new phone number for her. Seeing that picture made me miss the family, but I really missed Ava and wondered where she was now.

With the hope of contacting Belinda, I consulted the white pages of the Seattle telephone directory and called all the Barrows I could find. And then something wonderful happened—I found their mom.

When I asked for Belinda she was a little guarded and simply said that Belinda didn't live there; but once I told her who I was she instantly remembered me and asked if I wanted to speak to Ava. *What? Ava's here? In Seattle?* I was beside myself with joy and excitement. Of course, I wanted to speak to Ava. It had been three years since I'd last seen her, I was living with my dad, away from my mom, friends, and familiar surroundings, and I could use a friend here.

Ava sounded just as thrilled to hear from me as I was to find her, and we quickly made plans to see each other and catch up that weekend. She lived in a condo with her mom and little sister in downtown Seattle. Apparently, her parents divorced a few years earlier, which prompted the move to Seattle. She said she wasn't going to school or working right then and that her schedule was free to see me any time. I had a full–time job, so we decided to wait until Saturday to make the drive into downtown easier. I was so excited to see her that waiting until Saturday seemed to take forever; the week passed painfully slow.

Finally, Saturday arrived, and I carefully made the drive from the east side to the west side, which for me was terrifying because I had to drive across the Evergreen Bridge—a floating bridge, and I dreaded it. When I arrived at their condo, Ava's mom answered the door. She gave me a warm hug and said that Ava was upstairs, and I could just go on up and see her.

Seeing Ava for the first time in three years was a shock I wasn't expecting. I remembered her with straight, dark brown hair about shoulder length, a beautiful face with unblemished skin that didn't need makeup, and a sparkle in her young, bright eyes. The girl who bounded across the room shouting, "Tara! It's so good to see you!" as she hugged me exuberantly, had long curly, bleached blonde hair, heavy makeup, and hard, cold eyes; the sparkle was gone. She was still stunningly beautiful, but she had an edge to her now, and I could see that her innocence was no more. She also looked beyond her eighteen years.

Ava didn't notice my shocked reaction and began bombarding me with questions, "How have you been? What have you been up to? Are you going to school now? Working? Do you have a boyfriend?" She sounded like the Ava I remembered and soon we were reminiscing, laughing, and having a great time. Then she got an idea. "I want to show you around. Let's go out!"

Before I got a chance to reply, she said, "But first, I need to give you a makeover."

"What? Why?" I asked skeptically, as I didn't wear makeup at all, and didn't even own mascara.

"Come on. It'll be fun!" she assured me.

"Okay, um, I guess," I gave in.

Two hours later, I was walking down the sidewalk in a tight mini–skirt, push–up bra, tight top, leather jacket, clunky heels (I never wore heels) and so much makeup and hairspray I felt like Tammy Faye Bakker. Either that or dressed up as a cheap prostitute at a Halloween party.

Ava didn't look any better. However, she did have an agenda.

A car crept toward us and then stopped. We were in the University District—the "U District"—near the University of Washington. Both occupants of the car were wearing purple U of W sweatshirts and the passenger rolled down his window, motioning for us to come over.

To my horror, Ava walked right on over and began talking to the two guys. Then she looked over at me and asked if I wanted to get in the car with them. *Hell no I didn't want to get in the car! What was going on?*

The next thing I knew, the driver pulled his car over, parked and turned off the ignition. Both guys got out of the car and approached Ava. Again, she motioned me over, "Tara, come on! It's okay . . . these guys are cool."

"Hello! Don't worry, we don't bite," one of the guys said, grinning at me as I walked toward them. They were both smiling and greeted me with handshakes as though it were perfectly normal to stop on the side of the road and talk to two eighteen-year-old girls at nine o'clock at night. "My name is Nigel, and this is my friend Albert. We are exchange students from Fiji," he said slowly, in a thick accent.

"It's so nice to meet you! I'm Ava, and this is my friend, Tara. She's a little shy, but she'll be okay. Right, Tara?" Ava shot me a warning glance.

"Hi," I managed, wondering why this was so important to her.

We were near a park, so Albert suggested we walk over. He and Ava took the lead, already whispering and flirting. Nigel hung back and walked with me, trying his best to make small talk. He seemed nervous and I didn't make things any easier for him. When we got to the park, Nigel and I sat on a bench. I made sure I sat on the edge, as far away as I could get.

Albert and Ava said they'd be back in a few minutes and disappeared down a path, behind a big tree. I sat and stared at my feet. Finally, I looked over at Nigel and asked, "So, what's Fiji like?"

For the next fifteen minutes, twenty-two-year-old Nigel prattled on about his childhood and family in Fiji. He happily filled in the awkward silences while we waited for our friends to come back. I think he was just as relieved as I was that I didn't expect him to make any sexual advances toward me. Finally, looking slightly disheveled, Albert and Ava came back and she suggested we go home. Ava, my dear sweet friend, Ava, as it turns out was in fact a prostitute, and she was working her territory.

How stupid and naïve could I be? I needed answers and I needed her to start talking—NOW. She did as I asked and answered all my questions candidly. My head was spinning. She was from a good family and her two older sisters were successful; Belinda was a professional ballet dancer and Marie was a doctor in training. How did this end up being her lot in life at eighteen? Plus, she lived with her mom. How did her mom not see it? How could she not know what was going on?

Ava was a drug addict, a cokehead; she didn't always hook for money. She lost her virginity at age fourteen, never had a decent relationship, and was used to being treated like trash by guys; she expected it. Since the guys she dated only wanted sex, she decided, why not start charging for it? She worked on her own and told no one about it—until me. I think her little show and tell with me that night was a cry for help. Ava was in grave danger and I was determined to get her the help she needed.

"Ava, you're so much better than this! Please stop!" I pleaded. "It's not safe! Haven't you heard of the Green River Killer?"

"What? No, what are you talking about?"

"There's a serial killer in Seattle who kills prostitutes! It's all over the news. They call him the Green River Killer because he dumps a lot of his victims in the Green River. Women have gone missing from this very block! Geesh, Ava, you have to quit this or you're going to get murdered!"

"You don't understand. I've tried to quit but I can't," she nearly whispered. "I need the money. I need the fix. I can't do anything else. I have no skills, no education. I'm nothing." She implored me to understand with her eyes as she finally said, "Okay, I'll do it. I'll quit. But I need more time. Please, just give me more time. And promise me you won't tell my mom?"

Risking the loss of our friendship and knowing this was too big for me to handle, I did the only thing I could think of to make her stop—I told her mom.

A week later Ava's mom called and gave me the address of the Care Center Drug Rehabilitation facility where Ava was committed. She said they allowed visitors and Ava could use a friend. I tried to visit her, but they told me she didn't want any visitors. I tried a few more times, but then it was time for me to go to Miami for resident training, and I lost contact with her for a while. Fortunately, she was able to turn her life around. She eventually went to school for Cosmetology and became a hairdresser. She met a wealthy man, got married, and became a writer.

While Ava was in rehab, I spent my free time poring over the correspondence lessons as fast as I could. My eye was on the prize—resident training in Miami, and then traveling the world in my new career. Of course, just when my life was normal again, I had plans, and was happy—guess what happened? I got a letter.

8   here we go again

DEAR TARA,

Hi! Today was one of those rare days when I gathered all my belongings together and packed up to move. I re–read all your old letters. They made me smile and gave me a good feeling. Now I have a terminal case of melancholy. I'll bet you are dying to find out just why I'm packing (easily explainable). I JOINED THE ARMY. I wanted to (really). In fact, I'm the happiest I've been for quite a while. It is 3:00 a.m., I'm half–drunk, and Pink Floyd is playing on my stereo (quoting 'Pigs on the Wing' by Pink Floyd).

I still love my music, especially the lyrics. I sincerely believe that Utopia is a place where all the radio stations play Pink Floyd all the time.

Do you still care what happens to me? I know that I still care about you, even more than before (seriously). I want to know what you are doing and why you're doing it. As for me, I am now completely insane (I like it). I leave Monday for the army. Most of my friends have ex–communicated me for my decision. So has Lucy.

My daughter is nine months old now and is the cutest baby in the whole world. I decided to spare myself the cost of a divorce and not marry Lucy. I lived with her for nine months. She has admitted to me numerous times that she got pregnant on purpose. I no longer feel any guilt or punish myself for a mistake that I didn't make. I feel that now is the time for me to get on with my life. So it's Adios to Arizona. I love it! (Ha ha).

Tara, I realize that over the course of the last three years I have done little except make myself an ass in your eyes. All I ask is that you remember the enthusiasm we both had two years ago. I remember. Boot camp would be a lot easier to face with your reassurance. Almost like old times. I could almost cry with happiness at the feeling that sentence gives me.

Enough with the mushy stuff, write me! I'm a better human being now. I never really learned to express myself until I became insane. Please give me another chance. My life is different. The pain is gone. But, so are a lot of friendly faces. I need you. I'm sending this little thread design you gave me to prove to you that I kept the faith. I find it impossible to hold without smiling. I want it back please (now you have to write me!) I am 6 foot tall and weigh 180 pounds. My hair and eyes are still brown, amazingly enough. How about you?

Well, I must go for now. Please write me, Tara. I could use a friend.

    Love,

      Trey

P.S. Je t'aime (still)

Here we go again. *Do I allow him to once again turn my world upside down and let him back into my life? Or do I rip up this letter right now and never look back?* Well, if I did the latter, I guess this is where my story would end . . . of course I wrote him back.

And then the unexpected happened. I got a letter from *her*. Yes, that's right, from the mother of his child, Lucy. It was actually a nice letter with no animosity toward me. She just explained the situation as she saw it. I felt empathy for her. Not that I tried to hate her, I just didn't imagine myself relating to or liking her. Especially from Trey's portrayal of her being a scheming and manipulative liar.

She matter–of–fact explained how she had read my last letter and that she knew all about me. She said she was writing me because she didn't want me to get hurt again:

> *I hope I don't sound like some crazed wife or jealous lover and that this letter made some sense. I just want you to know that Trey loves me and is going to marry me when he returns from basic. I don't want you to be led on again. Please prove me wrong and write to Trey only as a friend, like he said you would. I hope we can meet each other someday and be friends. I know you'll always be a part of Trey's life, as well as mine.*
> *Sincerely yours,*
> *Lucy*

I didn't know if I wanted to be a part of either one of their lives right then. Had Trey lied to me? Was she lying about their impending marriage? Why did she really write to me? I didn't know what to think but felt I still needed to get to the truth—I needed answers. I wrote another letter. This one was worded carefully. I was not trying to be accusatory or judgmental, I just wanted answers. I sent the letter to his Army address and waited.

A month later, I received this letter:

> *Dear Tara,*
>
> *Here I am back at boot camp. I wasn't sure I should send the accompanying letter, but it's a good explanation (not excuse). I really hope you will consider writing me. I need you. I promise I will improve my honesty . . .*

> *Dear Tara,*
>
> *I received your letter about three weeks ago. I waited this long to answer it for several reasons, the main one being lack of any free time while in basic. I hope this clears up any questions you may have about my situation.*
>
> *Yes, Lucy does think I will marry her. She's wrong. She doesn't think I know she's pregnant again (without my consent). I do love her, but she's too much of an unstable partner to trust. I know my letter to you came at a time of need, but I asked for no commitments and I made none. I will admit that I wrote to you as more than a friend. I told you I loved you and I meant it. Though we may never be lovers or husband and wife, we will always be more than friends to me.*
>
> *My problem is that I would rather lie to someone than hurt them. I plan to stop that. Over the next few months my actions will seem cold and uncaring by most people (probably even you). I'm sorry. Life is very cold and uncaring at times. I am not leading you on. What I want from you is what you want to give. I'm not very good at giving, but now I will give you the truth.*

I love you because you loved me when there was no reason in my mind to love me at all. I love you because you are a survivor. I want you to be happy doing whatever you're doing. I still feel protective of you. I think we communicate very well with each other. I refuse to give up hope that our paths will cross again (possibly uniting).

This letter is meant to be explanatory. All emotions put forth into it are real. This is not a love letter. It is your right to decide how you feel, and act accordingly. Lucy and I must do the same. I feel no guilt for the actions I will take. I will write both of you. I'm going to need someone who will make me feel that I am needed. You can go on with your life, Tara, and I can go on with mine. Hopefully, someday we will both see that this wasn't just wasted time.

I then proceeded to receive three more letters from him, three days in a row. He was sending me a letter a day until I wrote back. I wanted to let him sweat it out a little. I didn't know if I should trust him again. I didn't want to get hurt again. But I still loved him, unconditionally, and forgave him of everything—I wrote back. This is his reply:

Dear Tara,

I was so excited to get your letter that I am now doing the insane. I'm writing this at 11:00 p.m. when our wake up is at 4:00 a.m. I joined the army because I felt my life had hit a dead–end. I wanted to do something new and adventurous.

I have no intention of misleading you. Lucy is now threatening to sue me for child support. Remember when I said my actions would be seen as cruel? Well, I can handle one accidental pregnancy, but when she chooses to intentionally get pregnant again and I've warned her of the consequences, then it is she who has made the decision.

I will pay child support, but Lucy and I are through. Write to ask her yourself, if you wish. She's now five months pregnant. I wish to God I'd learned my lesson the first time. I'm going to be a father twice over before I am 20 years old. Oh well, at least I don't have to worry about being sterile.

Take extra good care of yourself (for me).
Love,
*　　Trey*

He continued to write almost daily until I had received thirty letters in a month and a half. He wanted to earn my trust again. He wanted to show me he could stick to something. He slowly and surely started winning me back—wearing me down—until I fell hopelessly in love with him.

Dear Trey,

*Hi! I got two letters from you today! I always feel so good when I get letters from you. I love you so much! Yes, those words have quite an effect on me too. I've always had the feeling that we were destined to be together. Somehow I've managed to keep the faith. I believe in **us**.*

Lucy sent you cookies? Isn't there a saying, 'the way to a man's heart is through his stomach?' I honestly can say I don't know what to tell you about your situation. It's a delicate one and one that I cannot compare to anything I've been involved in. However you handle it, I will support you. But as far as suggestions or advice, you're on your own.

I LOVE YOU! I could say that a million times and never get sick of it. I think about you all the time. I'm always fantasizing about the future and how it will be to see you again. I guess I daydream a lot. Maybe someday, you won't just be a fantasy in my future; you'll be a reality in my present. For now, though intangible, you're about as real as they come.

You are the BEST letter writer I've ever met! I sincerely mean that, Trey. I feel very lucky just knowing you. When you're rich & famous, can I have your autograph? Seriously, it would be nice to see you again.

I turned in my written resignation at work Friday. Everyone knows I'm leaving now, the secret's out. My last day is Friday, March 15th. It's getting closer and closer. Four more weeks, what about you? Do you know your military orders yet?

I want to know all about your life! How are your mom and Chad? What does your dad do now? Do you like being a father? How does it feel? Do you like kids in general? What were you doing before you joined the army?

I care about you, Trey! I want to know everything I can about you. I'll do anything for you. Maybe someday we can spend some time together. We can get-to-know each other all over again.

Until that happens, I'll continue writing you and hoping.

I love you,
Tara

P.S. Take care of yourself! Don't let the Army work you too hard—if and when I see you, I want you to be in one piece. Promise me you'll come out of there alive, okay?

Many of his letters talked about the daily grind of military life, but he always made sure to end them on a personal note, usually very personal.

I love you. I am not a goal or a dream. I am real. I am yours if you'll have me. I can think of no reason for you to go through this all over again if you don't trust me. We won't ever have a chance if I can't earn your trust. I must be more reliable in turn. I wouldn't be up at 0330 writing you if it wasn't important. You may be independent, but you need someone. I want to be that someone. I won't tell you what to do or how to do it. All I can tell you is how I feel and what I want. I love you. I want you to be happy. I want to be with you. Whether or not you can be happy and be with me remains to be seen. Most of all, I want you to be happy. If I ever do something that hurts you, tell me so I can remedy the situation.

In another:

I love you. It kills me to write only those three words when I feel so much more. When you're in love, long distance communication is a bitch! You know what I mean. I know how you feel as far as trusting me goes. I'd be slow to trust myself also. I'll keep writing and telling you how I feel until there is no doubt in your mind. I love you. I want to be with you. I want you to trust me. I want this so much that I'm willing to wait and earn it. If I have to wait a long time, I understand.

Did you ever get the feeling we're destined for each other? I believe strongly that we are. Maybe I'm just feeling lucky.

You are one of the few people in the world I can communicate with on an equal basis.

Love,

Trey

9   my rose–colored glasses are shattered

THE LETTERS AND OCCASIONAL phone calls continued for two months until mid–March, and then it was time for me to leave for my resident training in Miami. Trey graduated from basic and was sent back to his hometown on recruiting duty for forty-five days before reporting to his new post in Texas.

While I was in Florida and he was in Arizona, we lost track of each other again. I feared he'd gone back to Lucy, so it was easier to give up this time. Besides, I needed to concentrate on my schoolwork. Now I felt like *I* was in basic training. Well, sort of. Classes began at seven thirty every morning, Monday through Friday, and didn't get out until five thirty. The days were long and intense. We had tests every day and were constantly studying. The course matter consisted mostly of geography, ticketing, computer reservations, airport and city codes and other airline industry trivia.

We studied hard, worked hard, and played hard. I was still eighteen and the drinking age in Miami was nineteen, but it didn't slow me down much. I shared an apartment with three other girls from the school, with diverse backgrounds and hometowns—a black girl from Chicago, a racist white chick from Delaware, a tough Latina–Indian from Detroit—and me. Made for interesting group dynamics—not.

Miami wasn't quite what I had pictured. It was warm and tropical, with palm trees everywhere, which was nice. But the bugs—ugh. I'd never seen so many bugs in one place before. We couldn't leave fruit or perishables out for five minutes.

They exterminated once a week and it still wasn't enough. I could put up with the flies, ants and mosquitoes—but I drew the line at flying cockroaches. That's right, the suckers had wings. Some of them were six inches long. Every time after the exterminators had been there, it sounded like we were walking around the apartment on potato chips. The dead roaches were under the carpet, thus crunching under our feet—it was so gross. Okay enough about the bug situation, believe me, I could go on. But you'd probably rather I didn't.

After I'd been there ten days, I started getting bummed that I hadn't heard from Trey yet. I called him from a pay phone and we talked for an hour. "I love you. I miss you," he crooned, in his velvety deep voice. "I'm saving my paychecks and all my leave time so I can visit you—wherever you end up."

I clenched the payphone tight in my hand and squeezed my eyes shut. It was so good to hear his voice. "I miss you too," I sighed. "They work us pretty hard here. I don't have any time off and I don't know where I'll end up. Right now, I have no idea what the future looks like. I just know I want to be a flight attendant with an airline—any airline."

"It's okay, we'll figure it out. You'll make a great flight attendant! I can't wait until you have a job and then you can get me free flights to anywhere in the world," he laughed.

"No, Trey, it doesn't work like that."

"I know, I'm just teasing you. Man, I am so sick of recruiting and filing. It will be better when I get to my new post. I can't stand it here anymore."

"Are you and Lucy getting along?"

"No. We pretty much avoid each other. I go over and help out with the baby when I can, but I'm not staying with Lucy."

Relief flooded my body. I guess a part of me didn't completely trust him because I was afraid he'd go back to her, since he was in his hometown. Besides, she was the mother of his child, whom he adored and talked about, and she was carrying his second child. I think my fears were reasonable.

In fact, I don't know if it's because I'd convinced myself he'd gone back to her, or if it was because I subconsciously wanted to get back at him in some way for hurting me, but whatever it was, I indulged in a vacation romance during my stay in Miami. I was naïve and oh–so–innocent.

Kevin Mead was top in our class, so we studied together—a lot. He was super smart, which impressed me. He was also black, which intrigued me. I grew up in an all–white neighborhood, went to a white school, and never personally knew any people of color—until my roommate from Chicago. Like I said, I was naïve. I had also lived a sheltered life in "Small town, USA." Naturally, I was curious about him, his culture, and his beliefs.

Kevin was different from me and I was full of questions about those differences, even stupid questions like, "Why do black people lay out in the sun when they're already tan?" Yet, he never laughed at me, just remained patient and kind. If he was humoring me, it didn't show.

My curiosity began to grow into affection for him, and he felt the same way about me. Eventually, we spent all our free time together and stopped hanging around our circle of acquaintances. My roommates gave me a hard time about him, and I began to realize that most people we met were against mixed–race couples. I'd never encountered prejudice before and did not take it well. Walking down the street together, we'd hear people yell "zebras" or "salt & pepper," usually infused with obscenities. Now I knew what discrimination felt like and I was outraged by it. How could people treat each other so cruelly? Apparently, my life had been a bit too sheltered. This was a very eye–opening experience for me.

Darla, my racist–and–proud–of–it roommate, informed me that her grandfather was a member of the KKK. Was that supposed to scare me? My reputation soon changed from "goody–two–shoes" to "class slut." I had become a social outcast and couldn't believe how two–faced and hate–filled these people were. And worse, they were my age. This was the mid–1980s—I thought the civil rights movement had passed.

Dad called with the news, "Your new baby sister was born!"

"Wow, that's great! What did you name her?"

"Jenny."

"Very cool. I can't wait to come back and meet her, just as soon as I'm done with resident training here. Just two more weeks!"

Upon graduating from the school, I found out the airline industry would never hire me as a flight attendant because I wouldn't pass their physical—which requires all employees to have full hearing in both ears. Having been a hundred percent deaf in my right ear since birth, this presented a problem. *Great, I couldn't have found out about this sooner?*

Instead, I was placed as a reservationist at a resort hotel in the Poconos, Pennsylvania. By this point, I had lost all contact with Trey. The resort of my employment was famous for their honeymoon suites, so couples were all around me, which got old and depressing fast.

I had no car, no TV, no social life, and spent most of my free time in my rented room on–site. I definitely had a lot of time to think. It was May, the weather was cold, and I was lonely. Plus, I hated my new job. I had a mean boss, and hotel reservations was boring. The stage was set, and the timing couldn't have been better when my sweet prince came for me, once again . . .

10 reunited

TREY HAD WRITTEN ME five letters but had sent them to my dad's address because he didn't know where I was. Dad took his time forwarding them to my mom, who in turn had to forward them to me. But in my dad's defense, he was busy with a newborn.

I met Jenny before relocating to Pennsylvania, when she was nineteen days old and I was a month away from turning nineteen years old. She was beautiful and precious, and I tried to imagine what it would be like if she were my baby. After all, Trey already had a one-year old *and* another one on the way. As I stared at the tiny bundle in my arms, I was more than glad she was my sister and not my child. I knew I wasn't ready to be a mother yet, and felt I understood why Trey had joined the army. The enormous responsibility of raising children must have been overwhelming for him.

By the time Trey's letters reached me, I received all five at once. No longer confused, I knew my heart belonged to him, and I felt ashamed of my Miami romance with Kevin.

Dear Tara,

Hi. I know this letter is long overdue and I hope you haven't given up on me yet. The last two months have been turbulent ones for me. I'm not trying to excuse my lack of communication, simply explain it. My new unit here keeps me very busy. Five days after I arrived, we left for a 15-day tactical exercise... I want you to know how devoted I am to you. Nothing can stop me. That is, provided that you can forgive me, yet again.

My newborn son weighed in at 7 lbs 9 oz and was 21 inches long. I haven't seen a picture of him yet, but Lucy says he looks just like me (she's playing with my emotions again). There is a lot of family pressure on me to marry her. I will not. I still love you. I will always love you. You are still on the top of my list of the best things in life. I want you so much (quoting 'Heaven' by Bryan Adams)

Tell me what you're doing now. Are you happy? I want you to be happy. Tell me what you need. I will do anything and everything I can to help. I think about you all the time. The song "Heaven" makes me think about you strongly. I imagine what it will be like when I finally do get to hold you 'here in my arms.'

Please write back. I don't know where you are, but I will continue to write to your dad's address and pray that he forwards these. I love you, Tara. Take care of yourself.

TNT . . . you light my fuse

Love,

Trey

Dear Tara,

Hi! I'm starting this letter while on my lunch break. This morning we had land mine training using real live M-15 anti–tank and M-16 anti-personnel mines. I was scared at first, but it gave me a lot of confidence in the equipment.

This part of Texas is right in the middle of tornado alley. I saw my first tornado about two weeks ago. It was 15 miles away. They're an awesome sight. I remember you writing about being in the Midwest before. Have you ever seen a tornado? Anyway, today's weather is the same as it was that day. I've been watching for them. The National Weather service has issued a tornado watch.

This is an okay post. They have lots of activities here. I'm on my company's softball team. We're 1–1 so far, I play first base. It's fun and it takes my mind off some of the day–to–day pressures. My hair is still very short, even by Army standards. We get a new first–sergeant next Monday. I hear his haircut policy is not so strict. I will grow mine longer (quoting 'Satisfaction Guaranteed' by The Firm).

Will you wait for me for years? Four years? That thought kills me. I need to be reassured or at least know how you feel. You know that I love you and I know that you love me. Now I want you to know how strong my love is. My highest goal in life is to see you again. I'm doing everything possible to have you by my side. It will be some time in the next four months, if your schedule permits. I will have saved enough money by then for airfare to take me wherever you are, and I will have accrued ten days of leave.

I love you! I can't wait to look into your beautiful blue eyes again and see the love and understanding. You understand me better than anyone I know, even my mother (especially my mother). I want to make you proud of me. I want to take care of you, protect you. I've become addicted to your love.

Do you mind if I take a sentimental look at the past? Do you remember our first kiss, when you and your mother said goodbye to us in Seattle? That was the first time I ever kissed a girl. How ironic that these feelings have grown from that one kiss. I know that was the origin of my love for you now. First impressions really are more accurate. You were the only girl for me then, and you're the only girl for me now.

I love you. I'll write again tomorrow. Be careful.

Love,
Trey

Dear Tara,

Hi! I didn't get a chance to mail yesterday's letter, so you'll most likely get both of these at the same time. I'm curious as hell to find out where you are and what you're doing. I hope you're not too far away. Not that it matters. I'll get to you no matter where you go. I hope your new job is living up to your expectations. Mine hasn't. If I had a choice, I'd get out right now. But I'm a soldier and I can live up to my commitments. It's not just a job, it's a good old–fashioned screwing.

Even if you don't write back, I will continue writing you. I'm very determined. I will allow nothing to stop me. I'm going to get to you, or get you to me. That's inevitable. I've let go too many times in the past. This is not going to be a repeat. This time I'm going to make it happen.

Sometimes I wonder why you're still so good to me after all the pain I've caused you. Why do you care for such an unstable and inconsiderate person? You've never done anything to hurt me, and remembering my behavior in the past still causes me to wince. And what's more, you make me feel special. I don't understand, but I love you for it. I know I have many faults and I'm trying to rid myself of them. I want to change for you, because you deserve no less than the best. I want you to do me a favor. When I start to mess up, I want you to tell me about it and not mince words. That may not be your style, but every now and then I need a good kick in the ass to wake me up. I don't mean to be inconsiderate, but sometimes I'm just not myself. I can change. I can talk about my problems now. I will do anything for you.

As much as I hate to admit it, at heart I am still just a boy. I have maturing to do before I can call myself a man. You are so much more mature than I am. I'm scared of losing you to a man, a real man. All my brains and muscles are no match for the maturity a man has to offer. Don't get me wrong; I do have a lot to offer. I will love you for the rest of my life. As far as personal improvements, things can only get better. The best is yet to come. I know I'm the one for you. I'm eager to prove how good I can be to you. Nobody will ever love you more than I do.

I've got to go to bed now. I love you. I know I will dream about you tonight. I'm looking forward to it. Take care.
   Love,
    Trey

Dear Tara,
Hi! Today has been a good day. I met my new squad leader. He seems to know his stuff, which is important because my life depends on him in combat. I love you. You should receive the letter I sent Friday in the next few days and who knows, I might get some mail from you before you get this letter. Well, return mail or not, I'm going to write until I strike terminal writer's block. I will allow nothing to stop me. My love is on the verge of overpowering. Stubborn like myself, it will adjust at your slightest whim. I'm still as patient and cunning as ever. Make no mistake about it, one way or another I'm going to get you.

I'm afraid it's time to say good night. I enjoy ending the day with a letter to you. I'm living for the day they shout my name at mail call. Oh, I did dream about you last night and I'll have another one tonight. I hope you don't mind. I love you. Take care.
   Love,
    Trey

P.S. Sorry this letter is so short but I don't have much free time tonight. I'll write more tomorrow.

Dear Tara,
Hi! So much happened today and I don't have much time so I'll try to include everything. My day at the range went well. I got to fire 200 rounds on

the M60 machine gun and two live 90 mm rounds as well. One round tore off the back–end of a pickup (at 750 meters)! I was the first one to hit it. I was ecstatic! My ears rang for an hour. We won our softball game tonight, 4–2. We are now 2–2 so far. Oh, I also had to help put out two grass fires caused by the ammo. We found a live dud at one site and beat feet out of there. It blew up five minutes later then we ran back and put it out quickly. I love you. I've got to get some sleep now. Please take care. I'll write again tomorrow.

> *Love,*
> *Trey*

Dear Tara,

Hi. I got your first letter today. It concerned me. All I could think about all day was you and your situation. I have some serious questions about us. Finally, I have one very serious proposition.

Don't you dare give up, Tara! I know you're tough enough to handle anything the world throws at you. Make the best of whatever you have and drive on. Reading your letter made me quit feeling sorry for myself. However, it didn't arouse an over–abundance of sympathy for you either. Look around you. Think of the freedom you have, all the different things you can do if you really want to.

"At one time I thought I wanted you, now I'm not so sure." I don't know what to say. That sentence made me want to cry. I've gone as far as rejecting you before. You didn't give up. I'm not going to either. All I ask is that you don't give up on me now. If you want me to leave you alone, I will reluctantly comply. I, on the other hand, know

*exactly what I want. I will tell you time and time
again, I want you.*

*What has happened to me has happened. So
what? Much worse will probably happen in my
life. I could fall out of bed tomorrow and die, so
why worry about Central America? Lucy has the
kids and as far as I'm concerned, they're hers.
She is an able mother. I had no part in planning
their conception. Should I allow her to force me
into marriage? No, I will help support them, but if
she thinks they need a father figure that badly,
she'll have to recruit one. I feel no guilt. I grew up
without my father. I never felt ripped–off.*

*What about you? When do I plan to spend
time with you? Well, you asked for this… I want to
marry you, NOW. I want to spend the rest of my
life with you. Of course we can make it work.
Consider that when you decide what you want.
This is no joke. Just say the word and I'll buy you
a round trip ticket. You can come down and stay
with me for a month or so. At the end of that time,
you can fly off to wherever you want, or we can
get married.*

*This offer will stand as long as I am alive.
Life here is not easy. I work long, hard hours.
There are no jobs for Airline Reservationists here.
It's not much of an offer, I realize. I love you and I
want to be with you for the rest of my life. If you
want me to call you and repeat this over the
phone, I will.*

*I'm already up for promotion in June. The
Army pays the cost for shipping a spouse and
furniture overseas for all soldiers grade E-4 and
above. My second tour will be overseas. How does
Germany sound to you? (Okay, so that last
paragraph was a cheap shot. I couldn't resist). I*

am up for promotion though. My squad leader
says it's almost a sure thing.
   How do you end a letter like this? I love you.
I'm sorry you are not happy. I hope things get
better for you. Don't feel pressured by my
proposition. I won't kill myself if you say no. But
do take it seriously. You have so many paths open
to you. I want you to choose the right one for you
(I'll keep my fingers crossed). Be careful, and
remember, if you need help any time, anywhere,
call me. I'll always love you.
  Love,
    Trey

  P.S. Please lighten up a bit in your next letter.

There was no "next letter." By the time I received his
sixth letter my resistance had dissipated. I was putty in his
hands. I made a long-distance call to the United States
Army Base at Fort Hood, Texas, and tracked him down.
He repeated everything he had written in the letter, just
like he said he would.

"Tara, I meant what I wrote in my letter. I want to
marry you! I've always known you were the one for me
ever since I caught my courage when we were kids. And
here I am catching my courage once more. I'm sorry to
have to do this over the phone . . ." he paused and cleared
his throat. Then in a softened voice he simply said, "Tara,
you're my best friend. I want to spend the rest of my life
with you. Will you marry me?"

Happy tears filled my eyes as I blurted, "Yes! Of
course I'll marry you!" And just like that, we were
engaged. I was giddy.

Just before he hung up, he said, "See you soon,
fiancée," and the line went dead.

As I mouthed the word 'fiancée' over and over I went into a sort of dazed stupor. We had made plans so quickly that it felt surreal to me. It was impulsive and maybe even rash, but I was beyond caring. *Perhaps I was the insane one now?*

Like I said, I was looking for a way out and here it was, my golden opportunity. I hated it in Pennsylvania. I'd spent my nineteenth birthday alone, feeling sorry for myself, and talking to my mom long distance for nearly two hours—collect. The job, the place, the people, everything there thoroughly depressed me. Besides, I was positive my boss conspired against me. I felt his unceasingly icy stares boring into my skull. The man positively hated me, and I have no idea why. I decided the logical thing to do was to follow my heart—and I did.

The next day I gave my resignation letter to my boss and booked a flight to Dallas. When I resigned, my boss took it well. He simply said, "The hotel business is not for everyone, Tara. You made a wise decision; no hard feelings."

I gave him a quick nod in reply. We shook hands, and I was out of there. Then I had to run some errands and close my bank account. I spent the evening calling my family and friends.

Mom was supportive and took the news of my engagement quite well. Her biggest concern seemed to be that I was leaving a job and didn't have another job to go to. Jack asked me questions about Trey and told me he wanted only the best for me. Then he added, "And keep your money to yourself!" I felt so loved, so cared for. I had the support of my family and friends as I got ready to embark on my next adventure.

The next day I packed everything I owned (which fit into two suitcases and a garment bag) and checked out. I took a taxi to the bus station, a Trailways bus from Pocono, Pennsylvania to New York City's Port Authority

Bus Terminal, and two taxis to LaGuardia airport (the first one broke down). On the bus ride, I enjoyed the scenic countryside vistas of deer, trees, and lush, green hills throughout New Jersey, as I stared dreamily out the window, imagining my new life with Trey.

At around ten o'clock that night I arrived at the TWA ticket counter travel–weary, but still upbeat. However, my mood quickly changed from weary to wary when I realized the ticket counter was closed. *Now what was I supposed to do?* My flight wasn't until the next morning and I couldn't walk around the airport, to kill time or look for a safe, cozy spot to sleep, with three heavy bags. I wouldn't be able to check my bags until the ticket counter re–opened at five thirty the next morning.

The terminal was deserted; I was alone and afraid. I wanted to just curl up in a seat and fall asleep, but I was worried my bags would be stolen while I slept. I began to look for a place to hide my luggage so I could get some sleep. I ended up locking my belongings in a bathroom stall in the women's restroom. I figured they'd be safe there for a couple of hours at least. After all, it was the middle of the night, and no one was around anyway. But I couldn't have been more wrong.

Fifteen minutes after I shoved my luggage into the stall and had found a semi–comfortable row of seats to lay down on twenty feet away, I woke to screaming, shouting and cursing, coming from the direction of the women's restroom. I cautiously walked toward the door, with great uneasiness, when one of my suitcases was hurled out like a projectile missile.

Suddenly, adrenaline and false bravery coursing through me, I marched into the restroom to confront my would–be luggage–napper (yes, all 101 pounds of me). "What the hell do you think you're doing with my luggage?" I yelled, as threateningly as I could.

"This is your luggage? You can't leave this in here! You stupid girl! Get this out of here! Go on, get it out right now!" yelled the burly cleaning woman, much more threatening and menacing than anything I could ever hope to accomplish.

She was furious with me and shouted expletives, trying to hurry me along, as she watched me pull my luggage out of there, and run as fast as my scrawny arms and legs could muster, my heart pounding so loud I could hear it beating in my head.

Thus, I was forced to spend the night in the terminal lobby sitting on my suitcases, stacked on top of each other, because I was paranoid they'd get stolen if I fell asleep—I slept with one eye open, so to speak. Yes, it can be done.

I boarded my flight at 6:25 the next morning. My final destination was to the waiting arms of my betrothed, in Texas, but I would have to take another bus from the airport in Dallas to the bus station in Killeen, another one hundred and fifty miles, before my journey would be over. Another long day awaited me; I was exhausted from guarding my luggage all night, so I slept on the flight as much as possible.

My bus finally pulled into the Killeen station just before four o'clock. Trey arrived via taxi about ten minutes later, enough time for me to freshen up a little and wash the sweat and grime off my face. It was a hot and humid June day and the air was oppressive. *This will take some getting used to,* I thought, as I sat on my suitcase waiting. I watched the taxi pull up, but couldn't be sure it was Trey, so I stayed where I was. As he got out of the car, while I stayed sitting on my suitcase, I sheepishly grinned up at him. My knees felt weak.

"How about a hug?" he asked, as he leaned toward me. When I stood up to hug him, I tripped over my garment bag. *Awkward!* I gave him a good hug and a quick kiss, but I didn't have a clue what to say to him.

"Sorry I'm so hot and sticky. I'm a mess and exhausted from two days of traveling," was about all I could manage.

We got in the taxi and headed toward Fort Hood, his army base. He gave me the grand tour while we waited for his friend, Freddy Miranda, to get off duty at five thirty. Freddy drove us to his house in a brown 1978 Chevy Camaro Z28, so I had to sit on Trey's lap. I savored that moment and reveled in the feeling of his warm body pressed close to my back. I could feel his breath on the back of my neck. This was real; we were finally together after all this time. In my reverie–induced euphoria I barely noticed that it was humid, 110 degrees outside, and I was drenched in my own sweat.

When we arrived at Freddy's house, a small, mint–green, one-bedroom cottage, he introduced me to his live–in girlfriend, Brenda Babbitt. We chatted and watched TV for a while, and then they went out for the evening. Trey and I were dead tired, so we took the two couch cushions and put them on the floor, side–by–side. Brenda gave us a sheet and blanket to use before she left. Once the makeshift bed was made up, I just looked at him like, *now what?* We were alone, and I suddenly felt modest and didn't know how to act.

He just smiled and said, "Well, I'm going to bed." He took off his t–shirt and pants and got under the blanket. I turned out the light, took off my blouse and skirt, and crawled in beside him, wearing a tank top and panties. I was trembling and very nervous. He kissed me ever so softly and held me for a while. He asked me if I wanted to make love, but I pointed out that we had no birth control, so we shouldn't. He agreed and softly tickled my back and shoulders as I drifted off to sleep in his 'spoon' embrace.

Earlier that evening Brenda asked us, "So, you two gettin' married? How'd ya meet?"

Trey and I exchanged a look. I took a deep breath and said, "Well, we've actually known each other since we were three. We were best friends when we were kids, but Trey moved away when we were ten. We kept in touch growing up, but—"

"Yes, we're getting married," Trey interjected, then put his arm around me protectively. I gazed at him quizzically as I pinched myself to make sure I wasn't dreaming.

Saturday, we had a BBQ at Freddy and Brenda's, and a few guys from the base came over. It gave me a chance to meet Trey's friends and get to know Freddy and Brenda a little better.

Freddy was a likable guy. At nineteen years of age, his black hair was of the short military–buzz–cut grade. He had dark brown eyes, brown skin, and a solid, muscular build of about five foot seven. Raised in Miami, Freddy (like Trey) had joined the army shortly after graduating high school, at eighteen. He was the third oldest of seven children in his family, and the first one to graduate from high school.

His parents emigrated from Cuba, lacked a formal education, and spoke little English. They all had their hopes pinned on Freddy to be successful, and Freddy did not want to disappoint. He worked hard and took being a soldier seriously, yet he had an affable personality. He was instant friends with everyone he met, and always the life of the party.

Brenda, on the other hand, was Freddy's polar opposite: she had shoulder length, dishwater blonde hair that was feathered and parted in the middle. She had a high forehead, light green eyes, nearly translucent pale white skin, and a small, thin, wiry frame. She was a five-foot-two bundle of volatile energy.

She tended to be hotheaded and told people she'd just met that she was a fiery hillbilly from Arkansas. Brenda left home at sixteen, and now, at just eighteen, had a wisdom that comes with a hard life. And she cursed worse than most truckers.

Freddy was manning the grill and called out, "Hey Tara, do you want a hamburger or a hot dog?"

"Um, I'll come over there and decide," I called back.

"Hey, hon? While you're over there, will you grab me a beer?" Trey asked.

"Sure babe," I winked at him. I walked toward the ice chest and my sandal fell off just as I stepped on a hot coal that had fallen out of the BBQ grill. "OWWW!" I shouted before I could control myself. Embarrassed and trying to be brave, but also being the incredible pain wimp that I was, I burst into tears anyway. I felt the pain was unbearable.

Trey rushed to my side, "Tara! Are you okay? Here, it's okay. Come on, I've got you now." He led me to a lawn chair then quickly got some ice. I began to calm down as he took care of me.

"Hey Tara, just walk it off! You're okay!"

"You're fine, that's nothin'!"

"Suck it up!" I could hear the teasing shouts and laughter of the guys, which made me want to disappear.

But Trey just leaned over and whispered in my ear, "I'm right here. I'll always be here for you." He somehow knew that I had a low pain threshold—and that this was no laughing matter.

A few hours later we all went to a local dance club. But my foot was still throbbing, and I was limping; dancing wasn't happening, not for me. Yet, Trey was unfazed, held me up and danced three slow songs with me anyway.

"Crazy for You," by Madonna, came on and I sang it in his ear, getting all mushy and sentimental. He paid attention to me like I was the only one in the entire place all evening; thus, an amazing 'first date.'

We had a long, personal and serious talk about sex and what it meant to us. We shared our sexual pasts and our expectations. I told him how I had lost my virginity at sixteen. It only happened once and I broke up with the guy the next day, but it happened. Once it's gone, you can't get it back.

I was nervous, and scared to have sex with him, and asked him to be patient with me—he would need to go slow and be gentle. I wanted him to know that I was not afraid of him but that I needed him to understand that certain things might trigger unpleasant memories. It was difficult for me to explain, to get the words out, but I think he got the message.

A few nights later, still at Freddy and Brenda's, Trey and I made love for the first time. We were on the couch cushions, on the floor, in the living room—and it didn't matter. I was finally with the man I had been fantasizing about for nearly five years, someone I had known for sixteen years.

I was nervous, but he was gentle and reassuring, and I loved him all the more for it. It seemed right, perfect, like how my first time should have been—with two people who are completely in love. And, by the way, *Wow!* No wonder there was so much hype around sex. Being with Trey was incredible. His body was a drug and I was hooked.

11   playing house

THAT WEEKEND WE bought a newspaper to look up rentals. We found a furnished, two–bedroom, singlewide mobile home for rent, just down the road from Freddy & Brenda's. The landlady thought Trey and I were married, and I didn't correct her. She was old, so I figured what harm would it do to let her think we were a moral couple living together in holy wedlock? Besides, we **were** engaged! She said we could move in the following Saturday.

Monday, Brenda took me to the Health Department to make an appointment to get on the pill; this was all new to me. Here I was about to play house and live like a grown up, engaged to be married, at barely nineteen, when I still felt like a kid myself. I had no idea what I was doing.

I stayed with Freddy and Brenda alone the rest of the week because Trey had to stay in the barracks a few more nights. He was required to get permission from his sergeant before being allowed to move off base. We visited him at the barracks Tuesday and Wednesday, and went to a picnic and softball game Thursday. They had sack races, boxing, heaps of food and beer, and kids all over the place. It was a fun, festive, family atmosphere. I tried to take pictures, but my camera died; it needed a new battery. Friday, we went to the lake, so the week went by fairly fast.

I woke up early Saturday morning with a mixture of butterflies and excitement—it was moving day. I was about to move into my own place with my fiancé; it was a bit surreal. Brenda drove me around to various thrift stores and flea markets, so I could pick up some used dishes, cookware, silverware, sheets, towels, and various necessities. I spent the remainder of the day cleaning the trailer, unpacking, and organizing to make the place as homey as I could.

The trailer was old and shabby, and the furniture threadbare and gaudy, so I had my work cut out for me. The sofa and matching chair were a worn-out brown plaid fabric–weave, the kitchen table was tan with rusty metal table legs, and the kitchen chairs were pea green vinyl with tears in the seats and some of the stuffing falling out.

There were also a couple of dusty old lamps, and the dressers were built–into the walls. Each of the two bedrooms had a box spring with a lumpy mattress on top, a twin in one and a full in the other. The kitchen housed a 1940s looking white refrigerator, gas stove top, and an old gas oven, with a small amount of mustard yellow Formica countertop space. Frankly, everything looked as aged and old as our landlady, Mrs. Strickland.

Our first night there we played monopoly with Freddy and Brenda, our first guests in our humble new abode. I lost quickly because I landed on Boardwalk and went bankrupt to Trey. I also didn't feel well and had a sore throat; I guessed I was coming down with a cold, so I excused myself and went to bed early. I listened to the cicadas singing as I felt their music lulling me to sleep, and I soon drifted off into a restless slumber.

The next day was Father's Day. I woke up at seven due to coughing, but Trey slept in 'til ten. I made him breakfast and a homemade Father's Day card that said I'd do 'anything' for him on his special day. I knew it would be a difficult day for him because his children were in Phoenix with their mother, and he hadn't even met his newborn son yet.

I wanted to be as supportive and understanding as possible. But he was in a strange and feisty mood; when I went into the bedroom to change, he came in and did a wrestling hold on me. Then he hid my shirt so I couldn't get dressed. He flirted and played games until we finally made love.

Later, he called his family from the payphone at the market down the street, because we didn't have a phone line yet, while I went to the Laundromat with Brenda. When I got back, he looked sad. He was struggling with his feelings about his children. He agonized over leaving them, "I haven't even met my son yet. He's already six weeks old. Hell, I didn't even get a say in naming him. His name is Steven, by the way."

What could I say? I just wrapped my arms around him and leaned my head on his shoulder. I gave him time with his thoughts and to grieve the time he was missing with his babies.

I was patient and understanding, and even tried to be objective. After a while, he opened up to me and shared his internal struggle, "I joined the army because I was stuck. Lucy and I weren't getting along at all, and I just couldn't take it anymore. But I miss my daughter terribly, to be honest, more than I thought I would. She was still just a baby last time I saw her. And now I have a son . . ." his voice trailed off and he held his head in his hands.

"Tara, I don't know what to do. I have to stay here because of my commitment to the army, but it's killing me. I want to see my kids. I want to raise my kids."

"Maybe you can get a pass or leave to visit them?"

"Nah, the army doesn't work like that."

"Maybe your mom could bring them to us for a visit?"

"And then what? I get to see them for a lousy weekend and then they go right back to *her*."

"We could fight her for custody. And I could adopt them when we get married! Trey, I want to help you raise your kids. I want to be a family with you—"

"Stop it, Tara. You don't understand. I mean, thank you, that's wonderful of you to offer, but there's no way we're getting those kids away from Lucy; not unless it's over her cold, dead body."

"That can be arranged!" I said in the most sinister voice I could muster, with a wink.

Trey laughed, but his smile didn't reach his eyes. He looked at the floor and sighed. I could see he was hurting, and clearly torn.

It broke my heart, but I had to say it. I had to say what we both knew had to happen. "You should be with her. You should be marrying Lucy, not me. You need to be with your children, and they need their father. They need you. I don't—not really. I'm just one person. I can take care of myself. I can't ask you to walk out on your family for me. That's too much to sacrifice; too many innocent lives affected."

He looked at me and I could see the pain in his eyes, but also the realization that I was right. After all, his mother had been pressuring him for months to "do the right thing" and marry Lucy. She was the mother of his children. They deserved a father. How could I compete with that? How selfish would I have to be to ignore that? I told him my being here was a mistake and that I needed to move out.

"What? No! You can't leave! You're giving up—wait—we'll figure something out. There has to be a way. I love you, Tara."

He convinced me to stay, to do a trial period so we could really get to know each other. Both of us agreed to put one hundred percent effort into the relationship. He needed this before he could make an informed decision about which path to choose. He said that at the end of a month, if we still wanted a future together, then he would tell Lucy, and marry me.

I was so in love with him, and love makes us do stupid things, right? I felt that if I lost him, I'd be nothing. I needed him; the thought of losing him was devastating. I was so confused … and so very young.

Trey understood me better than anyone, knew me better than I knew myself, and loved me anyway. He knew my deepest fears, worries and insecurities. He accepted my flaws, vulnerabilities and quirks, and never asked me to change. He knew the real me—and wanted me anyway. That was pretty heady stuff. That, and the fact that we'd known each other since we were three, that we had a shared history, made him difficult to walk away from.

I quickly got a job with the local weekly newspaper, *The Killeen Times,* as a proofreader. Apparently, all those A's in high school English paid off. It was a small staff, so I was also the receptionist. Later on, I got promoted to columnist after I wrote a news article about Trey's tandem parachute jump. It's a cool story, actually. Trey's mom was friends with Ted Strong, of Strong Enterprises. Ted was the inventor of the "tandem skydiving system" and a parachute manufacturer. He built a parachute that was big enough to carry the weight of two people strapped together, allowing the student to be attached to a tandem certified instructor. It was still a fairly new concept, and Trey got to try it out with Ted Strong himself. It was an exciting day.

My newspaper Editor–in–Chief loved the story, discovered I could write, gave me a raise and my own weekly column, called "Tara's Corner." I sent my columns back home every week and my family said that people would be shocked if they knew a nineteen-year-old wrote some of those articles, as they sounded so mature. Yeah? Well I didn't feel mature those days.

I often wondered what I was still doing there. Trey talked more and more about Lucy, and about his mom's pressuring him to marry her; his whole family was putting pressure on him. He wanted to support his children, but he was also feeling the obligatory strain of making them legitimate. Time was running out and he had to choose. I knew that if he chose me, it wouldn't be right. He'd always be haunted with abandoning his children. We would always live with that shadow over us.

We did the only thing we could do—we broke up. We decided that Lucy and the kids would come out in August and that Trey and Lucy would get married by the local Justice of the Peace. That way, he would go up in pay grades and be able to support a family.

But then he talked me into the preposterous. He asked me to stay—as his friend. He wanted me to meet her. I was still his best friend and he wanted me to meet his children. He somehow convinced me—and Lucy—that this was all well and good and normal. Yes, he was that persuasive.

Lucy called me the next day. She wanted to make sure the relationship was really over between Trey and I, and that he was actually going to marry her. The irony is that I liked her—she sounded nice on the phone, and she was hurt and confused. Funny, we might have been friends—if only she weren't about to take away the man I loved forever.

I was hopeless; the thought of never seeing Trey again was just too much to bear. I stayed, against my better judgment. Besides, we had a road trip planned that I didn't want to miss.

12   just friends

FOR THE FOURTH OF JULY, we drove to Muskogee, Oklahoma, for the USPA (United States Parachute Association) Nationals. Believe it or not, it was a fun weekend and we were adjusting pretty well to our new platonic relationship as friends. His mom was there, and Trey had been worried that we wouldn't get along, since she was so close to Lucy. I don't know what he told her, but she was incredibly nice to me. She made me feel comfortable and took the awkwardness away immediately. We all had a fun and festive time and Trey's tandem jump was definitely the highlight of the trip.

We slept in the back of a brown Chevy truck owned by Trey's army buddy, Bobby Patterson. By this time, we had talked endlessly about the fact that Trey needed to marry Lucy. He wanted to do the right thing, so we pledged abstinence.

Evidently, Trey had another agenda that weekend. When he invited Bobby to go to Muskogee with us, I thought he was using Bobby for his truck, so we could get a ride to the USPA Nationals. Bobby lived on the base, but he and Trey weren't that close, and I had never talked to him much before our little road trip.

Well, I was right about the using him for his truck part, but what Trey really wanted was for Bobby to move in with us. We weren't using the second bedroom, Bobby hated living on base, and Trey needed a ride to work every day.

He'd been riding with Freddy so far, but Freddy was sometimes late and a little unreliable, and Trey had gotten in trouble for being late a couple times, so he figured he needed another arrangement. Besides, Bobby had a twenty-inch color TV, compared to the fact that we didn't own a TV at all, and Trey thought it would be better for us to have another person around. He reasoned that if the three of us lived there as roommates, he wouldn't be alone with me as much, and thus not tempted to give into his desires. The lively discussion made for an interesting ride home.

"Hey Patterson, Miranda told me you hate living in the barracks," Trey began.

"Hell yeah I do! Man, I hate all that snoring. I can't sleep in a room with a bunch a guys snorin', it drives me nuts," Bobby quickly replied.

"What if you could live off base, like me and Miranda do, would you?"

"Depends."

"Depends on what?"

"Depends on if I had to pay rent or not, 'cuz I ain't payin' rent."

"Oh. Well, what if you had your own room and you wouldn't have to hear any snoring?"

While laughing, "It seems pretty clear to me that you need me more than I need you. Looks like I'm the one doin' y'all the favor. See, I don't *have to* move out. In fact, I can just get earplugs. But you don't have a ride!

Hell, you need me to get your ass to work every day. Am I right?"

It turns out that Bobby was smarter than Trey gave him credit for. They negotiated that Bobby would give him a ride every day, and not charge for gas, and Trey would let him live with us, and not charge for rent. They both seemed happy with the arrangement, but I was miserable.

Bobby was a privileged white kid from Missouri, with sandy blond hair and hazel eyes. At five ten, the 180-pound eighteen-year-old could have been moderately attractive, if it wasn't for his condescending attitude. He owned a 1978 Chevrolet Silverado 1500 classic truck, and a brand-new TV, and often made comments and snide remarks that quickly let me know he thought he was better than me. He also let us know that his family had money and that he had options when he got out of the army. So why does someone like that join the army in the first place? I had no idea.

A few days after Bobby moved in, and when both my roommates were at the base, I had to light the pilot light on our gas oven. It was around 5 o'clock and I was about to put a TV dinner in the oven. The guys took most of their meals in the mess hall on base, so I had to fend for myself.

I turned on the gas, hunted for a book of matches, found them, and struck the match bringing it to the pilot light. Just then the oven *blew up in my face*! I must have left the gas on too long. I caught a glimpse of my reflection in the kitchen window and saw that my eyebrows and eyelashes were singed off. Wait. *I had no eyebrows!*

In a dazed shock I called Brenda. She drove me to the hospital and they treated me for first and second degree burns in the ER. My right hand and face were burned, and my arm hair, bangs, eyebrows, and eyelashes were singed off. Whoever called Trey didn't give him any details, so he thought the accident was much worse and was panicked by the time he got there; I think he thought I was dying. When he saw that my injuries were minor, he was relieved of course, but a little annoyed too (he rushed and worried for nothing). Once they finished treating my wounds, I was free to go home.

Four days later I flew to Portland, Oregon to be a bridesmaid in my friend, Lisa's, wedding. I hadn't seen much of her since our Europe trip but we had kept in touch. *Great—a bridesmaid with second degree burns on her face, walking down the aisle.* Not one of my better days. Fortunately, all eyes were on the bride, and no one seemed to notice.

When I returned from Portland, my situation with Trey went from bad to worse. We suddenly argued about everything. I couldn't get along with him no matter what I tried to do. He was constantly picking fights with me. I think we were distancing ourselves from each other so it wouldn't hurt as much when it was time to part ways. I supported his decision to marry Lucy. I encouraged it, for the sake of his children. But letting him go didn't mean I loved him any less. It was agonizing.

After an adjustment period, the arguing stopped and we became good friends again. The physical aspect of the relationship had ended, but at least we were getting along. It was hard for me to just be friends, as I couldn't completely let him go; although I knew I had to. I just had this feeling that Trey and I weren't finished. I don't know why, but I refused to believe that I'd never see him again. I actually thought there might be hope for a possible future with him—still. Delusional? Idiotic? Perhaps.

As it got closer to the end of August, Trey and Lucy made plans and changed plans several times. She said because of her work obligations, she wouldn't be able to quit and move out until September. Trey still wanted me to meet her and especially wanted me to meet his children—and he was eager to meet his son, who was nearly four months old. I was strangely curious, so I agreed to stick around and meet them.

Trey and I were getting along exceptionally well. I still felt a profoundly deep connection to him. And occasionally, we would slip and let things get carried away. Like the time we saw "Rambo: First Blood Part II" at the movie theater. When we got home, we played strip poker. *Not helping!* Of course, one thing led to another, and no more platonic friendship.

I was still incredibly attracted to him. I tried to honor our agreement and remain only friends, but we were in close proximity to each other constantly. I felt so guilty, knowing he would be marrying someone else in less than a month. What were we thinking? Yet, nothing felt more right. My body responded to his every touch. Sometimes just being near him filled me with desire. He was forbidden, and I was weak. I couldn't get enough of him. I was a moth drawn to his flame, a junkie drawn to the powerful drug that consumed me.

I gave a month notice at work. It was harder than I thought it would be—as it turned out—I enjoyed my job at the newspaper. In fact, my job with the paper developed my love of writing and I decided to go into Journalism when I finally went to college (more on that later).

Meanwhile, September was an emotional month to get through, as we awaited Trey's impending doom to show up and take him away from me. Okay, maybe he didn't feel doomed, but I definitely did. The new plan was for his mom, Lucy and the kids to show up in two weeks, with a rented moving truck, and all of their furniture and belongings. Trey's mom was only accompanying Lucy to help drive and take care of the kids on the one-thousand-mile trek from Phoenix to Killeen.

Trey still wanted me to stay and meet them, as crazy as that sounded to me, and I still had my job to go to, until they found a replacement. Bobby insisted, "You couldn't pay me enough to stick around for this shit show!" and promised to move out the day before Lucy was scheduled to showed up.

We celebrated the beginning of Labor Day weekend with Freddy, Brenda, and a bunch of guys from the base Friday night, as it was also Freddy's birthday. We went to a local carnival and all that entails—the rides, the games, the cotton candy, and beer—lots of beer. It was easy to disappear in the big group, pretend to have fun, and blend in. No one noticed that I felt wretched and was heartbroken inside.

There was live music and Trey asked me to dance. While slow dancing with him, I couldn't shake the fact that our time together was dwindling. It just made me hold on tighter.

After Freddy and the gang left, we had the trailer to ourselves. Bobby went home to Missouri for the three-day weekend, so I decided to act on the opportunity before me. I tried to seduce Trey. At first, he didn't respond to my advances, but eventually he gave in. When we were finished, he acted like he was mad at me. I asked if he was mad and he said, "NO!" which meant drop it.

The next morning, Trey told me that our physical relationship had to end. "I'm going to sleep on the couch from now on, and I'll move into Bobby's room when he moves out."

I nodded and looked at the floor.

"Tara, I love you. You know I do. But we can't go on like this. It's too hard . . . I have to marry Lucy. The sooner I can wrap my head around that and accept it, the better it will be for all of us. It's not fair to you to keep leading you on like this when I have to marry somebody else. Please understand that I don't want to hurt you. It tears me up inside that I can't have you. Hell, after all I've put you through, I don't deserve you."

I knew he was right, but I didn't want to deal with it. I wanted to wallow in denial, so I went to my room, shut the door, and cried.

Brenda came over to ask if we wanted to go to the carnival again that day. She came in my room and found me crying. I told her not to worry about me, so she went into the living room and announced, "Tara's crying."

"I know," Trey said. "We just had a serious talk." After Brenda left, Trey came in the room and asked, "Are you going to be all right?"

"I don't know," I choked out between sobs.

He backed out of the room and left me alone the rest of the day, then went to the base to sleep in the barracks that night—partly to get away from me and partly because he had a four o'clock inspection the next morning.

When he left, I decided to take a hot bath. I thought it would calm my nerves. I couldn't have been more wrong. Instead, I felt myself on the verge of an emotional breakdown, wailing uncontrollably. I sobbed so hard I thought I was going to make myself sick. I had never lost it like that before. I scared myself.

I lay down in the tub with my head fully submerged in the water. I counted to ten. I contemplated drowning. *What would happen if I just opened my mouth and let the water flow in? If I just took a big gulp of it?*

Whoa! What the hell was I thinking? I woke up out of my stupor and realized that I had a strong will to live. My survival instinct kicked into hyper over–drive. I jumped out of the tub, splashing water everywhere, and took a long look at myself in the mirror. I was visibly shaking. Then and there, I made a promise to myself that *NO GUY* was worth this. *I don't care how wonderful he is! This is not worth killing myself over!* I had to get a grip.

That night, with Trey's scent all around me, it was nearly impossible to sleep alone in that bed. The next morning when I woke up my stomach was in knots, my eyes were bloodshot, and my head was throbbing.

When Trey came home that evening, we talked about what it would be like when I met Lucy. He brought up how excited he was to see his kids. After a while, it got late and we were tired. He asked if it was okay to sleep in the bedroom with me.

Once in bed, the conversation drifted toward sex. "I'm cutting it off because I think it will be easier on you in the long run," he said.

"My feelings for you aren't going to change, Trey. Whether we have sex or not doesn't change a thing. Just being *near* you is agonizing, knowing you'll soon belong to someone else, unbearable."

"I know. I'm sorry. I hate it too. Well, whatever you want to do then, it's your decision."

"I still want you," I whispered huskily. He pulled me close and hugged me tight. I covered his face with tiny kisses. We mutually made love and I thought my heart would burst my emotions were so raw. I wanted that moment to last forever. I wished I could spend every minute of the rest of my life with this man. I felt so powerless over my own future, and torn between doing what was right and giving into my heart. He needed me to be his friend, but I wanted so much more.

13   the beginning of the end

THE NEXT FEW DAYS dragged on, as I counted down the time. Work was distracting, which helped. Freddy and Brenda broke up. Freddy and Brenda got back together—drama all around. Trey told some of the guys at work about me, actually about the whole love triangle. Sergeant Landers seemed to think it was his sole responsibility to cheer me up. He befriended me and soon hung out at the house often. For the rest of the guys, I just became the butt of their jokes.

It was Monday night football and Trey went to Freddy's to watch the game. Sergeant Landers was there and didn't make any attempt to leave when Trey left. Half an hour later, Brenda showed up to use the phone. Half an hour after that, Trey showed up to get some whiskey, he said, for Freddy. Landers was still there and I could tell it bugged Trey. I know because he came back again an hour later, drunk—an hour before the game was due to end. Landers got the hint and split.

"I'm tired, I'm going to bed now. Goodnight, Trey," I said as I walked down the hall.

"You're going to bed already? Tara, why are you so tired? What did you two do together?" his accusing tone all too obvious.

"He wanted to talk, so we talked—that's all we did was talk. Goodnight, Trey." I went in the bedroom, got undressed, and got in bed.

Trey came in my room, turned on the light, got something off the dresser then gazed at me. He turned and left. He came back and stared again, unmoving, without a word. When he came in the third time, he studied me with sad eyes and finally whispered, "I love you."

"Come here and give me a hug," I said. Our embrace was long and tender. As we pulled apart I whispered, "Thank you, that was nice. I love you too."

He kissed me. He stood up and walked toward the door, "Can I have a pillow?"

"I gave you one."

"Can I have another one?"

"You need two?"

"You get two."

"Here."

"Did you give me the two shitty ones?"

"One each. Good night." He left. Two minutes later, he opened the door, stood in the doorway, and stared at me all over again. "Trey, what is it? What's wrong?"

"That mattress looks so comfortable. It's so much softer than the couch." He wanted to sleep with me, but I was determined not to let him. I was nice, but firm. He left again. Lucy called and they talked for five minutes. Then he went to his "room," on the couch, and stayed there. Thus, it was another long and sleepless night for me.

I could hear Trey tossing and turning in the living room. Apparently, he was having sleep issues as well. This whole resisting each other thing was obviously torturing both of us. *But what am I supposed to do? He's going to marry Lucy and be a father. I have to accept it and let him go.*

Tuesday was a long day at work for both of us. I wrote an article about revenge and Trey had an IG (Incorporated General) inspection. That evening we played solitaire. We were getting along well, and he even asked if he could sleep with me—he said he hated sleeping alone.

In bed he brought up Sergeant Landers, "What's going on with him? Why did he talk to you so long last night?"

"He said he has feelings for me. I told him I wasn't interested, and he just kept telling me how beautiful I was. He makes me uncomfortable. I don't want him to come over anymore," I said.

"Don't worry, I'll take care of it."

It felt good to know Trey was looking out for me. He put his arm around me and then things began to heat up. He slowly positioned himself on top of me as he kissed my face and neck. We made love and climaxed together; a shudder ran through my body. I whispered, "Thank you," wrapped my arm around him and fell asleep, the best night's sleep I'd had in weeks. What heartbreaking memories. *He is so incredible—but he's not mine anymore.*

Saturday arrived, Bobby moved out, and I was a wreck. I was having trouble accepting the reality that Trey's soon–to–be wife, the mother of his children, was due imminently. Yet Trey and I were getting along better than ever. There were no more games.

Since Bobby took his TV with him, we spent our evenings stargazing from the back yard, or hanging out on the couch, and having great talks.

Trey's brother, Chad, called and reported that Lucy had gotten a late start and wouldn't arrive until about noon Sunday. Thus, giving us an extra night together, so to speak. We played hearts and solitaire and listened to music on my record player.

"I know what you're thinking," he said. "You think that Lucy and I won't work out and I'll come back to you. Seriously, you might be right. But I love you too much to ask you to wait for me. I can't expect you to put your life on hold like that. No, I have to try to make this work."

An Eagles song was playing in the background. Trey said, "If I start this over, will you promise to listen to it?"

"Okay," I managed. The song was "Wasted Time." He started it over and turned it up. It was sad and meaningful for both of us.

When the song was over, I looked up at him. "Did you understand that?" he asked me.

"Yes," I replied. "Don't think for one minute that you wasted my time. I have no regrets. I'm thankful for what precious time we were able to have together. I'll never forget you."

He was sitting on the chair, I was sitting on the couch, and we looked deeply into each other's eyes, speaking volumes without a word. Suddenly, I noticed he was sitting on my camera. By reflex, I reached out for it.

"I love it when you get on your knees like that," he smiled at me. I took the beer from his hand, put it on the table and crawled onto his lap, straddling him. I wrapped my arms around him and hugged him tight and held him as long as I could.

"I love you, Trey."

"I love you." We remained in a long, compelling embrace, just holding each other, afraid to let go. At last, I tried to break away, but he held on to me. I hugged him again. When we did part, his head was down; he wouldn't look at me. Then, I saw a tear on his cheek. I gently kissed it away. I brushed another one with my finger. I was at a loss for words, so I hugged him again. I couldn't cry. I was beyond tears. I told him that everything would work out.

"It has to!" I felt so helpless. I climbed off his lap, not because I wanted to, but because my legs were cramped from sitting in that position for so long and my left foot had fallen asleep. I got up, sat on the edge of the couch and put my hand on his knee. He put his hand on mine and we sat there holding hands. I felt so close to him— and so sad.

"Ready to go to bed now?" he asked softly.

"Hmm, do I get that fifteen minute back rub you owe me?" I quipped back.

"I'll mail it to you with the rest of the money I owe you." We went to bed and made love. Each time I thought would be our last. I lay with my head on his chest and we fell asleep together.

Sunday morning, D–Day had arrived. I woke up, went to the kitchen and had a bowl of cereal. When I came back to the bedroom, I climbed in bed with Trey and said, "I'm cold." We snuggled close until our desires overtook us. He pulled me on top of him and we held each other as tight as we could, kissing longingly.

We remained locked in a tight embrace, when I joked again about the fifteen minute back rub he owed me. We chatted and laughed, and then he began massaging my legs, butt, back and shoulders, while I was still lying on top of him. "Relax," he whispered. I put my head on his shoulder and completely submitted—he was in full control of my body. Time seemed to stand still.

"How was that for a back rub?" he smiled slyly. I had no words. He was so gentle, so tender and loving. He knew exactly what my body craved—gave of himself completely, to please me. He made love to me, in every sense of the word. I felt so close to him, like we were one. I loved him so much.

Trey got in the shower and I cleaned up the house. We had no idea when they would show up. We were jumpy and nervous, as they could arrive any minute. I had to prepare myself mentally. Our moods varied throughout the day, but we seemed strangely close. We were affectionate, happy, sad, despondent—a roller coaster of emotions—waiting for a phone call or a knock on the door. It was an emotionally trying day for both of us.

By four thirty that afternoon, we were getting worried. They were in a U–haul truck somewhere on the freeway. Were they all right? Wouldn't they call if they were going to be this late? Lucy finally called at six and said they were still four hours away. She told Trey to tell me to mess up my hair because she "looked awful."

We were tired. I went to lie down when Freddy and Brenda stopped by. I just wasn't in the mood for company and stayed in my room. After they left, Trey joined me. We couldn't keep our hands off each other. It was like some magnetic force drawing us together. Hugs, kisses, lying in each other's arms, pretending to sleep. I wanted to spend every last second of every hour that I possibly could with him.

"We're crazy, aren't we?" I observed. He looked puzzled but knew what I meant. We knew Lucy wouldn't be there until ten and we took full advantage of our last hours together.

He held me as I melted in his arms. I took off his shirt and let my hands explore every inch, every muscle, as though I were blind and seeing and feeling him for the last time. I wanted to remember him exactly how he was at that moment, and my hands acted as the sensors that would imprint his image on my brain for eternity.

Lucy called again at ten. She said they were still two hours away. He asked me to try not to look so sad. What was I supposed to do, be ecstatic that his fiancée was coming to take him away from me? Strange, that on this day of all days, I felt closer to him than ever before. How ironic that we were close until the very end, and even at our closest and most intimate the day his fiancée was on her way here to marry him. We were getting restless by eleven, fatigue and weariness taking over. We tried to get some sleep, but it was impossible. We sat together on the couch and waited.

I was spending every available second possible with him. I knew that soon enough, he'd be taken away from me forever. We were eerily silent, lost in our own thoughts, and tried to get some sleep. It had been an emotionally draining day, and I knew the night wasn't over yet.

Just when it seemed I had finally dozed off, close to one a.m., I heard a truck pull up—they were twelve hours late. *Thank you, God, for giving me extra time alone with him.*

I nearly fell off the couch and announced, "They're here." I was too dumbfounded to say anything else. We turned on the kitchen light and Trey went outside to greet them. I peeked out the window then ran and sat on the edge of the chair as they walked in; I was fidgeting and anxious. Lucy and I hardly spoke to each other. Trey's mom was the icebreaker, I was so thankful she was there. She gave me a big hug and his twenty-month-old beautiful little girl crawled onto my lap. I even held the baby. It was all so surreal.

I left at two a.m. and spent the rest of the night on Freddy and Brenda's couch. Unable to sleep, my mind kept torturing me with thoughts of Trey and Lucy together in my bed, on my sheets, using my lamp and alarm clock—especially after we had been on that bed that very day. I cried myself to sleep. Little did I know I was forming a habit that would continue for the next five weeks—nights were always the worst.

14 Lucy

IT'S MONDAY, September 16th. I'm depressed and I hate her. My first impression of Lucy was not a positive one. She wasn't friendly toward me at all. *Gee, I wonder why.* Perhaps she felt threatened? True. But I didn't like her anyway. I was jealous, hurt, and mad. I think meeting her was a bad idea. How did I allow myself to be talked into this?

When I got home from work, Trey's mom was asleep on the couch. She woke up when Trey, Lucy, and the kids came home and took family photos in the front yard. I felt like an outcast. I said goodbye to Trey's mom and left them alone, then she got in the U–Haul truck and made the drive back to Phoenix.

Trey left Lucy and me alone together—on purpose. He knew if he were around, we'd never talk, so he ate dinner on the base. She put the kids down for a nap and was in the living room folding laundry. I came in and tried to make pleasant small talk, but it was awkward. Then she just decided to launch into it, "I know you and Trey had a relationship, Tara, but it's over. I know you think that he loved you, but he's with me now. I know everything. He tells me everything. So be the friend he says you are and nothing more, okay?"

"But he does love me," I said under my breath. And then, "I don't understand why you would want to be with someone who doesn't love you. Why did you keep relentlessly pursuing him when he broke up with you—multiple times?"

"Because he's the father of my children! And he will love me. You'll see! I'll make him love me. We will be a family and my kids will have their dad and there's nothing you can do about it. I am the mother of his children! He chose me! You are not a threat."

"I know. You're right. He chose you. I hope you're happy."

"Thank you. We will be! Look, I know you've been a good friend to him. But he was confused, and he came to you at a low point in his life when we weren't getting along. I'm sorry he hurt you, Tara, but you don't understand. Trey and I always planned to get married. You were never a threat, just something he needed to get out of his system. He loves me and he loves the kids. You're just his friend."

"But—?"

"No, I know he cares about you, and I'm sure he always will. But it would be best if you just forgot about him and left us alone."

"Don't you have another child, Zoey, is it? By someone you met before Trey? Why aren't you with him? Where's your Zoey now?"

"She's staying with her grandma, his mom, for a few weeks, back east. And he's sick."

"Oh? Back east where?"

"In Virginia."

"What do you mean by he's 'sick?'" At this point, I was beyond being polite.

"Well, when we were together, he went kind of crazy. He's mentally incompetent and unable to take care of Zoey. I have full custody. But his mom wants to be in her life so I let her stay with them for part of this summer."

"Wow, that must be hard for you, for her to be away from you for so long. How old is she now?"

"She'll be five next month. Yeah, I miss her terribly. She has a big personality and can be really dramatic sometimes—heck, maybe she'll be an actress, ya know? Trey and Zoey don't get along very well, which is part of why I sent her over there for a while, while we get settled in here. She'll be back in a couple weeks."

"An actress huh? Cool. I was in a couple plays in high school. It was fun . . ." *What am I supposed to say now?* I was surprised how forthcoming and transparent she was. I knew she was two years older than Trey but didn't realize she'd had her first child at sixteen. And here she was at twenty-one with three kids under age five. I actually felt sorry for her.

Lucy bore somewhat of a resemblance to me—brown shoulder length hair, styled the same way (straight with feathered bangs) similar bone structure, and coloring. The main differences were our eyes (hers were brown) and her curves (I had no curves).

That night, I stayed on the couch—it was hell. All my stuff was still in the bedroom. I imagined them having sex. I woke up from a bad dream crying. I just wanted Trey to hold me and tell me everything would be okay. I was so lost and afraid. I couldn't go to my best friend for comfort because he was in my bed with Lucy! I wanted to die.

Tuesday morning Trey came into the living room at 5:30 to put on his boots. He was sitting in the chair, next to the couch, when I woke up. Lucy followed him out and sat on the floor in front of him. She was wearing a revealing nightgown with plenty of exposed cleavage.

You'd never know she just popped out a kid; she had a great body. She watched him as he put on his boots, and then moved to the arm of the chair to sit beside him. They stood up together and she kissed him as he walked out the door. I didn't appreciate her little display of affection, which no doubt was for my benefit. She went back to bed and I attempted to get a few more z's myself. Since the baby had cried all night, I was definitely sleep deprived.

I went to work, wrote my last article for "Tara's Corner," and got home around four. Brenda was at our trailer bugging Lucy with personal questions. I glared at her and she left. Trey got home looking sad. He proceeded to drink heavily, then challenged Lucy and me to a game of hearts. The game started out fun, with Trey being in the lead. On our final hand, somehow the queen got in Trey's pile. No one knew how it got there so Trey accused us of cheating. We declared the hand unfair and were going to re–deal, but he got upset.

"Give it to me, it doesn't matter, I'm losing anyway," Lucy demanded. Trey protested. She said, "I don't want to argue. You're right, I'm wrong, let's keep playing." He got mad and yelled obscenities as he walked out the front door.

Lucy and I were stunned by his sudden outburst and began comparing notes. Trey was standing by the window, listening to our conversation. He burst through the door, outraged. He said we were conspiring against him. He asked why we could talk so candidly about him but couldn't talk *to* him. He demanded to know what we were talking about and felt left out. He thought we were telling evil secrets about him. He referred to me as "her" and talked only to Lucy—about me, in front of me.

"You've been acting like a bitch! And she (pointing at me) won't even talk to me," he shouted.

"Sit down, I'll talk to you," I said icily. He actually sat down.

"What do you want to know?" asked Lucy. "I have nothing to hide."

"Talk then! Tell me everything! Why are you two being so chummy? Why did you take Tara's name off the mailbox? Why are you acting like such a fucking bitch? Go home, Lucy! I don't want you here. Go back to Phoenix! I don't want to marry you," he finally paused, panting and red faced.

"Give me the money, I'll go right now," Lucy was livid. "Trey, you're such an asshole!" she shouted as she threw a beer can at him. They said things just to hurt each other. I was uncomfortable witnessing all this volatility and felt trapped. They both had scary tempers. I excused myself and went outside. As I closed the door, I heard her on the phone with Trey's mom.

"Trey says he doesn't love me anymore. He doesn't want to marry me and wants to send me home." I heard more yelling and banging around, so I took a walk around the block. I had never seen Trey so angry like that before. It seemed to me that they brought the worst out in each other. Lucy was violent and scary and threw whatever she could grab. It was like watching some bad TV movie, and I wanted no part of it. I went to Freddy and Brenda's and slept on their couch.

The next morning, I woke up late for work. Even though I had already written and submitted the last article for my column, I still worked as a proofreader, and covered the phones during lunch. I hurried to the office and had a horrible day.

When I got home, the house was a disaster, and no one was there. I went to Brenda's. She was babysitting while Trey and Lucy were at the Justice of the Peace—getting married. *After the fight they had last night? Wow. Whatever.*

Both babies were wet and crying. *Way to go Brenda.* I took them back to the house, changed them, fed them, and vowed never to leave my own children with Brenda should the situation ever arise.

The dining room was piled to the ceiling with boxes, a dresser, bed, couch and tables. They weren't able to cash his mom's check, so they couldn't put the stuff in storage. The reality of my situation suddenly hit me hard. Since I had an ounce of pride left, I decided I needed to get out of there *right now*.

I called my grandma, who lived in Wichita Falls, Texas, about a four-hour drive away, and asked if she would come get me. We quickly made plans for her to pick me up Saturday morning. She didn't need directions, since she'd already visited a couple months earlier, when Trey was on a bivouac for training purposes. She told me she loved me and that she was looking forward to seeing me soon. I hung up feeling loved and buoyed enough to get through the next few days.

I went back into the kitchen, found my suitcases, and began throwing my stuff into them. They came home, and Lucy left again to go grocery shopping. Trey walked into the kitchen and asked if I was mad at him. That was a mistake—I exploded. I could see the pain in his eyes, with tears beginning to form. He turned and left the room.

I followed him—I was on a roll. "That's it? You have nothing to say to me?"

"What do you want me to say?"

"The truth!"

"Tara, I love you. I'll be heartbroken when you're gone. I'll miss you."

Showing no mercy, I retorted, "You've got a funny way of showing it."

"Would it help if I said I was sorry? You know I had to do this. I had to marry Lucy—for the kids."

"I know, but it doesn't make it any easier. I hate this."

"She needs me more than you do. This is not a marriage based on love; it's a marriage of convenience. I don't know how long it will last. I really do love you. I'll write to you."

"I know this isn't easy for you either. I'm sorry I ruined your wedding day. So, is it okay if I give the groom a hug?" We hugged, and then he showed me the marriage license. Yep, it's official.

According to Lucy the next day, the happy newlyweds did not consummate the nuptials. I couldn't help but feel a tiny bit of smug satisfaction; I'm almost ashamed to admit it. Lucy had to take Trey to work because we needed the car, but she couldn't find the keys. They were arguing again. I rolled my eyes, went in the bedroom and found the damn keys—second place I looked—under Lucy's purse, on the floor. I was quite pleased with myself. Trey and Lucy were not amused.

That night Bobby and some of the guys from the base came over to watch a football game with Trey. Bobby taunted me and asked, "How's the happy family?"

I wanted to kick his teeth in. The guys seemed to think the whole scene was pretty damn funny and they all left with big grins on their faces. Lucy and Trey got friendly on the couch. PDA I did not need. Trey asked if something was wrong and I just glared at him.

"I'm tired and I want to go to sleep. You two are sitting on my bed." Lucy got up and left, and I began putting the sheet and blanket on my couch bed. I told Trey that nights were the worst.

"Do you want me to tuck you in?" he teased, and patted me on the back as he strode off down the hall. I cried myself to sleep yet again.

It was finally Friday—my last day at work and my last night in Killeen. Work was uneventful and disappointing; my boss wasn't even there. My co–workers went out to lunch and left me there to cover the phones for an hour and a half. I felt like no one cared. When it was time to say goodbye, they wished me luck, we exchanged addresses and promised to keep in touch. It didn't feel like I was leaving though, just made me more miserable.

When I got home from work, Lucy wasn't speaking to me. *Great, what did I do now?* I apologized for whatever offended her and we got along better. I packed and gathered all my stuff, which was difficult because one of my suitcases was still wedged in between Lucy's furniture in the dining room. I had squeezed behind a mattress and box spring to get to the trapped suitcase when I overheard Trey tell Lucy he was going to a high school football game. I yanked the case hard and hurled it out, climbing out over the mess as quickly as I could.

"Where are you going?" I demanded.

"To a football game."

"Why?"

"I haven't seen a game in ages, and I want to see one," was Trey's monotone reply.

"But it's my last night here!" I wailed, my whole façade crashing down. Trey looked at Lucy, shrugged, and walked out the door. I sobbed pathetically. My cover blown, I apologized to Lucy and tried to make up a story about my fragile emotional condition. I don't think she bought it and frankly I just didn't care anymore. Trey came back ten minutes later because the game had been moved, due to rain. I couldn't face him, so I got my raincoat and told Lucy I was going for a walk.

It was dark and raining heavily and I didn't have an umbrella. I secretly hoped I'd get run over or murdered and put an end to my suffering—it didn't happen. I walked around the neighborhood, in the rain, in the dark, crying and feeling sorry for myself for nearly an hour. I couldn't face them, just couldn't handle it anymore. I was falling apart, but I was also soaking wet and freezing, so I pulled myself together the best I could and went back to the trailer. I wanted to be alone, but I had nowhere to go.

Lucy asked, "How was your walk?" like nothing had happened. We all played make believe and pretended our lives were normal. We played the board game Risk, and Trey won.

I went to the bedroom to finish gathering my things and searched for my gold pearl pinky ring, a gift from my mother. I remembered leaving it on the dresser. It wasn't there. I loved that ring. The band swirled around the pearl like arms embracing it. I couldn't find it anywhere.

Lucy stomped in, "Trey wants to talk to you, to say goodbye. He sent me in here. He wants to kiss you." She was pissed. I didn't care anymore. I was equally pissed because I couldn't find my ring and practically accused her of taking it.

I walked out to the living room to talk to Trey. He told me he loved me, said he'll miss me, blah, blah, blah. By this point, I was emotionally numb, just sort of shut down. He said he needed to go to bed. I watched dry-eyed and dead inside as he walked down the hall.

I woke up early Saturday morning, took a shower and got ready for my grandma to pick me up. She arrived at 9:30 and I began loading my stuff into her van. Trey was still asleep. I went in the bedroom and took a picture of him sleeping. Lucy followed me, naturally. I asked her if I could have a few seconds alone with him, to say goodbye. She reluctantly left the room. I gently woke him up.

"I'm leaving now. This is goodbye . . . well, I don't know what to say, so I guess I better go."

"I'll walk you out," he said. He got up, got dressed in front of me, and we walked out together to the living room. I could only imagine what must have been going on in Lucy's mind right then. I ran down the alley to say goodbye to Freddy and Brenda. They gave me big hugs and we promised to write to each other.

As I was walking back, the mailman was there. Trey went out to greet him and I heard him say, "Does Tara still live here?" I walked up to him and said I was Tara. My mail was a phone bill. Perfect. Trey took it from me and said he'd take care of it; that was nice.

We stood on the sidewalk facing each other in silence. Lucy was standing in the doorway with the baby in her arms and toddler at her feet; my grandma was sitting in the van with the sliding-door open. We had an audience.

"I love you, Trey." I whispered, almost inaudibly.

"I love you."

"Take care."

"Keep in touch. Good luck with everything…" he stepped toward me. We hugged, kissed, and parted.

"Well, this is it," I sighed.

"Yeah."

"I'll write to you."

"We'll always be friends. I promise to write too. Be strong and **have faith**." As he said those last words, "have faith," he squeezed my hand. At that moment I knew our paths would cross again someday—they just had to. I couldn't imagine never seeing him again. *When?* Only time will tell.

I wrote him one last letter and tucked it in his pocket as I let him go for the last time.

> *Dear Trey,*
> *Well, this is goodbye…I hate goodbyes.*
> *When I came out here last June to start a life with you I was selfish. I was jealous of Lucy and wanted you all to myself. I didn't understand why you chose her over me. I didn't believe you when you told me you loved me, didn't understand some of the choices you made. But, you have made your decision, and now you have to live with it. You*

have two beautiful children and a wife who loves you. They are special, Trey. Take good care of them; they've endured a lot for you.

Even though I'm hurt right now, I don't regret being with you. We've had some precious moments together that I will always cherish. You know I'll never forget you. But, you have a new life now, one that doesn't include me. Good luck with your new life, Trey. It was fun while it lasted.

My only regret is that there aren't two of you...it seems we still have so much to offer each other, there's still so much growing and exploring—time went too fast. Somehow I feel unfinished with you, still. I felt like we held back from each other, each one afraid to fall too hard.

You're my fantasy. You're someone I dream about running away with to some exotic, foreign land...a place to forget all our worries, troubles and anxieties, and just be us. Where we don't have to answer to anyone else, and we just do what feels good, for each other and ourselves. Does a place like that exist? I know I'm a dreamer, but in being with you, some of my dreams came true. Through you, I got to live a part of my fantasy.

Too bad the timing was off. I know we could be great together. Maybe we'll meet again in another life?

I'll always care about you. Be good. Take care. Have a wonderful life...and I do wish you happiness.

> *Goodbye Trey. I'll always love you,*
> *Tara*

P.S. You still light my fuse. And please smile when you think of me. I love your smile.

15   so this is college

AFTER I LEFT Trey, I stayed with my grandparents for a month and visited family in Wichita Falls. I had to figure out what I wanted to do with my life. I needed to make some major decisions about my future. Yet, I was in no mood to think about anything; I was heartbroken and despondent. I spent most of my time weeping, alone in their guest room, and feeling sorry for myself.

When I wasn't being a recluse or grieving excessively, I was lying on the couch and watching TV, the epitome of laziness. It was that type of day when my Uncle Tim stopped by to talk to me, really talk to me. My grandparents gave me space to wallow in my despair, and tiptoed around my fragile condition, but not Uncle Tim. He strode across the living room and turned off the TV as he said, "Sit up."

Uncle Tim was only ten years older than me because my grandma had him when my dad was twelve years old. Tim had thick brown hair, gray–blue eyes, and an easy smile. He was an intimidating figure at six foot four and 220 pounds of muscle, but he had a tender heart and would give the shirt off his back to a stranger. At twenty-nine, he was a college graduate and a successful businessman and entrepreneur. In fact, he was launching his own company in the Aerospace Industry and I highly respected and adored him. Needless to say, when he said 'sit up,' I sat up.

Uncle Tim proceeded to ask me a series of questions about my hobbies, interests and goals. He asked what my aspirations were. He asked where I saw myself in five, ten, even twenty years. Finally, he asked, "Tara, why don't you want to go to college?"

"Because my high school guidance counselor told me not to," I whined. "She said I wasn't college material!"

"Really?" he laughed. "That's ridiculous! You're going to let a little thing like that hold you back? Of course you're college material—"

"But I'm not smart enough."

"Yes. You are."

"But what if the classes are too hard? What if I fail? What if—"

"Stop right there. Promise me you won't ever let anyone crush your dreams again. You can be anything you want to be, Ta Ta (his pet name for me). Anything! Going to college is about more than just figuring out a major or a career. Going to college is about figuring out who you are as a person; it's about growing and learning and making lifelong friends. It will prove to your future employers that you have what it takes to stick with something for four years, and it will set you apart."

He was patient with me as he addressed my fears, one by one, until they had dissolved into excitement. Uncle Tim changed my life that day—right then and there I made the decision to go to college. He gave me the gentle shove I needed and I vowed, one way or another, to make him proud of me. That day, I promised myself that I would graduate from a University in four years. *And Mrs. Tank can bite me!*

I soon discovered that it was too late to apply to any college, anywhere, for fall term. After all, it was already mid–October. I was also homesick, as I had now lived away from my mom for more than a year. I had ventured out on my own and failed; it was time to go back home with my tail between my legs and ask forgiveness.

My mom and Jack took me in, forgave all, and loved me unconditionally. Actually, they didn't need to forgive me because they weren't mad at me in the first place. I was the one who needed to forgive myself. They gave me my old room back, but now I shared it with Mom's enormous drafting desk, because she was using the room as a home office. However, it was a small price to pay for free room and board.

I enrolled in the Winter Session at Portland Community College, with classes beginning in January. In the meantime, I got a job as a cashier at Fred Meyer and saved all my money for tuition and books. I had to prove to my family that I was serious about college, which meant paying for the bulk of it myself. I had sold my car when I left for Miami back in March, so I took the bus to work and school, and began looking for a cheap car to buy, eventually settling on a yellow 1978 Toyota Celica.

Living at home again had its pros and cons. After being out on my own I had developed certain habits and routines of independent living and had to make a few adjustments. Still, I enjoyed being around my parents again and was thankful for a place to stay while attending PCC.

I adapted easily to college life. In fact, I loved it. It was nothing like high school. All my fears about not being smart enough, good enough, or able to fit in and make friends quickly dissipated. My uncle was right about everything—a wise man indeed. Not only did I enjoy my classes at PCC, I even sat in the front row and participated (*gasp*). I had been quite shy in high school and pretty much only spoke when spoken to, in my acting class, or on stage. I even auditioned for the play and got a lead.

My major was Journalism and I wrote for the school newspaper. It was a paid position. The newspaper staff wasn't part of a class; it was run as a business mostly after school. I had found my niche.

Eventually, I even met someone. I had grieved and pined over Trey for six months and it was time to get interested in the opposite sex again. His name was Chris McCarthy and we met at play rehearsal in January. He was older than me, at twenty-four, while I was still nineteen. He was studying Massage Therapy. Chris was always on the lookout for willing participants to practice his newly acquired skills on, and had no shortage of volunteers. It was quite common to find him in the middle of a group of people waiting for their turn for a shoulder rub. Obviously, he was ridiculously popular, and had great hands. Who doesn't like free shoulder rubs? He was also absolutely nothing like Trey.

Chris had an exuberant, bubbly personality, and was outgoing. He was always optimistic and loved life— perpetually in a good mood. His positive, carefree attitude was infectious and drew me to him like a magnet. I needed to stop dwelling on the past and stop being so negative, and Chris was just the person to teach me how to let it go. At five foot seven with shaggy brown hair and coppery brown eyes, he was a mischievous bundle of energy and we began dating in March. Life became fun again and he kept me laughing constantly.

Of course I told him about Trey and he understood my pain. He said it helps to remember the pain, for without pain we wouldn't know how incredibly special it is to be happy. My pain has helped shape me into who I am today. Chris taught me not to dwell on the past, but also not to bury it. He told me about the one who broke his heart too—Malia. Ironically, she sounded like me. *Hmmm, should I be concerned about this? Nah.*

Chris and I dated exclusively for three months. We even held an intimate little ceremony when he officially asked me to go steady. He made a big deal out of having a girlfriend and made me feel special. We put invisible rings on each other's fingers and sealed it with a kiss.

During that time, when I wasn't at work or in class, I was with Chris. Sometimes I wondered if I spent too much time with him, but we enjoyed each other's company tremendously, never fought or argued, and when we weren't together, we missed each other. Plus, it was thoroughly enjoyable to hang out with him, and he made me feel good about myself. Therefore, I came to the conclusion that, no; we were not spending too much time together. He even helped me buy the Toyota because he knew more about cars than I did, and he wanted to make sure I didn't get a lemon.

The only thing I worried about while seeing Chris was that my grades might suffer due to a lack of studying. Surprisingly, they didn't. I managed being a full–time college student, two part–time jobs, being in college plays, and having a boyfriend; miraculously, my grades consisted of straight A's.

After three months together, Chris got a summer job in Newport Beach, California, with a buddy of his, more than a thousand miles away. We didn't officially break up when he left, but decided a break would give us time away from each other to think about what we really wanted. He felt that he didn't have my "whole heart" because he thought I was still in love with Trey.

"When you're finally over him, then maybe you can fully be with another. Sometimes when you're with me you seem distant and detached. I don't think you really love me."

"What? Of course I do. I do love you," I insisted. But even though it was hard to admit, I knew as I said the words that Chris was right. I still loved Trey.

He also said that he had grown restless in Portland and felt he needed a change; he said he needed to take a spiritual journey and that he couldn't do that in Portland. He needed to go somewhere to find himself. He was searching for something when we were together; he said he didn't feel whole.

Now that it was summer, and Chris was gone, I had more time on my hands, so I got another part–time job. I got hired as a telephone Interviewer for a marketing research company. In other words, I became one of those annoying people that called people during dinner and asked them to take twenty–minute surveys. Hey, it was a job and I needed to make as much money as possible; I had three more years of college to pay for.

In August, a friend of mine from an Acting class at PCC, Lori, was moving to Pasadena and asked if I wanted to drive down with her; she said it was a long drive and she could use the company. In fact, she was so worried about making the drive herself that she bribed me with the words "free ride" and "I'll pay for your meals."

Being the broke college student that I was, I decided her offer was too good to refuse and I also wanted to seize the opportunity to visit Chris in Newport Beach. We had been writing to each other and called occasionally but had never mentioned my visiting him. I wasn't sure how he would react but decided to surprise him anyway.

Lori and I left Portland at four o'clock Sunday morning and drove straight through to San Francisco, with only brief fast food, gas & restroom stops, and got there at 5:15 p.m. We stayed with her friends Sean and Elaina and crashed early.

The next morning, we left San Francisco at six thirty and arrived in Pasadena at two that afternoon. I had to restrain myself from rushing to the nearest phone and calling Chris right then. Lucky for me, when we arrived at Lori's new apartment, it had phone service because she was moving in with a roommate who already lived there. After brief introductions, I couldn't contain myself any longer and asked to borrow the phone.

"Hello?" answered his friend, Ron.

"Hi, is Chris there?"

"Yeah, hold on, I'll get him."

"Hello, Tara?" Chris inquired.

"Hi, how'd you know it was me?"

"Oh, Ron guessed. What's up?"

"Well, um, Lori asked me to help her move. She's moving to Pasadena and we just drove down. Um, surprise!" I exhaled as I blurted it all out in one big breath.

"You're *here*? In California?"

"Yeah."

"Oh, wow. Hey, that's great. How long are you staying?"

"Oh, I don't know; a week or two. It kinda depends on you."

"Oh. Where are you again?"

"I'm in Pasadena right now, but Lori said she can take me to Newport Beach if you want."

"Great! How about we meet in Huntington Beach? I'll bring Ron, and you and Lori can have dinner with us."

"Okay, I'll ask her. Hold on," I exuded, as I could no longer contain the excitement in my voice. Lori nodded agreement, I wrote down an address and we hung up.

Chris's friends were great, very hospitable. They said I could stay as long as I wanted, and they had an extra bed in the loft at their beach house. Everyone was friendly and made me feel right at home. Everyone that is, except the only one I cared about—Chris.

I went down there hoping we'd get back together, but I could not have been more wrong. Two days after my arrival he started picking fights with me, and we argued constantly. He was definitely not acting like the Chris I knew at all. He was cruel, and it confused me.

Then one night he took it too far. We had spent the day at the Balboa Fun Zone, an amusement park and video arcade on the Balboa Peninsula, with his friends. He asked me to go for a walk with him, just the two of us. We hadn't been alone together since I'd gotten there, so I quickly said yes before he changed his mind. I'd had a bad feeling that he hadn't wanted to be alone with me but didn't understand why. At least now maybe I'd get some answers.

He wasted no time telling me what was on his mind, "I want you to go home. This isn't working out and you need to go home—now."

"I don't understand. What did I do? Why are you telling me this—"

"I don't want a relationship right now. I thought I made that clear to you. I thought I wanted to be your friend, but I don't. Go home, Tara! You shouldn't have come down here."

"What?"

"Why are you so nice to Ron all the time? It seems like you like him. Do you like him? You talk to him more than you talk to me. You two are always so chummy!"

"What? No! Where is this coming from? You're jealous of my friendship with Ron? He's your best friend! Of course we wouldn't do anything!"

"I don't trust you anymore, Tara. You're not affectionate and you don't open up to me."

"Chris, you're not making any sense! You told me to give you space, you said you just wanted to be friends! Now you want me to be affectionate with you? I don't understand what you want from me. Plus, when I try to talk to you, you tell me I'm talking about myself too much and I'm boring you! I can't do anything right!" I shouted at him indignantly. I was hurt and confused and didn't understand what brought this on—the criticalness, the mixed signals.

I ran back to the beach house by myself, went to the loft and tried to make sense of everything he'd just said. An hour later, he came up, apologized and said he really wanted to be my friend, and would I forgive him?

He said that he didn't want a relationship, that he just wanted to be friends, but then he would analyze *our* relationship. For someone who said he didn't care and didn't want to get involved, he sure spent a lot of time rehashing and psychoanalyzing any shred of affection we may have still felt for each other. He was acting crazy and I'd had enough. Luckily, his friend's Aunt was driving back to Portland and said I could get a ride back with her. *Perfect. It's over.*

Classes started up again at PCC and I was determined to get all my General University Requirements out of the way so I could transfer to Washington State University, in Pullman, Washington, the next fall. I changed my major to Broadcast Journalism, from just Journalism, and was excited to attend the Edward R. Murrow School of Communication at WSU. I wanted to be a TV News Reporter. I was going to be the next Connie Chung.

Chris came back from California and called me. He said he wanted to see me, but I couldn't imagine what he could possibly want from me. I wished he'd just leave me alone. He was the one who kept saying he didn't want a relationship, and he was so cruel when I visited him in Newport Beach.

We met for pizza a few days later. He had a scruffy mustache and beard, which looked stupid because it was growing in patchy. We made small talk for a while and then he confessed that he had gotten back together with Malia, before he went to Newport Beach, at the beginning of the summer.

What an ass! He lied to me. He let me visit him. Want to hear the best part? He said that if I really loved him, I'd fight for him, and that I wouldn't give up. *Are you kidding me? Malia can have him! Truly unbelievable.*

I called him a liar and a womanizer. No way was I going near *anything* resembling a 'love triangle' again. I'd like to think I learned something from my experience with Trey and Lucy. I wasn't about to go down that road again.

16   turning twenty-one

SPRING CLASSES AT PCC were in full swing; I was still working part–time at Fred Meyer, had a lead in the play, and not dating anyone. I stayed busy but was restless for the next milestone. My routine at PCC was getting tedious and I couldn't wait to get out of there and move to Pullman. I was also eager to move out on my own again and turn twenty-one—in a ceaseless rush to be a grown–up.

The weekend of my twenty-first birthday my dad flew me up to Seattle because he considered it a rite of passage to take me bar–hopping now that I was of legal drinking age in the state of Washington. What he didn't realize was that the drinking age was nineteen in Florida and only eighteen in Texas. I had already been to bars legally, so it wasn't a big deal to me. But he seemed excited to share this milestone with me, so I went along with it to humor him.

Still, I was eager to turn twenty-one. It seemed like such a magical age to me; one I couldn't wait to reach. I had daydreamed, planned, and set goals for this mysterious age, thinking that once I became a full–

fledged adult I would somehow be able to solve life's puzzles.

On Saturday Dad had a small family party for me with cake, candles, ice cream, presents—all the usual stuff. When the party wound down, he announced that it was time to take me bar–hopping. He took me to three bars, and I ordered a drink at each one. Why? Because Dad said he wanted me to experience the thrill of showing them my I.D. Because it was exactly twenty-one years since the day of my birth and it deserved to be celebrated and commemorated with a *"look out world, I'm legal"* attitude.

We got home at one thirty in the morning, no longer my birthday, and I was buzzed enough to want nothing but sleep. When I woke up eight hours later, I had a headache and thought to myself, *this is it, the party's over. I'm twenty-one now and it's time to grow up.*

I spent the rest of the weekend putting together two one thousand–piece jigsaw puzzles with my half–sister, Nicole. Nicole was my dad's daughter from his second marriage and six years younger than me. I flew home Monday night.

On the flight back to Portland I thought about the weekend, how it felt unproductive, and ended too soon. I hadn't accomplished anything, except fitting a bunch of little pieces together to make one big piece—ugh.

By the time the plane landed, I was in a terrible mood. My nineteen-year-old theatre friend from PCC, Mike, picked me up at the Portland airport. We had been in a play together and he was proving to be a true friend. He greeted me exuding all the tail wagging happiness of an excited puppy, with his big, dopey smile and warm hug. I wanted to hit him.

"Hey, Tara! How was your weekend? How do you feel, birthday girl?" he asked, as he grabbed my bag from me, ever the gentleman.

"I feel like I just found out there's no Santa Claus," I said dejectedly.

"What? What are you talking about?" he asked incredulously, as we made our way toward the baggage claim area.

In a blank monotone I continued, "Like I've just been symbolically *de-virginized*. I mean, this is something I've looked forward to for a long time and now that it's finally here, it's a big letdown, a sort of innocence lost. I feel betrayed in a way, that is, about turning twenty-one. I'm not a kid anymore; I'm an adult now. I can do anything; go anywhere. I can drink alcohol and gamble—so what! What's–the–big–deal–who–needs–it!" I gestured wildly, as passersby gawked at me.

"Tara, I don't understand. You should feel free! You are no longer inhibited by the under-twenty-one laws; you are no longer in your parents' clutches."

"Free? Yeah, sure, I feel free. I have the freedom to pay rent, taxes and bills; I have the freedom to spend money on alcohol and gambling; I have the freedom to be an adult burdened with responsibilities and duties.... But this is not why I wanted to be twenty-one—I thought life's problems would vanish; instead, they just intensified."

"But don't you feel any different? Any older?"

"Hell no! I still feel sixteen. I feel like I've been ripped off; all those years I didn't enjoy my childhood because I wanted to hurry up and grow up—enter grade school, junior high, then high school; get my driver's license, graduate, vote, go to college, drink, graduate college, buy a house, have a career, get married and raise a family. You know, the American Dream!"

"Okay, but those are important goals. I mean, if everyone thought like that, we'd all go to college and become productive citizens, right?"

"Wrong! We've been brainwashed. When we were kids, grown–ups pushed us with admonishments like, 'Act your age; be a lady; don't get dirty; be mature; be responsible; be smart; use your common sense.' They said things like, 'Wait 'til you get older, then you'll understand,' or, 'older and wiser.' Well, I don't understand, and I'm not sure I want to either! If that's what being a grown–up is all about, I don't want any part of it. Now I'm expected to do something with my life— make a difference. For what? What's it all for? WHY?"

"Tar, everybody feels that way sometimes. I don't have all the answers, nobody does. When we get older, we don't magically find the answers."

"Yeah? Well, guess what? Life doesn't get easier either, it just goes faster. I wish I could be a kid forever. I want to go back to the days of ignorant bliss. I spent too much time dreaming about the future instead of actively being involved in the present. The carefree, responsible– for–nothing days of childhood are gone."

"But it's not too late, you're still young. Just slow down and live in the present and maybe your next ten years won't be as short–lived. You can't relive the past or go back and correct your childhood mistakes, ya know."

"I know, but what about all the broken promises? What about my shattered dreams, my unfulfilled goals, all the things I never got, but always wanted?"

"Hey, it's not too late. Geez, don't be so dramatic! You can still achieve your goals, but now maybe you have different goals. Sure, you probably never got that swing set you had your eye on, but you got over it. So now you want other kinds of toys, and who's to stop you from getting them? After all, you *are* twenty-one, mommy can't tell you, 'No, Tara, it cost too much.' That's your decision now."

"Yeah, I guess you're right."

"'Life is a mystery to be lived, not a puzzle to be solved.'"

"Right. It wasn't any fun solving those jigsaw puzzles anyway," I chuckled. "What's the point? I make my own decisions now and I can still be a kid at heart."

Suitcase in hand, Mike and I left the baggage claim area and rode the escalator to the airport parking lot. On the way home that night I saw a shooting star. I made a wish.

17   wazzu

"I AM OFFICIALLY a Washington State University student! The campus is beautiful, I'm taking 18 credits, have time to work on the Chinook Yearbook Staff, be on a co–ed softball team, date, and be a little sis at a fraternity. My dorm roommate, Heather Matthews, is really nice, and I've met lots of new people, and am making new friends. I absolutely love it here!" I wrote in a letter to my Uncle Tim, thanking him for that college pep talk he'd given me two years earlier.

It was true, I did love WAZZU, but it wasn't an easy road to get there. My parents couldn't afford to pay my tuition and between paying for PCC, buying a used car, and insurance, I'd spent all the money I'd earned so far. I applied for grants, scholarships, school loans—anything I could get my hands on. I was able to get a low–interest student loan, but I still needed to come up with three thousand dollars by August fifteenth. There was no way I would come up with that kind of cash conducting telephone surveys.

The only job I could think of where I could make a lot of money in a short amount of time, with my age and qualifications, was waitressing. I had a couple of waitress friends and they said they earned way more in tips than in wages. Unfortunately, I wasn't even qualified to do that because I had no previous waitressing experience; every place I applied to turned me down. The irony was not lost on me—I was stuck in a catch-22.

I'd finished classes at PCC, it was summer, and time was running out. I was already enrolled in fall classes at WSU, but I'd never be able to go if I couldn't come up with the money by August. I was getting desperate.

Combing the classified ads in the Sunday newspaper, *The Oregonian*, gave me the craziest idea. I quickly dismissed it as preposterous, there was no way I could do that, but the idea grew and festered in my mind and I couldn't shake it. Finally, I got up the nerve to call the number in the ad. After a quick phone interview, they wanted to see me in person.

I applied for a cocktail waitress job at a topless bar in downtown Portland. However, even they wouldn't give me a waitress job without experience. I couldn't believe it. But they did make me an offer for another job . . .

That summer, with less than two months to my August 15th deadline, I had a job as a topless dancer. And you know what? I earned every cent of the money I needed for college before the deadline. I told you, one way or another, I was going to college—I meant it.

Student life at WSU was different from PCC. For one thing, campus life in Pullman was much healthier—no one smoked. Being in a smoke–free environment cleared up my constant colds, allergies and asthma. I also sold my car before moving to Pullman, so I walked everywhere and was the healthiest I'd ever been.

WSU's campus was breathtaking with its beautiful brick buildings, lush greenery and trees, and scenic vistas of rolling green hills and the Blue Mountains. I lived in a dorm on campus, which made walking to classes a breeze. The students were welcoming, and I made friends easily. The social stigmas and cliques of high school were gone, and people were just people; I loved it. My professors were cool and seemed to genuinely care about their students. I enjoyed most of my classes, and college life was good.

Many doors opened for me, and I mean that in the most literal way; these doors opened to parties, mostly frat parties. I didn't belong to a sorority because I didn't think Greek life was the right fit for me. But some friends did talk me into the "Little Sister/Big Brother" program at one of the fraternities, Phi Sigma Kappa. I liked the idea of having a 'big brother' because I'd never had a brother and always wanted one. Plus, they had strict rules about not dating your brother/sister and I felt it was a safe way to bond with a member of the opposite sex, possibly making a lifelong friend.

My big brother, Zac Graff, was a great guy. He stood six foot one, 235 pounds, with brown hair and eyes, and I looked like a small child in comparison. He played strong safety, a defensive back position, on WSU's football team.

Zac was an absolute gentleman who respected and followed his fraternity's rules. We got along great and both had the same Broadcast Journalism major, so we often studied together at the frat house, and I got to know some of the other guys too. I soon grew quite comfortable at the house and felt like a little sis to many of the other guys there as well.

They had many big brother/little sister events that were fun to attend, as well as the traditional "keggers" that fraternities seem to be known for. I didn't really like the taste of beer, so often I would carry around the same cup all night and sort of sip at it. This worked well for me in that I wasn't pressured to drink, didn't drink too much, and still had a good time without suffering the consequences of a hangover the next day. However, there was one party that changed my life, and my relationship with my big brother, as well as the fraternity, forever.

It was a Saturday night in mid–November, a week before Thanksgiving break, and the guys had a fiesta party—with tequila and margaritas. I quickly discovered that I liked margaritas. I was beginning to feel a buzz and my friend, another little sis at the house, Suzie, said she was tired and wanted to go back to the dorm. I wasn't ready to leave yet, so I told her I would find Zac and he'd make sure I got back okay. Assuming I was fine and in good hands, she left.

"Hey, has anybody seen Zac?" I asked to no one in particular. I began walking around, searching the party, when I felt a tap on my shoulder.

"Hey Tara, I heard you were looking for Zac?" It was Chet, a senior friend of Zac's whom I had just met that night. "I just saw him a minute ago. He's upstairs chillin' in my room. I'll take you to him," he smiled broadly and put his arm around my shoulders to guide me upstairs.

"Oh! Are you sure he's up there? It's okay, you don't have to take me; I can find it," I stammered as I felt him practically pushing me up the stairs.

"Oooh Tara, had a little bit to drink, huh? Watch out for those steps! Ha ha. Yeah, he's up there. Come on, it's just a little further. It's okay, I've got you."

"No, I'm fine. I'm not stumbling, you're pushing me," I protested.

"What? Don't be silly! You're totally drunk! Don't worry; Zac will take care of you. We're almost there… easy, easy. Ah, here we are!" He pushed me through the door and told me Zac was just around the corner. I entered the room, which also had a ladder that led to a loft. I scanned the empty room quickly and saw no trace of Zac, so I climbed the ladder and called out his name.

Nothing. Then I heard the door shut and lock, but it didn't register in my head.

I climbed back down the ladder declaring, "He's not here. I need to leave, I have to go find Zac." When I turned around, Chet was standing there naked, a peculiar sadistic look in his eye.

"Oh my God, you're naked! What's going on—?"

Chet raped me that night. When he finished, he left the room and left the door wide open. I put my clothes on, walked downstairs and out the front door. I walked back to my dorm alone, shaking, in shock, and with tear–filled eyes. I tried to make sense out of what had just happened to me.

When I got back to my room and turned on the light, it woke up my roommate, Heather. She saw the condition I was in and was suddenly wide–awake, asking me questions. She called the police and they made me go to the University Hospital, where the Dr. examined me for a rape kit and took my clothes as evidence. By this time, it was well past two o'clock in the morning and I was exhausted. But I still had to fill out a police report; the night just wouldn't end.

A month later, after being questioned by the Pullman Police several times, one counseling session, and being excommunicated from the fraternity (even Zac had stopped talking to me) I dropped all charges. The police said it would be difficult to make a conviction stick because it was my word against his and there were no witnesses. Chet told them that we'd had consensual sex; he said I was a slut and a liar and that I was easy. He said he had no idea why I would accuse him of rape.

The police said the fact that I had been drinking only incriminated me more because it meant that I was not of sound judgment. They implied that I didn't remember things correctly, as they actually occurred. They said that

I probably did give consent, that I brought it on myself and that I had no business being in Chet's room. In a nutshell, that I had "asked for it" and it was somehow *MY FAULT*.

I lost friends over this. Everyone judged me, believed the rumors, and looked at me differently. Friends tried to minimize it, pretend it didn't happen. I became a social pariah, an outcast. I just wanted to disappear, even wanted to quit school. I was humiliated beyond anything I'd ever imagined, and I felt so alone. I missed Trey desperately. I felt he was the only person who would have stood by me, who truly cared about me.

I went to just one counseling session. Talking about it only made me feel worse. I felt ashamed and was angry that I let it happen. The police said there were no signs of a struggle; his skin was not under my fingernails and there was no evidence that I resisted or fought back. That stung. I couldn't explain why I didn't try to fight him off. I couldn't make them understand that I was PARALYZED WITH FEAR; that I couldn't move. And I couldn't help but be angry with myself for being such a helpless victim.

By this point, I just wanted to lock it away and pretend it never happened, move on with my life. If the case went to court it could drag on for months, and I didn't want to be the poster girl for date rape. Yeah, that's what they were calling it. Only, it wasn't a date. Whatever, I just wanted it to be over; I wanted my life back.

The clincher? They seemed to be more concerned about HIM than me. The police told me that if I pressed charges it would ruin Chet's life. He was preparing to graduate in December; he had a fiancée in Seattle waiting for him; he had a bright future and a wedding to plan. Was that something I really wanted to do to him? Did I want to be responsible for ruining a man's life? I allowed them to bully me into letting him get away with it. What about my life? I felt like nothing. What about his fiancée? Didn't she have a right to know what kind of man she was about to marry?

It was a dark time for me and I had to decide if I was going to let this consume me and drop out of school, or come back with my head held high the following semester. Luckily, Christmas break was about to start and I had some time to think about it. I wrote this entry in my journal:

"There's no justice. The prosecuted go free and the victims get persecuted. One month ago, on the 13th of November, a senior member of Phi Sigma Kappa fraternity raped me. I pressed charges and was ready to take it to court, but it was an uphill battle and I didn't want to ruin his life. I dropped the charges.

I was a little sis at that house and now I'm being excommunicated from it. I'm being punished for something I didn't do. What's worse is Zac is turning on me. He's friends with the fucker who did this to me! I feel so low right now; so cheap and used. I don't know what I want anymore—from life, from anything. My values and ideals have completely changed. I don't even know if I want to be here next semester, I have to fight through this thing and I don't know how. I'm so incredibly scared. I feel so alone—so lonely. I miss Trey so much. Every guy I meet here is a total asshole. No one understands me!

I have no one to turn to. I feel so isolated, so cut off from the world. I'm such an outcast. I don't belong here. Where do I belong? Is there a life for me? Where? What the hell am I going to do with my life? I need a sense of direction. I need to have a goal—to be motivated, inspired—to be going somewhere with my life! Not nowhere! Am I crazy? Am I going off the deep end? Is this Hell? Have I died? Am I in eternal purgatory? I need answers! Not more questions!

I feel so much stress and pressure to excel in life—to graduate from college—to make good grades. To have a career, raise a family—make everyone proud of me. I'm 21 fucking years old and I'm wasting away! I'm so terrified! I'm not happy. When does it get better? Does it get better? Is this how I'm going to feel for the rest of my life? How long am I going to live? Will I ever be happy? Is it worth it?"

18   my surprise visitor

HELLO SECOND SEMESTER! Yes, I went back to school after Christmas break. Did I mention I was a Theatre minor? I am not minimizing depression or what happened to me at all; I just want to acknowledge that I had a tendency toward the melodramatic, so please don't be alarmed about the journal entry. Besides, I'm a survivor, remember? That day after the bathtub incident in Texas I made a promise to myself—I meant it.

Spring semester came and went, and I got through it. Some friends stuck by me, others drifted away, and I made a few new ones. I kept my head down and concentrated on my studies. Then in April, guess who called me?

For spring semester, I moved to a single room (no roommates) in the same dormitory, McCroskey Hall. Having been raised predominantly an only child with my own bedroom, as it turns out, I valued my privacy and needed my own space.

One Friday afternoon, around four thirty, as I was on my way home from racquetball class, I heard my phone ringing from the hallway just outside my door. I fumbled with the key in the lock, slammed open the door and lunged for the phone—it was Trey. I think my heart stopped beating. He was in town and wanted to see me. He said he was living in Seattle now. I gave him directions to my dorm, slammed down the phone and raced for the shower. I had just played racquetball for an hour and was sweaty. No way was I going to let him see me like that. I got ready as fast as I could, cleaned up my room, and the phone rang again. He was downstairs in the lobby of my building.

My room was on the second floor and the walk down the stairs to the lobby was excruciating. I was nervous, excited, scared, shocked—I didn't know if I wanted to jump for joy or cry with renewed grief from my earlier pain. It had been three years since I'd last seen him. I always hoped I'd see him again, but I never thought it would happen like this. I walked through the lobby door, saw him, and froze.

"Hi, don't I get a hug?" he asked with that casual, sideways smile. We hugged, and then I awkwardly walked him back up to my room. It was uncomfortable at first. I was tense and still struggling with the pain of losing him three years earlier.

Trey pulled the chair out from my desk and took a seat while I sat on my bed. I just sat there and looked at him for a few minutes, processing that he was actually *here,* sitting in my room, at my dorm, on my college campus.

I took in the sight before me and noticed that his hair was much longer (no more military buzz cut) he was more muscular, maybe even taller, and he looked older. He was now a twenty-two-year-old man.

"What are you thinking?" he asked.

"I'm thinking I can't believe you're actually here. I'm thinking I have a million questions, and that I haven't heard from you for *three years!"*

"Ask me anything. What do you want to know?"

"Okay. For starters, why didn't you write to me like you said you would?"

"Lucy asked me not to. I wanted to respect her wishes and I really tried to make things work with us. It wouldn't have been fair to any of us for me to keep in touch with you. I wanted to for my own selfish reasons, but I realized I had to let you go. And if my marriage was going to stand a chance of surviving at all, I had to commit to it. I had to try to forget you."

"Why are you here now?"

"Honestly? I haven't been able to go a day in the last three years without thinking about you. I constantly wonder where you are, what you're doing, and if you're happy. I never meant to hurt you, Tara. All I've ever wanted was for you to be happy. It makes me so sad when I think about how much pain I've caused you over the years. I can never make that up to you—and I am so sorry."

"But, I mean, how did you find me? Why are you here?" I was determined to stay detached, yet fighting back tears. *Damn emotions!*

"Our moms still send each other Christmas cards every year. My mom told me you were at WSU now. I've kept tabs on you all along. Once I got to Pullman, I looked up WSU in the phone book, called their directory assistance, and got your number."

"But you live in Phoenix. You told me on the phone you live in Seattle now? What's going on? What about Lucy and the kids?"

"Lucy and I are separated. I moved to Seattle temporarily to give us both some time to figure things out. I'm staying with my dad right now, but I'm looking for a job. I just moved up here last week," he paused. "Tara, when I woke up this morning, I didn't know I was going to see you today. It's my day off and I was out running errands. I drove by a sign that said, 'Pullman 280 miles.' The next thing I knew, I turned my car toward that sign and headed east—and here I am."

My head was spinning; it was all too overwhelming to take in. I was happy to see him and presently unattached, but it had taken me years to get over him. I didn't need to be distracted with complications and be sucked back into his world again. Finally, I gathered my thoughts enough to say, "I can't do this. You can't just come into my life and turn my world upside down and hurt me again. I have to focus on my studies. School and my career have to be my number one priority right now. I don't have time to be in a relationship—with anyone.

"Besides, you're not even divorced yet! You're only separated. What if you get back together? I don't— I don't know if I can trust you."

"Maybe this was a mistake. I'm sorry. I shouldn't have come. I'll go away and leave you alone . . . if that's what you want."

"No, of course not. You drove all this way just to see me. I'm glad you came. I just can't do a long-distance relationship again. It's too hard. And you have to figure out what you and Lucy are going to do."

"She cheated on me."

"Ha! There's some irony! Oh, sorry, it just slipped out. Go on."

"It's okay, I deserved that. Lucy met some paramedic named Dave and they've been sneaking around behind my back for who knows how long. She hates my guts. After you left, she never trusted me again. Whenever we fought or argued she always threw your name in my face. She made me burn all your letters, and the pictures too. I have nothing left, nothing except my memories. Tara, I'm sorry things turned out the way they did. I still love you. I never stopped."

I was a mess. He was sweet, remorseful, and vulnerable. My resolve was weakening. It was also getting late and we were hungry. Since I lived in an all-girl dorm, I offered to go to the dining hall and bring food back for us. We were allowed male visitors, it was just easier if I got the food and came back. I didn't want him to attract attention, and I didn't want a bunch of questions from the other girls later.

I grabbed a couple burgers and some fries from the dining hall next door, typical college food, and hurried back. It was already dark, and Trey mentioned he didn't want to have to drive back to Seattle in the dark. "Could I spend the night? I can sleep in this chair if you want me to? I just worry about driving back so late. It's nearly a six-hour drive and I'm exhausted as it is. It's been a long day."

"Uh sure, you can stay here. But no one can see you. We're not allowed to have boys here after ten o'clock at night and I don't want to get in any trouble." I got up, went to my closet, and got out my sleeping bag. I threw it on the floor and said, "Welcome to my guest room!"

"Hey, cool. It beats this stiff chair!" Trey smiled and unrolled the sleeping bag while I went to the bathroom and brushed my teeth. Of course, the bathroom was down the hall and shared by ten other girls. When I was sure it was empty, I motioned Trey down the hall to hurry. Surprisingly, he was quite stealthy, and nobody saw us.

We both got in our respective beds and began reminiscing. The old feelings came flooding back in a tidal wave and before I knew it, he was in my twin bed with me. The dam burst, and my resolve was gone. We shared a magical night and a wonderful memory but made no plans for the future. The next morning, I walked him to his car, and he was gone.

Once again, I had to forget about him and do what I came to Pullman to do—finish college. I couldn't let anyone derail my plans, not even Trey. Besides, he wasn't even divorced yet. I'd be a fool to get involved with that love triangle disaster again. I told him to give me a call when the divorce was final.

19   watermelon

I STAYED IN PULLMAN that summer and enrolled in summer session to get a head start on the next school year, because my goal was to finish college in three and a half years. Looking back, I'm not sure why I was in such a hurry to graduate, but I was. (Truthfully, I felt guilty for taking a gap year. In my mind, I was a year behind my fellow classmates, feeling I should graduate in 1988 instead of 1989). They closed the dorms over the summer, forcing me to find other housing.

Luckily, my new friend whom I had just met in a Communications class, Julie Madrid, was staying for the summer too, and she already had an apartment. She said her roommates were gone for the summer and I was welcome to stay with her, but I had to be out before her roommates got back in the fall. We were the same age and she was also taking summer classes—to get ahead, or catch up, depending how you viewed it.

Julie and I got off to a slightly rocky start and I learned a valuable life lesson: never eat your roommate's food without permission. We were in a summer class together and she had a waitressing job at Pelican Pete's. She worked long hours and was exhausted when she came home late at night.

One particularly hot afternoon, and without air–conditioning, I came home from class while Julie was at work. I was hungry and began foraging for food. I opened the fridge and saw a tantalizing watermelon, cut into cubes, and stored in Tupperware. I stared at it for a while, knowing I shouldn't eat it, but it taunted me, so I figured a few missing bites wouldn't be noticed.

As I kept eating the deliciously juicy watermelon, I justified to myself that I would go to the store the next day, and replace it, so I wasn't really stealing Julie's food. I couldn't stop eating it and began to feel guiltier and guiltier with each bite. Before I knew it, the container was empty. I quickly washed it, put it away, and hoped she wouldn't notice until I'd gotten a chance to go to the store and replace it.

No such luck. When the five foot three, tawny–haired, pretty twenty-one-year-old walked in an hour later, she headed straight for the refrigerator. I stayed in my room and pretended to be studying. I heard loud shouting, followed by the sound of the refrigerator door slamming shut.

"TARA! Did you eat my watermelon?" she yelled from the kitchen, not even bothering to see if I was home first. I opened my bedroom door and meekly slunk toward the kitchen. I was busted and all I could do was own up to it and apologize. But she was having none of it.

"Yes, I did. I'm sorry!" I apologized. "I'm going to replace it, I promise. Tomorrow I'll go to the store, get another watermelon, and cut it up just like yours was. It's just that—"

"That's not the point!" she yelled, leveling her gaze at me with her big blue eyes. Then she softened, "You don't understand. I don't care if you borrow stuff or eat some of my food once in a while. But not like this! The whole time I was at work I was picturing that watermelon and how good it was going to taste when I got home. I cut it up before I left for work just so it would be ready for me, so I wouldn't have to do anything but come home and eat it. It was the expectation of knowing it was in the fridge waiting for me. AND NOW IT'S NOT THERE!"

I felt awful. I would have gone to the store right then to replace it, but it was dark, and I didn't have a car. All I had was a Vespa moped that I used to go back and forth to campus.

I did replace the watermelon the next day, but Julie didn't talk to me for a couple days. I made a terrible first impression on my new roommate, and it took a little while to gain her trust. Thankfully, she wasn't the kind of person to hold a grudge, and after a week or so, we became fast friends. And a couple of weeks after that, we even laughed about it.

Summer flew by quickly, and as agreed upon, I found another place to live before fall semester. I moved into a duplex about a mile off campus with a sister and brother, Becca and Pete Schneider, who were looking for a third roommate to help with expenses. I enjoyed the extra autonomy that living off campus provided. However, I did miss the dining hall food. None of us cooked; we lived on a budget and subsisted mainly on Top Ramen, pizza, peanut butter & jelly sandwiches, boxed Mac & cheese, Spaghettios, and milk & cereal. It's a wonder we survived.

I focused on my studies and didn't date at all. I told myself it was because I wanted to concentrate on school and do the best that I could in my major. The school had its own cable TV station, and we produced a nightly newscast called Cable 8 News. It was very rigorous, and therefore easy to tell myself that I didn't have time for anything else. I also had a part–time job on campus, working in the Communications office, after classes, four days a week. It was a demanding schedule, but I'd had demanding schedules before. Honestly, I think I just needed time to heal, and kept boys at a safe distance. However, there was one boy who was an exception, the one who, try as I might, I just couldn't forget.

It was November of my senior year and I got a letter from Trey. It was addressed to my old dorm but found its way to me at the duplex. My class–load was heavy and intense, and school was my top priority. I definitely wasn't involved with anyone. He said he needed a friend. His divorce was pending, Lucy had shacked up with the paramedic, and he was going through a rough time. Who was I to refuse him?

We exchanged a few letters and by Christmas break had made plans to see each other again. It just so happened I was going to my dad's that year, who lived fifteen miles from Trey. He said he was living on a houseboat and working as a pantry chef at The Rusty Pelican, on the marina.

I hitched a ride from Pullman to Seattle with a friend from school. She dropped me off at my dad's house at 4:20 p.m. on a Thursday. Since Dad was still at work, I quickly called The Rusty Pelican to find out Trey's work schedule. They said he had the day off. I called his place and he sounded surprised to hear from me. He said he wasn't expecting me until Friday, but that he'd love to see me. I told him I'd visit later that night if my dad let me borrow his car.

Dad let me borrow the car and I arrived at The Rusty Pelican around eight thirty. Trey met me there and took me to his houseboat. It was a bit awkward at first and we made small talk, not knowing what to say to each other. I was also cold and kept my coat on. Then I saw his photo album and began to look at pictures of his kids; that broke the ice and we were soon more at ease with each other. We went back to the restaurant and Trey bought me a drink, introduced me to his work buddies, and we had fun dancing to a live band.

A slow song came on and Trey asked me to dance. He placed his hand on the small of my back and pulled me close to him. I nuzzled my face in his chest and breathed in his scent, feeling his taught muscles beneath his t–shirt, as our bodies moved as one to the rhythm of the music. I closed my eyes and let the familiar memories rush in, desire taking over as the old sparks lit up again.

When the song ended, I pushed him away, confused and conflicted about my feelings. I had promised platonic friendship. He said he needed a friend and I didn't want to let him down. I was light-headed, and I told him I needed fresh air. It was freezing outside when we walked back to his houseboat. I felt chilled to the bone, my teeth chattering.

"Go in my bedroom and get under the blankets," he ordered, as soon as we got inside. I didn't argue. I jumped under the covers on his bed and he brought in a portable space heater. Then he climbed under the covers with me and we began to warm up—in more ways than one.

"No, Trey, we shouldn't. I don't want to confuse you. Remember, you asked me to be a friend. Your letters made it clear that you wanted this to stay platonic between us."

"Yeah, you're right. Thanks for reminding me. But you smell so good, and you feel so good, and . . ."

Our willpower soon gave way and we made love, falling asleep in each other's arms, and waking up at ten the next morning.

I stayed until two in the afternoon and was worried that my dad would be mad that I hadn't brought his car back yet. He had another car he could drive, but I didn't have permission to keep his car this long, so I was worried. As soon as I got back to the house, I called Dad at work and he wasn't mad. In fact, he asked me to pick up Jenny, my three-year-old half–sister, from a Christmas party and babysit her while he went on a date. He was fresh off the divorce from Carolyn, Jenny's mother, and was just starting to date again. Naturally, I was all too happy to help.

Saturday night it was foggy outside, and my dad wouldn't let me drive to Trey's. He said I'd have to wait until Monday. I didn't argue too hard because I had a sore throat and was getting a cold anyway; I went to bed early. The next morning, Trey called me and told me to watch the Seahawks game. Surrounded by pillows, blankets, tissues and throat lozenges, I sat on Dad's brown leather couch in my pajamas, robe and slippers, and watched the game by myself while Dad and Jenny were at a friend's house watching the game in a more festive atmosphere.

Monday, on his day off, Trey and I exchanged Christmas presents and he took me to Spaghetti Factory for dinner. I bought him an aquamarine earring stud for his newly pierced ear, and a red sweater. Red was my favorite color and I believed everyone should own a red Christmas sweater. He gave me gray knit gloves, since my hands were always cold.

By this time, we both had colds, so we were quite the pair, coughing and phlegmy. Nice picture, huh? Since we were both sick, we decided I should go back to Dad's. Trey walked me out to the car, kissed me and sent me on my way. We didn't say goodbye because he said he'd call me Friday.

Dad had to cancel our ski trip because of my cold. He said he didn't want me to get worse. I coughed all night. *Some Christmas vacation this turned out to be.*

Trey called me Friday afternoon and we tried to say goodbye. It was torture. "I love you, Tara."

"I love you too."

"I have to get back to Phoenix soon. It's time to finalize the divorce with Lucy and I miss my kids. I'll try to visit you in Pullman before I head out. I promise to keep in touch."

"Okay, me too."

"Hey, don't sound so sad."

"Right, of course. You either."

"We'll keep in touch. It will be okay."

"Yep. Call me when the divorce is final."

"Okay. I love you. Goodbye."

"Bye."

He didn't visit me. Time passed, and I soon graduated from WSU. I moved on with my life and he moved on with his.

20   flash forward

TWENTY YEARS LATER, I found myself going through a divorce and thinking of Trey, wondering about his life. Where was he? What was he doing now? Was he happy? What was his daily life like? Was he *(dare I think it)* single? The last time we saw each other, we were twenty-two. I thought that would be the last time I would ever see him again.

My mind drifted to a simpler time, a time when I was young, and the world was full of possibilities. I allowed myself to think "what if." What if Trey had never met Lucy all those years ago? I couldn't help myself. I let myself go there—how different things might have been. What if we had stayed neighbors as kids? Grown up together? Gone to the same high school? What if we had gotten married? How would my life be different today?

'What if' and 'if only' are dangerous words. Why, after all this time, was I still obsessed with this man?

Don't get me wrong, I'm not complaining. The last twenty years have been good to me. I have a beautiful daughter whom I love more than anything. I have a job that I enjoy. I've loved and lost and traveled. But I can't stop that nagging feeling, that incessant wondering, what might have been?

Could a second chance at first love be possible? Was I kidding myself? I decided to find out.

But to answer these questions in a way that makes any sense, I need to fill you in on a few highlights of the last twenty years. Ready? Here we go.

21   the real world

I GRADUATED in May and moved to Bend, Oregon, for a Reporter Internship at KTVZ. It was nothing like I thought it would be—it was one hundred times worse. I was not cut out for hard news—it chewed me up and spat me out. I remember our professors used to say, "If it bleeds it leads." But I didn't really get it until I was out there, out of my little WAZZU bubble, in the real world, reporting real tragedies—car accidents, wild fires, robberies, stabbings, murders, death, and destruction. News sucked. I wanted to do fluff pieces all the time, like the local cat show, or a human–interest story. My producer shot down all my story ideas. She told me I didn't have the stomach for hard news, and I wasn't about to argue with her.

Starting as a first year TV News Reporter in a small market meant paying dues and working up the ranks. Working evenings, weekends and holidays for minimum wage meant no social life. Plus, I went home to my little attic bedroom that I rented from a young, hippy couple, dejected every night because I couldn't leave work 'at the office.' I couldn't become a desensitized robot that just reported the facts. And frankly, I didn't want to. I didn't want to lose touch with my own humanity. Reporters can be so calloused. Like the time a five-year-old girl was hit and killed by a car on a residential street, and the reporters shoved microphones in her mother's face, just for that coveted sound bite. Disgraceful. This is what I wanted to be? No thank you!

When I figured out that I didn't want to be a TV News Reporter after all, what was I going to do with my brand new college degree that said Broadcast Journalism? I had to come up with a plan B, and quick. So there I was, a college graduate without a plan, who, much to my chagrin had to race through college in three and a half years because I was in such a hurry to be out in the 'real world.' *Yay, what irony.* It was time to reassess my aspirations.

I still wanted to utilize my degree, just not in news. Hoping to pursue a career in corporate video (more money, evenings, weekends and holidays off, and nobody had to die) I moved back to Seattle and got a job at Boeing—again. This time I was angling for a highly coveted position in their motion picture/television department. They had their own television station that broadcast all things Boeing company–wide and I was determined to be part of it.

However, it was nearly impossible to break in. BMP/TV had no openings and I was told they usually hired from within the company first. I figured my best shot was to do something as comparable as possible in another department, and then transfer in when a position opened up.

Fortunately, I was able to get a job as a Tour Director at Boeing's 747/767 final assembly plant in Everett, leading tours of the airplanes being built. By the way, the Boeing factory is the largest building by volume in the world, at 472 million cubic feet. In fact, did you know that a 747 uses ninety gallons of paint that weighs around

550 pounds? It's true. I learned all kinds of amazing fun–facts about Boeing airplanes and rattled them off four times a day, on ninety-minute tours.

Even though I viewed the job as a stepping–stone into BMP/TV, I enjoyed working at the Tour Center. People and tourists from all over the world came in large groups to take the tour and I met many nice people from far away countries I'd only dreamed of visiting. Sometimes we'd get guests who tried to ask questions we couldn't answer because they wanted to "stump the tour guide." It turned into a friendly competition among my co–workers and I to see which of us could fill our heads with the most airplane trivia.

And the most often asked question? "How many parts are in a 747?" A 747-400 is comprised of six million parts.

22   chateau ste. michelle

IN CASE YOU DIDN'T KNOW, Boeing is a large company, with many employees. In fact, besides the federal government, Boeing is still the largest employer in the state of Washington. Therefore, it was pretty much a given that I would eventually meet someone I wanted to date, right?

I was renting a cozy one–bedroom house in Everett, near work, and starting to get lonely. Even though I met literally hundreds of people at work every day, I didn't have much of a social life. I was on the phone with my grandmother one day, when she called me an old maid. She said she was surprised I hadn't found a nice boy in college to marry. She even made a joke about my going to college to get an "M.R.S." degree. Great, at barely twenty-four, I was already feeling family pressure to find a man.

And then I met Aaron Dryden. He worked at Boeing too, but thirty miles away, at their Bellevue Computer Services office. He brought his cousin to take the Boeing tour, who was visiting from Hartford, South Dakota, and a huge airplane enthusiast. All through the tour, Aaron kept making eye contact with me, and I thought he was cute. After the tour he asked me some random question about planes just as an excuse to talk to me, and then boldly asked for my phone number. I gladly gave it to him and wondered how long I'd have to wait until he called.

He called me that night. I was surprised to hear from him so soon, but quickly realized he strayed from the path of 'normal.' For our first date, he asked me to meet him at Gas Works Park in Seattle, Saturday morning at eleven o'clock sharp, and added, "Bring your bike." Let me just tell you right now—*Best. First Date. Ever.*

It was a beautiful, rare and sunny eighty-degree day in August. I pulled up next to Aaron's car in the parking lot and got my bike out of the back. Aaron wore an over–sized light blue Hawaiian print shirt, black and white polka dot shorts, a light blue bandana rolled up as a head band, white socks and black biking shoes. Tan, with wavy dark blond hair, hazel eyes, and a slight–built frame at five foot six, you can imagine how intimidating he looked when he reached down, rubbed his thumb on his bicycle chain, and then smeared the black grease under both eyes. Taking in the spectacle before me, I couldn't suppress a giggle.

Undaunted, he quickly smeared the grease under my eyes too, then, with a mischievous twinkle in his eye, said, "Let the bike ride begin."

"Where are we going?" I implored.

"You'll see," he grinned back at me as we got on our bikes. I followed him down the bike path that led out of the park.

We rode fifteen miles to the Chateau Ste. Michelle Winery in Woodinville. It was idyllic. We took a tour of the winery, bought a bottle of Blush Riesling, crackers and cheese, and settled down to a lovely picnic luncheon on the lush green grass. We were then treated to a free performance of *A Midsummer Night's Dream* at the winery's amphitheatre, to which we drank a newly purchased bottle of Chardonnay.

We were giddy and giggly from the wine, but thought we better head back, so we clumsily mounted our bikes and teetered back down the path toward Seattle. We'd ridden less than two miles when Aaron stopped. We parked our bikes at the edge of the path and walked down the bank to the Sammamish River. Next thing I knew, he pulled off his socks and shoes, helped me take off my socks and shoes, grabbed my hand, and we both jumped in. We had a great time laughing and splashing around; he had me laughing so hard tears were leaking out of me! He was absolutely hilarious. I don't remember laughing that hard in a long, long time. Aaron was just what I needed.

The ride back to our cars proved daunting. Being the light weight that I am, I was not prepared to bike while intoxicated, which of course made Aaron laugh even more. I'm sure we made quite a scene as the other bikers passed by wary of us.

By the time we got back to our cars we were dry, sober, and hungry, so we stopped at Dick's Burgers and had burgers, fries, and shakes. After dinner I waddled off to my car and drove home smiling, thus ending a perfect first date.

Aaron and I dated about four months and got along great. He was warm, wonderful and witty, and nothing like Trey. He was easy going and kept me laughing on a continual basis. But he wasn't serious, that is, about me. I didn't think it bothered me until I had one of those scary, close call, life–altering moments that changed my perspective.

There was a rare, freakish Arctic snowstorm in the Seattle area, with black ice all over the freeways. The trouble with black ice is, it's invisible, so when a driver hits a patch of it, the unexpected loss of traction causes a high risk of skidding or spinning out. As luck would have it, I was on my way to Aaron's from work in my cherry red 1989 Toyota Corolla SR5 (that I bought as a college graduation present to myself). The traffic was bumper–to–bumper gridlock due to the weather, and I had to pee horrendously. I'd already been sitting on the freeway for two hours when it began to pick up a bit. Anxious to get to a toilet and relieve my bladder, I sped up only to drive over a large patch of black ice.

Suddenly, I spun out of control, hit a cement pole, and became airborne. My car flew into a ditch, and landed on the passenger side, wheels in the air, on the right side of the freeway. The driver's door was stuck shut and the passenger door was on the ground.

I don't know how long I waited until help arrived. It could have been fifteen minutes or fifty (this was before cell phones, so calling 911 was not instantaneous). I think I blacked out, because the next thing I remember was the Jaws–of–Life prying open my door to extricate me; then the paramedics put me on a board with a neck brace because they didn't know the extent of my injuries. I was rushed via ambulance to the nearest hospital and was overcome by two thoughts.

Thought number one: I still had to pee and felt my bladder was going to burst. I was in serious pain and contemplated just letting go and peeing in my clothes. Then I actually tried it. I couldn't go. I had some mental block and wasn't able to just lay there and pee. When I got to the hospital, I told the nurses. They gave me a bedpan and I still couldn't go. Talk about your issues! Eventually, someone gave permission to let me get up and use a toilet, with assistance. It actually hurt to pee at first, but then the relief was almost euphoric.

Thought number two: Life is too short to play games. I knew I wanted to get married and have children someday.

I also knew that was not going to happen with Aaron. He was a great guy and we had a lot of fun together, we just weren't the right ones for each other. We cared about each other deeply and I considered him a great friend, but we weren't in love. I knew what real love was. *Maybe I was subconsciously still waiting for Trey?* Aaron and I parted amicably.

My injuries consisted of a few minor cuts and scrapes, and I had to wear a neck brace for two weeks, but I didn't have to stay overnight in the hospital. Fortunately, it was Christmas break and I was able to spend it recuperating at Mom's, in Stonewood. One of the perks of working at Boeing was that they shut down over Christmas and everyone got the week between Christmas and New Year's off.

While at Mom's, I reassessed my life in Seattle. The Tour Center was a dead–end and getting tedious; I could recite the entire tour while practically sleep walking. I had been in contact with the department head at BMP/TV and I knew people who knew people there. I had to face facts—there were no openings and I wasn't going to get in there any time soon. My relationship with Aaron was over. Life in Everett, in my tiny house by myself, was boring and lonely. I was homesick. So, there it was.

With the help and encouragement of my close friends from my theatre days at PCC, Pat and Shawna Decker, we came up with a plan to get me out of Seattle and back in Portland for good.

23   a fresh start

I GAVE my boss at the Tour Center a month's notice. He was great about it and wrote me a nice letter of recommendation for my next endeavor. It was pretty scary leaving a job for nothing, but again, with Pat and Shawna's generosity and support, I took the leap of faith that I would be able to land on my feet again. They said I could stay with them as long as I needed.

My car had four thousand dollars in damages and was deemed un–drivable, so my last month at Boeing I carpooled with a co–worker. Ready for the kicker? Apparently, I had paid my car insurance premium renewal three days late. According to them I wasn't technically insured the day of the accident; they declared that my policy had "lapsed." *Are you kidding me?* The insurance company refused to pay a penny. Luckily for me, my mom's next–door neighbor owned an auto body shop and agreed to fix my car at a discount, and with a payment plan. Unfortunately, he was doing it as a favor, on the side, so it took him three months.

Pat and Shawna were barely out of the newlywed stage, having only been married a year and a half, when they said I could stay with them. I met Shawna at PCC five years earlier and was maid–of–honor at their wedding. I definitely didn't want to be the third wheel. I was motivated to get a job as soon as possible.

Within two days of moving back, Shawna got me a job at the company where she worked, Synergy Consulting, downtown Portland. I was a mail clerk, filing and sorting the mail. It was a temporary position and not ideal, but it was something while I continued to look for something better.

It felt good to be back in the area again. I enjoyed being in close proximity to my mom, and Shawna and Pat were great friends. It was nice to have people around who cared about me, and the loneliness I felt in Everett was now gone. I rode to work with Shawna most days, or took the bus when our schedules were different. I began digging myself out of debt and saving to pay for my car repairs. I was very thankful—I had a job, a place to live, good friends, and my car was being fixed. I felt like I was going to be okay. And then I met a guy—things were definitely looking up.

I was set up with Danny Rook at a Portland Trailblazer basketball playoff party—Rip City! The party's hostess, Shelly, a co-worker, had been telling me for weeks that she knew the ideal guy for me, but I was reluctant to be set up and didn't want to go on a blind date. She told me the party would be perfect because I could check him out without risk, and he'd never be the wiser. He had no idea he was being set up; he just came to watch the game with friends.

There we were, it was game one of the play offs and the Blazers were playing the Seattle Super Sonics. It was a high–scoring nail biter and the Blazers lost. After the game, a few of us went to Dublin Pub to forget about the loss. Danny came too, and we finally started talking to each other over a couple beers, after furtive glances and subtle flirting during the game. When it was time to leave, he walked me to my car, we exchanged phone numbers and he gave me a brief kiss.

He was strikingly handsome with chiseled milk white skin, straight black hair and ice blue eyes. A lanky six feet tall, heads turned wherever he went. He was charming, thoughtful and highly intelligent, and I was intrigued from the moment I looked into those piercing eyes.

We'd been dating for just three weeks when he surprised me with a large bouquet of twenty-five balloons for my twenty-fifth birthday. Their buoyancy rivaled my own as I gleefully held onto my balloons with a fierce grip and a jaw–splitting smile. Yep, I was floating on air. Danny also met Mom and Jack and we celebrated my birthday with dinner at TGI Friday's, then cake, ice cream, and a Blazer play–off game at their house. It was definitely a birthday to be remembered, even though I didn't feel twenty-five.

Danny was one year older than me, and a painter by trade. He could paint anything: interiors, exteriors, commercial, residential, faux painting. He was excellent at his job and took pride in it. He enjoyed texturizing and faux work, and would often create mini–murals all over the walls in his house, practicing and perfecting his craft. It was always fun to see what new creation would be there each time I visited. Next to a faux marble would be a wallpaper texture, or painted bricks, or distressed wood look; he was remarkably talented.

After we'd been dating a few months, my mom hired Danny to paint her house. I offered to help and was relegated to cleaning the gutters, which turned out to be a disaster. First of all, Danny was a perfectionist (which seems like a good thing until you're the one working with him and all he does is criticize your work). Second, I fell off the ladder two hours into my job and scraped up my shin. And third, I burned my arms with bleach, had to call the poison center, and ended up covered in burn cream after a long hot shower. For some reason, Danny never took me on any more of his jobs. *Gee, I wonder why.*

He was also the most obstinate, pigheaded, frustrating and challenging person I'd ever met. Nearly every conversation turned into an argument or debate. He loved to argue. But he argued logically and was so articulate that I didn't have a chance of winning an argument even if I was the one who was right. Even though I disliked arguing with him, he had a way of pulling me in, and we often had stimulating debates about deep philosophical topics that lasted hours. The problem was, he never backed down, thought he was right even when he was wrong, and rarely apologized for anything.

But he also had a kind and generous heart. Shawna, Pat and I were forced to move because the owners of the house we were renting wanted to sell it. It was time for me to move out anyway, and when I had trouble finding an apartment, Danny offered to let me stay with him for a couple months until I found a place of my own. He lived in a four–bedroom house with a roommate, Steve, and they had room for me—temporarily of course.

Two weeks before moving in with Danny, I started a new job at a video production company, as a Production Manager. Although the job title sounded more impressive than it was, I enjoyed working there. Unfortunately, the job only lasted four months. Nearly everyone was laid off when another company bought them out in a hostile takeover.

Meanwhile, Danny and I had been together for nearly three months and I was about to move all my stuff in, albeit temporarily, in a week. I was aware that he hadn't told me he loved me yet. One night, in a moment of vulnerability and panic I asked him about the words we never say.

"You don't tell me how you feel," I nearly whispered.

"Don't I show you?" he retorted back, sounding annoyed.

"Yes, but I'd like to hear the words—"

"What words?"

"Never mind, just drop it," I said as I rolled over and eventually fell asleep, feeling irritated.

Two days later, while dining at our favorite healthy Mexican fast food place, Macheezmo Mouse (with the best Boss sauce ever) Danny blurted out "I love you," in between bites of his wet burrito.

Moving day arrived on a Saturday and Danny had to work, so my parents helped me move my stuff out of Pat and Shawna's garage, and into Danny and Steve's spare room upstairs (they didn't have a garage). While I was in the middle of unpacking and organizing, Steve's family visited—my first night there, and his sister wanted to spend the night. I was exhausted and in no mood to make small talk with strangers, so I excused myself and went to bed.

I spent the next day cleaning and reorganizing the kitchen. I wanted to unpack and use my dishes because none of their dishes matched, and they were chipped and ugly. Plus, they didn't cook much, so their kitchen was a disaster. After all, they were two single guys in their twenties, so yes, their house looked like a messy bachelor pad.

THREE WEEKS LATER, Danny and I were strolling through Lloyd Center mall when we wandered into a pet store and saw a seven-week-old Netherland dwarf bunny. She was a tiny ball of dark silver-gray fluff and we loved her instantly. Since she was gray, I suggested we name her after Bugs Bunny. Danny liked the idea, but changed it slightly to Buds Bunny, as a joke to reference his penchant for marijuana. We built an elaborate home for her in the sunroom, a fully enclosed sun porch that had been carpeted and turned into a small room, which was perfect for our little Buds bunny.

Living with Danny had its ups and downs, but it was never boring. He was one of those people who had such a high IQ that it made him socially anxious. He was hyper-aware of everything, over-analyzed situations most people thought nothing of, and rationalized things logically ad-nauseam. His mind was constantly working. Of course, he was aware of this. His solution was to self-medicate with marijuana. It calmed him down and helped his mind relax a little. He often referred to himself as a 'functioning stoner.'

One weekend we drove up to Mount St. Helens (three hundred miles round trip) to shoot video of the devastation from the catastrophic volcanic eruption eleven years earlier. I was able to borrow a video camera and some equipment from work and we thought it would be cool to go up there and record what we saw. I later edited the footage into a mini–documentary and sent it to his family in Minnesota.

The day trip itself was fun, but on the way back we got in a fight about something stupid, which carried over when we got home. While I was in the kitchen making spaghetti, Danny came in and grabbed a bunch of the just drained pasta out of the pan and threw it against the wall. Then, for added effect, he threw some at me.

He yelled and screamed like a tantrum throwing two-year-old. "I don't even want fucking pasta! This is too al dente! Can't you make anything decent? This is shit!"

I was shocked and disgusted by his behavior and decided the best way to get him to cool down was to not even engage him at all. I left the mess, skipped dinner, and went upstairs to take a shower. *Trey would never treat me like this. What am I doing with this guy?*

While washing my hair, I heard the door open, shower curtain slide back, and as I blinked the shampoo out of my eyes, there was Danny in the tub with me—fully clothed, down to his converse tennis shoes, looking sad and pathetic and full of apologies. Yes, life with Danny was anything but boring.

Two weeks later, after more fights and bickering, he told me to move out. "I won't tolerate your poutiness anymore! You've stayed too long and worn out your welcome. This was never supposed to be a permanent arrangement, Tara. I'll help you find a place."

Some of my "poutiness" was attributed to the fact that work was stressful with the hostile takeover happening, and I knew I was getting laid off. Fortunately, one of my clients owned a small video production company and offered me a job as a production assistant/receptionist. Like I said, it was small. It was a reduction in pay and a demotion, but it was a job. We set up a formal interview, and within two weeks, I lost one job and started another—the next day.

Three weeks after Danny told me to move out, he helped me move into a one–bedroom apartment three blocks away, then showed up again at nine thirty that night to watch "Star Trek" while I was still unpacking boxes. We continued six months longer as girlfriend and boyfriend, living three blocks away from each other. He kept Buds Bunny at his house, but I had visiting privileges.

Things got better between us after I moved out; we argued less and focused more on spending quality time together and planning fun activities. We went on ski trips to Mt. Hood, near Sandy, and Mt. Bachelor, in Bend; hiked in beautiful forests and arboretums throughout Oregon; and even went to a 'big cat farm' out past Molalla where I got to hold live cougar cubs. That was an unforgettable experience. I wore my WSU Cougars sweatshirt, of course, and we got to see cougars, jungle cats, and their cubs.

To hold a twelve-week-old cougar cub in my lap was indescribable. I could see the claws, feel the muscles and power, and was amazed at this beautiful wild creature looking up at me, fearless and trusting. I was incredibly moved. The same day I was playing with baby cougars, my WSU Cougars and the UW Huskies were battling it out in their annual rivalry football game, the Apple Cup. Naturally, Aaron decided to call me that night to rub it in that the Huskies won. But after seeing, holding and petting real, live cougars I didn't care one bit. It was totally worth missing the game.

After three months with the small video production company, a nasty recession set in, and I got let go right after the morning staff meeting because my boss said he couldn't afford to pay me anymore. *So, it's time to get another job. Again. Geez, is this the story of my life or what?* The next day I stood in line at the unemployment office for nearly two hours. Did I mention it was December? Recession, plus Christmas, plus being unemployed, plus dysfunctional relationship, equaled low self–esteem. What did I do to combat the unemployment blues? I got a kitten.

While attending a cat show in Portland with my mom, I fell in love with an eight-week-old red Somali kitten (a long-haired Abyssinian). He had a bushy long tail and striking red fur, just like a fox, so I named him Foxy. He instantly became my constant companion and even enjoyed riding in the car, so I took him up to Seattle for Christmas with me and he captivated my family with his striking looks and crazy kitten antics. Danny liked him too and I often took Foxy with me over to Danny's house to play with Buds Bunny. They were cute together, and a welcome distraction from my job woes. Sadly, when Danny's six-year-old niece visited, she fed Buds Bunny chocolate, and he found her dead the next morning (the bunny, not the niece).

The next three months consisted of job hunting, a few interviews, breaking up with Danny, getting back together with Danny, becoming just friends with Danny, and other minutia of day–to–day unemployment and the effects of having a yo-yo boyfriend. I was miserable, seemed to have a chronic cold that I couldn't shake, and felt sorry for myself generally every other day. And in the back of my mind, Trey was always there. *What was he doing? Where was he now? Was he happy?* Then one pivotal phone call changed my life—*thank God!*

Mid–March I got a call for a job interview from PayLess Drug Stores corporate communications video production manager. The company was thirty miles away and I had applied for the position back in December. When they told me there were no openings at the time, I had no idea they kept my résumé on file—I was elated!

Three interviews, a physical and drug screen, and two weeks later I celebrated my first day at my new job, in the PayLess Wilsonville headquarters video production department. I got there early, left late, and drove thirty miles each way. It was a long but rewarding first day. So far, I loved my new job and I had a great boss. A month later, I moved into an apartment less than a mile from work because I loathe commuting.

25   my creepy stalker guy

WORKING AT PAYLESS was fun, fast–paced, kept me busy, and a great distraction from men. Plus, it was a novelty for my friends and family, and many of them wanted a tour of the impressive state–of–the–art television studio and control room. We were set up just like a working TV station, with all the cameras, lights, sets, monitors and equipment. We even had a satellite receiver and were able to broadcast live video teleconferences to all of our store managers—to a retail chain of 1,038 stores.

We also produced the employee training videos, which sometimes constituted filming in a store after hours. Thus, I put in some crazy long shifts, as we'd often be filming all night, while the store was closed to the public (one time I worked straight through from ten in the morning to five o'clock the next morning—nineteen hours). Our department consisted of three full–time employees and we only hired freelancers when we had bigger shoots, so I often performed the duties of eight crewmember jobs rolled into one. This made the job exciting and I loved the variety, but it quickly consumed my life—I had no free time.

After repeatedly turning Danny down for dinners or movies because I was exhausted, he drove down and visited me at work. I gave him the tour, and the worst thing he could think of to point out was, "There aren't any windows." Yes, I suppose it was a bit of a bat cave, but I was usually too busy to notice.

Things naturally faded away between Danny and me until we eventually lost touch. It was easier to just let it go, rather than a big dramatic ending. Thus, our year together was over.

I had moved into a one bedroom, one bathroom, eight hundred and fifty square foot apartment that felt roomy and spacious compared to the three–bedroom, one bathroom, nine hundred seventy square foot house I grew up in. The bedroom was spacious, and the kitchen had lots of counter space and cabinets—I loved my new place. It was my refuge, and it was less than a mile from work. For me, it was perfect.

Eventually, the pace slowed down at work and I managed to settle into a comfortable routine. I even found time to socialize and my well–meaning (married) friends wanted to set me up on blind dates. *Ugh.* It turns out I had a 'type.' I was attracted to guys who weren't able to commit emotionally. They were scarred by a past relationship, emotionally unavailable, or just immature; yet, I was attracted to them like a moth to a flame. *Hmm, I'm no psych major, but does Trey have anything to do with this pattern?*

Perhaps I thought I could heal them, or make them feel again, who knows? I often quoted a saying that became a sort of mantra of mine, "Hurts have taught me, never give up loving. Be willing to take another risk and chance—otherwise tomorrow may be empty." I don't know who said it originally, but it helped me through some dark and lonely times.

Speaking of lonely, I somehow managed to acquire two more cats. When I started working again, I felt bad for leaving Foxy alone all day, so I got him a kitten. She was a timid, scrawny gray tabby I found in a foster home for rescue cats. She had a harsh little cry, so I named her Mio, Chinese for meow.

A few months later, I found a Siamese mix, three-week-old kitten, abandoned in a cardboard box at the grocery store, with a sign taped to it that said FREE. She was severely malnourished and flea-ridden; a tiny thing that didn't even weigh a pound. Naturally, I couldn't leave her there to die, so I took her home and nursed her back to health, with the plan to find her a good home.

Of course, I fell in love with her and ended up keeping her myself. I named her Tia. So there I was, living in an apartment with three cats, Foxy, Mio, and Tia—*yikes.* I sometimes joked with my mom that I would end up one of those crazy old ladies with fifty cats—who lives alone. *Gee, I'm off to a great start with three, aren't I?*

My new job at PayLess was great, and every day was a new adventure, but they also *paid less.* Therefore, when my muffler broke and I discovered I owed taxes (pay back for collecting unemployment) I took a few print modeling jobs to get out of debt. I knew a talent agent who agreed to represent me, because I often used her Agency to book actors for our training videos.

At first my boss at PayLess was okay with it, but then she decided it interfered with my hours working for her. She said it was a conflict of interest and I couldn't do the modeling anymore. By then I had earned enough to pay my taxes.

While we filmed a training video at the Wilsonville store, one of the actors I hired for the shoot flirted with me. He was striking with shockingly white hair and pale blue eyes, so I was intrigued, but he was forward, borderline aggressive, and insisted on taking me out for coffee after the shoot. I protested, citing I shouldn't date the talent, but he wouldn't take no for an answer. While I admired his confidence and charm, I also felt a little strange around him, but couldn't pinpoint it. Against my better judgment, I met him at a diner nearby. But I ordered a 7up since I didn't drink coffee.

Adam Gillman stared through me with piercing eyes; the kind of stare that made my skin crawl. "So, Tara, tell me about yourself," he said, in between sips of his coffee. "Did you grow up around here?"

"Yeah, I did, not too far from here actually. What about you?"

"Me? Oh, I'm from New York. But I already know all about me. I'd much rather talk about you!"

I squirmed uneasily in my chair. His eyes followed my every move. What was it about this guy? There was an air of creepiness about him I couldn't shake off. I heard an unmistakable voice in my head say, *'Why didn't you listen to your mother and go with your gut?'* I had to get away from this guy and I had to do it fast.

Thinking quickly, I blurted out, "I'm sorry to have to cut this short, but I have to go back to work. We're up against an editing deadline and I really have to get back."

"But we just got here. Relax for a minute. You haven't even finished your 7up."

"I know, I'm sorry. I just didn't realize how late it was. Thank you for the 7up, but I've gotta go," I insisted as I stood up.

"Well, at least let me walk you to your car. What kind of gentleman would I be if I didn't properly escort out the pretty lady?"

I nodded in defeat, turned and walked toward the door with Adam on my heels.

When we got to my car, I again thanked him and reached for the door handle. He reached out to hug me, so I hugged him back. But instead of letting me go, he forced a kiss then shoved his tongue in my mouth. At first, I was just grossed out, but then I got scared. I backed away with a smile, tried not to show fear, and waved goodbye. As I peeled out of the parking lot it never occurred to me that the nightmare had just begun.

Adam called me later that night and told me he was falling in love with me. The next day, he personally delivered a dozen roses to my work. The day after that, I saw his car in the parking lot of my apartment complex when I went home for lunch. He knew where I worked, he knew where I lived, and he called me at home and at work repeatedly. I told my boss and the security guards where I worked, and even called the police. I had a stalker and I was terrified. I also called his talent agent and she told me everything she knew about him, which wasn't much.

At first, the police said there was nothing they could do. They told me to stop answering my phone and to give them the tapes if he left messages on my answering machine. When I didn't answer the phone, Adam left messages. Eventually, the messages got threatening and harassing, and he often called in the middle of the night. I turned the tapes over to the police. Pretty soon I saw his car everywhere. I was afraid to be alone and had to be escorted to and from my car by a PayLess security guard every day.

About a week later, a police detective in Tigard called to warn me that there were other complaints against Adam Gillman, and that the Portland police had been monitoring him. They were waiting for him to incriminate himself enough for them to make an arrest.

Then Adam called and left a message saying, "I know you called the cops, I know everything. I am going to sue the hell out of all of you for character defamation. You're a lying little cunt and you need to be punished."

My mom bought me mace, and Jack, a former police officer, loaned me his snub–nosed 38 special. He said that if my stalker broke into my apartment and I shot him, it would be self-defense and I wouldn't go to jail for it. *Are you kidding me?* I didn't want to shoot anybody!

The detective called back two days later, saying they were ready to arrest him for another crime, but that he wasn't home, and they couldn't find him. The detective asked if I could stay somewhere else until they found Adam, just as a precaution for my safety.

I stayed with my parents that weekend until I finally got the call Sunday afternoon that they caught him. They said I was safe now and that I could go back home. Adam was going to be behind bars, hopefully for many years. I cried with relief and gratitude that I had my life back.

26   baby track

SHORTLY AFTER THE WHOLE STALKING THING, I got sick; what began as a cold turned into strep throat. The doctor I went to prescribed amoxicillin, a common antibiotic used for bacterial infections. I got my prescription, went home and fell asleep. The next morning, I woke up with a swollen and puffy face. My eyes were swollen nearly shut. I also had a body rash, hives and a red, hot, fat face. I called work, described my symptoms, and our department secretary drove over, got me, and rushed me to the hospital. They took blood tests and confirmed that I am now allergic to amoxicillin. *Great. What more could go wrong? Is someone trying to kill me?*

By the time my one-year anniversary with PayLess rolled around, I was ready for a vacation. I went on a road trip with my best friend from college, Julie, who was now a TV News Anchor in Yuma, Arizona. Julie and I met at WSU and I lived with her one summer (remember the watermelon incident?) while we took a required Communications class together. We were both transfer students, had family in Seattle, were the same age, and had the same major. When we graduated from college, we stayed close even though we didn't live near each other.

I flew to San Diego and she met me at the airport. We stayed with a friend of mine from high school that night, then hit the road early the next morning and made our way to the Grand Canyon. We drove nine hours to Flagstaff, checked in to a Motel 6, and then hit the Grand Canyon bright and early the next morning.

Wow! There are no words to describe it accurately. We hiked all over the West, South, and East Rims. It was beyond majestic and reminded me of a movie I rented a week before my trip called, oddly enough, "Grand Canyon." There was a line in it that stuck with me about how insignificant we are next to the Grand Canyon. Looking out at the vastness of it all, in the midst of all those years of rock formations, I could hear the movie line.

Danny Glover's character said, "Hey, you know what I felt like? I felt like a gnat that lands on the ass of a cow that's chewing its cud next to the road that you ride by on at seventy miles an hour." *Yep*. I figured, life is short, play hard and strive to be happy.

With that in mind, and feeling nostalgic, I called Trey from a phone booth outside a roadside diner in Flagstaff, about ten o'clock at night. Julie and I had been reminiscing about our first loves over dinner, and I suddenly longed to see mine. The fact that I was in Arizona (where he lived) when this feeling overcame me was not lost on me. The fact that I had zero sense of Arizona geography did not deter me. Naturally, I assumed as soon as I called him that he would want to rush right over and see me.

Leaving Julie in the diner, I took a last swallow of my beer, took a deep breath and headed outside. With the liquid courage from the two beers I'd had with dinner and a handful of quarters, I marched over to the phone booth in the parking lot and opened the telephone book. He wasn't listed. I looked at the front of the phone book and it said 'Flagstaff.' *Hmm.* I was pretty sure Trey still lived in Phoenix and this phone book didn't include that city. Undaunted, I picked up a quarter, deposited it into the coin slot on the phone, and dialed directory assistance.

"Directory Assistance, what city please?"

"Phoenix," I barely whispered, trying to find my voice.

"What name?"

"Yes, I need the number for Trey Thompson please. The first name is spelled T R E Y."

"Thank you, one moment." I waited as she looked up the number. "I have the number now; would you like me to connect you?"

"Yes please." I heard the phone click a few times, then ringing. My heart thumped so hard I thought it was going to burst out of my chest. I cleared my throat. More ringing.

Finally, on the seventh ring I heard a sleepy, deep male voice answer, "Hello?"

"Hi, may I please speak to Trey?"

"Cough, cough. Yeah, this is Trey," he said, sounding irritated.

"Oh, um, hi. I'm sorry to bother you; it sounds like I woke you. I'm sorry. I shouldn't have called. I'll just let you go back to sleep, okay? Bye—"

"Wait. Tara? Is this Tara?"

"Yeah. Uh, it's me. I didn't recognize your voice, you sound different. How are you?"

"Wow," he paused. "I'm fine, I just have a cold. Um, I can't really talk right now. Man, how long has it been?"

"Nearly five years. Why can't you talk? Is someone there . . . with you?"

"Yeah," he sniffed. "My wife."

"Oh!" completely shocked, I took a moment, sighed, then asked, "When did you get remarried? I'm sorry. I shouldn't have called. I wasn't thinking. I was just wondering how you were that's all. I just wanted to hear your voice and know that you were okay."

"Tara? What's wrong? Why are you calling me?"

"Well, it's just that, I'm here, in Arizona."

"Here? Where, exactly?"

"Um, visiting the Grand Canyon with a friend. I'm in Flagstaff. I thought maybe I could see you. But that was stupid. I mean, um, I didn't know you were married again."

I heard a slight chuckle on the other end, "Tara, do you know how far I live from the Grand Canyon?"

"No."

"I'm over three hours away. It's at least two hundred miles to Flagstaff from here."

"Oh. I see. I didn't know." There was an awkward silence, and then I asked, "How are you, Trey? Are you happy?"

"I'm a dad again. My wife and I just had a baby girl, which is why I'm asleep before ten o'clock at night."

"Oh wow, congratulations. That's great," I managed, as I felt my heart breaking once more.

"It's good to hear your voice Tara. Are *you* happy?" he implored.

I wanted to tell him no, that I was miserable and lonely and missed him terribly. Instead, with false bravado and a fake smile plastered to my face, I babbled, "Yeah! I've got a really good job working in video production, so I'm using my degree. I was a Reporter right after college, but I didn't really like it, so I got a job in corporate video. It's great! Besides, it pays better and has better hours, and, oh yeah, and I get weekends off."

"Good for you, that sounds great," his voice, a flat monotone. "Well, I really do have to go now."

"Okay. Congratulations again on your new marriage and the birth of your daughter. Take care of yourself, okay? And know that I'll always care about you."

"Thanks. Me too."

"Goodbye Trey."

"Bye."

I hung up the phone, went back into the diner, and told Julie all about it, through mournful sobs, and feeling heartsick. "He's married *again!* I just can't believe it. I thought he was going to look me up when he divorced Lucy!"

"Wow, I'm sorry Tar. That sucks," Julie empathized.

"Why didn't he find me? Does he even think about me anymore? What's wrong with me? WHY can't I get over him? I have been absorbed in some delusional, storybook fantasy of Trey showing up at my door, rescuing me from my life, and the two of us living happily ever after. Julie, I'm sick. I still have dreams about him. I can't get him out of my system no matter what I do. I still have this weird idealistic, romantic notion of how true love is supposed to be. And Trey is the model I compare to every guy I meet. I've put him on some kind of pedestal of perfection—the one that got away."

"Sounds like a classic case of Cinderella Syndrome. Have another drink and call me in the morning," she smiled. "But seriously, you can't sit around waiting to be rescued. You've got to get out there and put Trey behind you. Don't be so hard on yourself. You're still young and have plenty of time to meet the right guy. You will, you'll see."

The next morning, we got up early and drove to Sedona, headed toward Julie's house in Yuma. We stopped and enjoyed the sites of the picturesque tourist town, with its stunning red rock formations and cool looking red dirt. It was truly a dazzling backdrop amidst the quaint western town.

After spending eighteen hours on the road with Julie, and talking about everything imaginable, our voices were so hoarse we could barely speak. By the end of that trip, we knew everything there possibly was to know about each other. When I had to go back to work, I was sad to leave because I knew I would miss her terribly.

My second year at PayLess was a bit turbulent. There were a lot of shake–ups in management and our parent company, Kmart, decided to sell us. Eventually, we were purchased by Thrifty and became known as Thrifty PayLess. This caused numerous layoffs and re–organizations in our management structure, as the Thrifty employees moved into PayLess headquarters. My manager quit, and our VP of corporate communications was fired. I was given more responsibilities, and a promotion to Associate Producer.

The video production department was down to two— just Rick Parker, Senior Producer, and me. We were shoved under the corporate communications umbrella. We felt like the ugly stepchildren. Most people kept under the radar because we were all afraid we'd lose our jobs.

Therefore, we had team spirit building workshops and morale boosting activities—*yay*. For Halloween, I was strongly urged to participate in the company's festivities, which involved dressing up as the Professor from Gilligan's Island because our combined departments didn't have enough men. Since video was under communications, I was not given a choice of which character I'd rather dress up as (I would have made a much better Mary Ann). Nevertheless, we won second place in the company costume contest.

One particularly frantic and harried day, a freelance grip dropped a 4k softbox (heavy studio light) on my forehead. He was on a ladder and I was helping him; next thing I knew, I was lying on the floor and someone called

911. I had to get a CAT scan, and ended up with a concussion and a horrendous headache, which the doctor referred to as "brain pain"—*lovely*. He said I needed to be monitored for twenty-four hours. My friend and a freelancer we used often for shoots, Matt Adler, took me to my mom's house. It was a Friday, so I spent most of the weekend on Mom's couch and feeling sorry for myself because I was wasting my weekend—I had to cancel a date.

My social calendar was surprisingly full, considering the majority of my friends were men, due to the predominantly male workforce in my field. It was nice to have guy friends though; they gave me interesting perspectives on dating and the male psyche. They were also great at helping me with little odds and ends and repairs around my apartment. And it was great to have a date when I didn't 'have a date.'

Matt and I often went to parties together, the movies, hiking, the beach, bike riding, and even skiing. Hanging out with Matt was better than a date because we had no expectations and never felt the need to impress each other. He was my date for the Halloween parties and New Year's Eve. We had each other's backs and kept each other from being lonely.

Matt took me to a friend's housewarming party, and I chatted with a woman who was about my age, twenty-eight, and holding a nine-day-old infant. She asked if I wanted to hold her baby while she got some food in the kitchen.

I must have sat on the couch holding that baby, mesmerized, for the next two hours. She was so tiny, so precious, and so adorable. Suddenly an overwhelming sensation came over me to reproduce! It was crazy how badly I realized, at that moment, that I wanted, no, *needed* to have a baby. It was like a spell was cast over me and I couldn't think straight. You've heard of the proverbial biological clock? Well, mine was ticking so loud that my ears were ringing. Matt had to practically pry the baby out of my hands and drag me out of that party.

I didn't understand what had happened to me that night, I mean, it's not like I'd never held a baby before. I guess I just realized that I was nearing the end of my twenties, and *very* single. I'd been mostly dating guys that didn't warrant a second date. Was I just picky?

I even considered that I didn't need a man to raise a child and looked into the possibility of getting a sperm donor—for about five minutes. In spite of all I went through with Trey, I was still an idealist and a romantic at heart. I wanted the whole package: love, marriage, and family. Was that such an unrealistic goal?

Coincidentally, a few days later, I was in the office of my new boss, and former co–worker, Rick Parker. Out of the blue he asked me, "What are your goals, Tara?"

"I want a family, like you. I want to be married and have children," I confessed. Rick had a wife and two beautiful children, ages four and six, who had visited him at work before. Apparently, I coveted his life more than I realized, because I clearly wasn't thinking about the consequences of my unguarded candidness.

"Yeah, uh, okay," he said, clearly thrown. "But, I uh, meant your career goals, here with PayLess?"

"Oh," I blushed as I looked down and tried to disappear into the wall behind me. There was no recovering from that. *What was I doing, sabotaging my job?* Here I was, in a job I enjoyed, in my chosen field. I had drive, ambition and career goals. Why couldn't I tell Rick that? What was wrong with me? I had become so consumed with thoughts of getting married and starting a family that I told my boss about it. That was a mistake I would end up paying for.

Sure enough, a few months later, Rick called me into the conference room and Sean from Human Resources was sitting at the table. It was three o'clock on a Wednesday, and they told me that my position was being eliminated, as were hundreds of others, due to the Thrifty PayLess merger and the need for corporate downsizing. They said I had two weeks left, and that I would receive a severance package. I'd just been laid off after three years of loyal and dedicated service.

Less than a year later, Rite Aid acquired the entire Thrifty PayLess chain, and PayLess was no more. Rick and all my former co–workers were out of a job too, and the corporate headquarters in Wilsonville, Oregon, was dissolved.

27   mistakes, blunders, and mishaps

WHAT DOES ONE DO when one finds one's self unemployed again? Take a vacation, naturally. I'd already had it planned, and the plane ticket was non–refundable, so I visited my BFF, Julie, again. This time she lived in Savannah, Georgia, and worked as a TV News Reporter/Anchor. Naturally, it was time for another road trip.

We drove from the Savannah airport to Orlando the first night. It was good to see her again. It had been nearly two years, and yet it felt as though we hadn't missed a day. We just picked back up right where we left off.

We hit Epcot Center in Kissimmee, Busch Gardens in Tampa, St Petersburg, the Gulf Coast, and Clearwater, all in Florida. On the way back, she showed me around Hilton Head Island, Beaufort, and Hunting Island, all in South Carolina. It was beautiful, and I had the best shrimp burger ever on Hunting Island! Another road trip success.

Unfortunately, it was time to go back home and face the fact that I was unemployed again. While flipping through the want ads in the Sunday *Oregonian*, I saw an ad for sheltie puppies. My grandparents always had collies when I was growing up and I'd loved them dearly. A Shetland sheepdog (sheltie) was basically a miniature collie, right? Being the impetuous, emotional idiot that I was back then, I answered that ad (instead of the ads for jobs) and was the proud owner of an eight-week-old male puppy that night, which I named Kenji. I justified it by telling myself that I had time to train him properly, so that when I went back to work, he'd be fully housebroken and trained. Needless to say, my cats were less than thrilled.

My next brainiac move was that I hadn't read my lease for the apartment in which I'd been living for the past three years. It clearly stated "NO DOGS" in bold writing. My apartment manager found out about Kenji in less than a week, and two weeks later I was served an eviction notice. Undaunted, I began the search for an apartment that allowed dogs.

When I didn't have any luck finding one, I turned to the roommate–wanted ads and found a family in Troutdale who had a room for rent. They not only allowed dogs, they even had a dog run in the back yard, and said they loved animals. They didn't own any pets at the time, so I felt like I had struck gold. I moved in without a second thought.

Before I lost my job, I had an opportunity to go to Australia with a friend. I strongly considered it, but I would have had to quit PayLess because they didn't grant leaves of absence. While weighing the pros and cons with another friend, he said he didn't think I'd go to Australia because my mom wouldn't approve.

When I told her what he'd said, she looked at me lovingly and said to me, "You will always have my approval in everything you do. I am proud of you because of the way you are. I am proud of your corporate job and I'd be just as proud if you went to Australia. I approve of what you do and who you are. There's nothing you could do that I would not approve of because I approve of you—your beliefs and principles—you are my daughter and I am proud of you."

Those words and unconditional love from my mother consoled me over and over as I pondered how quickly I had made such a mess of my life. It felt like doors were slamming in my face everywhere I turned. Video production companies told me I was overqualified, others weren't hiring, and most ads I applied to didn't even call me in for an interview. Plus, I was sick for a month.

First, I caught the flu from my roommate's kid. He was six years old and threw up all over the hallway in the middle of the night. The kids were loud, whiny, and nosy. They went in my room when I wasn't home and let Foxy out of the house—he was missing for three days. I had to give Mio to a friend before I moved because she began attacking Foxy for no reason I could figure out. She loved her new home and environment and became very affectionate with her new family. Perhaps she didn't want to share anymore and preferred being the only pet?

I didn't realize what I was getting myself into when I had agreed to move in with a family. This caused me a great deal of stress, and my flu soon turned into bronchitis, which turned into allergic rhinitis, and then walking pneumonia. To say my life was a mess was an understatement.

After a month of living with the family from hell, my friend, Sheila Jin, whom I had met when working at PayLess, graciously offered me her basement until I could get back on my feet. Sheila lived in a beautiful, newly constructed custom home on two acres of land, with her husband, Ray, and their beautiful eight-month-old baby girl, Ciarra, in Ridgefield, Washington. The basement was unfinished, but it had a bedroom and bathroom with a shower, so I had it pretty good. Plus, I had my own private entrance and there was a huge yard for Kenji.

Foxy and Tia liked it too, and Foxy soon became quite the mouser.

However, as Kenji grew, I quickly discovered that my sheltie puppy was not, in fact, a purebred sheltie. His coat was short (the long hair never came in like the breeder said it would) his feet were enormous, and he wouldn't stop growing.

I called the breeder to complain, but she denied it and wouldn't take him back; then she avoided my calls. I filed complaints with the American Kennel Club, Clark County Dog Club, and the Better Business Bureau. I had a case, but taking her to court was an uphill battle and not one I was capable of fighting at the time. She eventually took Kenji back, but her check bounced, and I never got my money back.

It was another low point for me, and I began to question my judgment and mental state, especially my gullibility. How had I allowed myself to be conned into buying a mixed–breed dog? Why hadn't I done research on the breeder? And so on.

Plus, Kenji was a sweet puppy and I felt terrible about giving him up. But I was also unemployed and living in my friend's basement, and in no position to be a large dog owner. As I said goodbye to Kenji an odd thought popped into my head, *I wonder if Trey has any pets?*

28   my knight

JOSEPH SPENCER came into my life at the worst possible time. *Or was it the best possible time?* Unemployed and living in Sheila's basement, I didn't have any self–esteem and didn't feel I was good relationship material. I had been living there for nearly three weeks when Ray's friend stopped by. I barely met him, and we hadn't even talked to each other, but I thought he was very attractive.

It turns out Joe thought I was attractive too, and he asked Ray about me.

He called me the next day. He had a super sexy phone voice—broadcast quality *and I should know*—deep, but not too deep. I could listen to that voice for hours. He was also articulate, charming, witty, funny, and easy to talk to. We made plans to meet for dinner the next night at The Dragon King Chinese restaurant in Vancouver, Washington, and I eagerly anticipated our meeting.

I spent nearly three hours getting ready for my big date. Not unusual, you say? Well it was for me. I sort of prided myself on being a natural minimalist and could get ready in fifteen minutes for almost anything, and I rarely wore make up. But this time, I went all out and was even a bit daring. I showed up to the restaurant wearing a tight, black leather skirt! The look on his face was priceless.

Joe was dressed in a collared, white button–down shirt and black slacks, as he was meeting me after work. At five feet ten, with an athletic build, he was very easy on the eyes. He was boyishly handsome and looked younger than his age, even though he was only twenty-five.

The fact that he was three years younger than me concerned me at first, but he quickly assured me that our age difference was not an issue. With big, deep brown eyes, thick eyelashes, eyebrows and medium brown hair, a slight chin dimple and mischievous smile, he was a sight to behold. Picture a young Tom Cruise, "Top Gun" era, and you're getting close, but Joe was even better looking—I couldn't stop staring.

"Hi Tara, it's great to see you again," he said with an easy smile and a quick hug. We were seated at a booth and he immediately commented on my leather skirt, "When I told you I really like black leather and that I have a leather couch and chair, I didn't know you'd show up wearing my couch."

It was an instant icebreaker and we had a good laugh over it. He commended my bravery and humor to pull off such an outfit on a first date and I think I won a few points that night. He had a quick wit that was difficult to keep up with, as well as a dry sarcasm that reminded me of Chandler Bing, a character from the TV show, "Friends." Needless to say, I could barely eat my dinner because he had me laughing so much.

We enjoyed each other's company greatly, and when we finished dinner, Joe suggested we keep the evening going somewhere else for dessert. I readily agreed, so I hopped in his car and we drove to downtown Portland to the Brasserie Montmartre. On the way there, I discovered he had a Disney music CD and asked if I could play it. He said sure, and we instantly became six-year-olds, singing at the top of our lungs to the old Disney classics—it was liberating.

The Brasserie was a French, jazzy restaurant with great ambience and live music. They had white butcher paper and crayons on top of their linen tablecloths; naturally, we grabbed some crayons and began doodling. The conversation soon turned a bit serious, and with dramatic flair Joe cleared off a spot in the middle of the table and listed the words, "Sex, Drugs, Rock 'n roll, Religion, Politics, Relationships, Marriage, Children," in big letters. Then we went down the list one–by–one and covered every major topic—both his views and mine. As we moved onto the next topic, he checked off the word.

It was incredible. We covered all the taboo subjects on our first date; all the stuff they say not to talk about—*especially* on a first date. I was quickly finding out that Joe was not like anyone I had ever met before.

We discovered not only did we have a lot in common; we also had the same values, morals, and similar beliefs and philosophies. Plus, we had weird stuff in common— the kind of stuff that doesn't really matter but is not something you'd expect to have in common with a stranger.

Like, our moms both got married at age eighteen and birthed us at nineteen; they've been married three times; we're not close to our biological fathers; we're close to our moms; we have step siblings and half–sisters; we had the same major in college; we were both TV News Reporters, yet got out of the TV news industry for pretty much the same reasons; we don't drink coffee, like nuts, or country music . . . and the list goes on.

We learned more about each other in just a few hours than I'd learned about some guys in an entire relationship. He drove me back to my car, I gave him a hug and we went our separate ways.

When I got home that night and told Sheila about it she said, "He sounds too good to be true. What's wrong with him?" Honestly, I was a little worried. He seemed so perfect. *Too perfect?* I didn't want to question it because after only one date I was already developing feelings for him. I was toast.

The next day, Joe called around five to tell me that he had a "really, really, really good time last night," and that he was looking forward to seeing me again. He was being honest and open and saying all the right things, without playing any mind games—refreshing. He was exactly what I'd been looking for, and it scared the hell out of me.

When I hung up the phone, I felt like I couldn't breathe, and I didn't know why. I tried to explain what it felt like to Sheila, but it didn't come out right. We summed it up to the fact that I'd never had a normal, healthy relationship and now that the possibility of one was staring me in the face, I didn't know what to do about it. I caught a glimpse of what real intimacy might be like with Joe and I wanted to run and hide.

It had been seven years since the last time I'd seen Trey, and two since I last heard his voice. Dating, for me, had been a series of unfortunate events. No one was good enough. None of the men I met compared to the image that was seared in my mind. I had unknowingly held Trey to an impossible ideal, and set myself up for failure because no one would ever come close to the Trey I had invented in my mind. Even as I met and was getting to know Joe, memories of Trey haunted me.

The next day, Joe called twice. We talked about nothing in particular, but it was reassuring to hear his voice, such a nice voice. After I hung up the phone, I felt better about us. I started reading a book, *Are You The One For Me?* It helped put some things in perspective about my childhood, my relationship with my dad, and why I choose the men I do. According to the book's author, I'd never had a "healthy relationship" before. She said it has to do with our programming from childhood, but that we can still learn how to change and reprogram our relationship mentalities. Being a child of divorce, I definitely wanted to change my 'relationship mentality' and not take the same path my parents did.

Finally, it was Friday night, June 23, and time for my second date with Joe. It was a beautiful sunny day in Beaverton and we met at six, at Cucina! Cucina! Italian restaurant. The hostess seated us outside, next to Rod Strickland, from the Portland Trailblazers, and two of his friends. But I didn't notice until they left, when Joe said, "You know that was Rod Strickland who just walked by us, right?"

"Really? Oh, wow. No, I didn't recognize him. I guess I only have eyes for you," I said, rather sheepishly. The truth was, I wasn't very observant to begin with, but I also wasn't as big of a diehard Blazer fan as Joe, and probably wouldn't have recognized him anyway, unless he was "wearing a jersey, dribbling a basketball, and on TV," Sheila teased me later.

During dinner, Joe placed a gift bag on the table, next to my plate, cleared his throat and declared, "I feel bad about meeting you right after your birthday and I wanted to do something about it. So, on this day, exactly one month *after* your birthday, I thought we could celebrate, and I got you a little something."

"For me? Wow, that is so thoughtful. Thank you—"

"Open it."

I reached into the bag, pulled out the tissues, and discovered a volume one Disney CD (to which he owned volume two). It was the perfect gift, and would remind me of our first date and singing in the car together forever. We locked eyes and I could feel my heart flutter.

After dinner, we went to his place, made sandwiches for our rafting trip the next day, walked in the park near his condo, and talked about past relationships, our faults, sex—all kinds of fun "getting–to–know–you" topics. At 10:45 p.m. he walked me to my car, and we hugged for a long time. It felt great just to hold him. Then he asked, "Do you want me to kiss you good night?"

"Do you want to?"

"Yes, but I don't want to rush things—"

"This isn't the first date anymore, it's okay," I grinned up at him. He leaned down and kissed me softly, slowly at first. Then I pushed my body hard against his as the kiss turned passionate. He pulled away, smiled and said something about seeing me tomorrow. I was distracted by the fact that I was breathless and panting, and finding it difficult to concentrate on anything. I mumbled words, got in my car and dreamily drove away. What a first kiss! What a great second date. I was giddy.

The next morning, he called at 6:15 to make sure I was up. I was. In fact, I had tossed and turned all night, too excited to sleep, in anticipation of our action–packed day together. I met him at his condo at seven and we were on our way. We followed his friend Scott to Sandy, Oregon, met the rest of the group, about twenty people, and headed to Maupin singing Disney tunes all the way. Once there, we unloaded the rafts and supplies and were in the Deschutes River by 11:45. It was a popular and crowded spot, and we started off like bumper boats. But I was with a skilled river guide, lifeguard and water fight protector. I felt safe, and lucky to be with such a great guy.

The rapids were fun, and Joe maneuvered us through them with ease. The only problem I had with the day was all the water fights. Every time I dried off, they'd drench us again. But other than that, the day was nearly perfect. There were six people in our raft, two other couples and us. They were younger and drinking, but only one got obnoxious. He was easy enough to handle so it wasn't a big deal. When I got stressed about the water fights, Joe would just say, "Hakuna Matata! No worries," and I'd suck it up, smile, and not let them ruin my day. It was only our third date and he already knew how to make me feel better. I loved his positive, easygoing attitude—it was contagious, and my cheeks hurt from smiling all day.

The next day, we went to a park, lay on a blanket under a tree, and took turns reading to each other from the book, *The Rainmaker,* by John Grisham. I enjoyed being read to; I think people should read to each other more often. The day after that we saw "Batman Forever," and the day after that Joe took me to dinner at the Shilo Inn. In other words, we saw each other every day for a week. And it would have continued that way, but he had to go on a three-day business trip.

Our time apart only made us miss each other more, and we talked on the phone every night, whether he was on a business trip or not. We quickly moved into the "boyfriend/ girlfriend" stage without even questioning it, and a mere month after we met, we said those three little words. He was the best thing that had ever happened to me and we were moving very fast.

Three days before Joe told me he loved me for the first time, I wrote him a letter declaring my love for him but didn't give it to him. I guess I just wanted to hear him say it first. Or maybe I thought it was too soon and I didn't want to scare him off, but the point is, I fell in love with him, and I fell fast and hard. Here's that letter:

Dear Joe,   *July 19, 1995*

Do you have any idea how much I love you? The thought of losing you made me realize that I love you more than I thought possible, that everything feels so right with you. I can't imagine my future without you in it.

*I love you, Joe! I know that now. It's very clear to me, an epiphany of sorts. Actually, it's a relief not to have to hold it in anymore. I've admitted to myself that I'm in love with you. The next step is to tell **you**. Are you ready to hear it?*

I would do almost anything for you. I feel I'm just bursting with love to give—and I want to give it all to you. I feel so strongly about us, so positive. I know what we have is special, and rare, and precious. I want to protect it. Nurture it. Help it grow. I want us to defy the odds, to rise above our broken homes and dysfunctional families and see that it really can work. I've been cynical for too long. We have the key ingredients for a successful and happy life together (connection, chemistry, compatibility, commitment) and lots of love.

Three days later, while camping on Government Island with Joe's family, he said those three words, and I was definitely ready to hear them. We were standing outside our tent, gazing at the Columbia River, about to go inside and put on warmer clothes, when he just blurted, "I love you, Tara."

"Really?" I stammered. *Come on! What a stupid thing to say!* He wrapped me in his arms, which allowed me to compose myself. I leaned back, looked into his eyes, and said strong and clear, "I love you too."

29   i do

TWO MONTHS after Joe and I met, he asked me to move in with him. I moved from Sheila's basement to Joe's condo in Beaverton. And two months after that, we got engaged. Yes, we were moving *very* fast. I was also freelancing as a production coordinator for commercial and industrial film and video production companies, which involved some travel, and Joe traveled often with his sales job. Yet there we were, still getting to know each other, and living together with demanding, somewhat chaotic schedules. But that didn't stop us from moving forward full–steam ahead.

In October, we took a four-day weekend trip to New Orleans because Joe had tickets to the Miami Dolphins vs. New Orleans Saints game at the Superdome. He was an avid Dolphins fan and liked to see them play live whenever he got the opportunity. Unfortunately, the Dolphins lost that game, 30–33, but that was never the intended highlight of the trip. He actually had a different kind of goal scoring in mind.

We were at the Top of the Dome revolving bar and restaurant for a cocktail before dinner, and having a casual conversation about housecleaning and laundry, of all things.

"I know we've both been busy lately and that I can be kind of messy sometimes, so thanks for picking up after me and for doing my laundry; laundry can be such a drag," he said.

"I don't mind doing your laundry," I smiled back at him.

"Oh good, would you mind being my wife?" he said casually, with a twinkle in his eye.

"Would I—? Wha—? Um, that's not something to joke about," I faltered.

"I'm not joking. Tara, will you marry me?" he asked as he whipped out an engagement ring from the front pocket of his jeans.

In shock and staring at the ring, I stammered, "Yes. YES!" He put the ring on my finger and I was so stunned that I had to tell the first person I saw. As a cocktail waitress neared our table, I jumped up and shouted, "Look, we're engaged!" and shoved my ring in her face, beaming at her. I beamed at everyone that night—dazed with delight, astonishment, excitement, love—and high hopes for our bright future together.

We had a lot of fun celebrating our newfound engagement in the French Quarter that night. I was with my knight, my hero, the man I loved and adored, and planned to spend the rest of my life with. This was definitely a great start to my fairytale dreams coming true.

The time that followed our brief six-month engagement was a whirlwind of activity. We sold the condo, went house hunting, had an engagement party with our families, bought a house, packed, moved, unpacked, and managed to plan, shop for, and book all things wedding related, while holding down full–time jobs and sticking to our budget. I don't know how I was able to get everything done in time, let alone preserve my sanity.

We moved to a lovely three-bedroom house in Vancouver, Washington, and I got a sales rep job for a local toy company. I met with florists, caterers, reception halls, bridal shops, and bridesmaids; made endless phone calls and ran endless errands, all during lunches, after work, and on weekends.

One such errand involved going to a paper supply store downtown Portland to pick out the stationery for our wedding invitations. My mundane task soon turned into a near panic attack when I heard a chillingly familiar voice at the front of the store.

I stood in a row of paper displays toward the back, perusing cream swaths. A distinct male voice said, "Do you carry typewriter ribbon here?"

I froze. The salesclerk answered the disembodied voice as I peered around the corner. I spotted a man with that shockingly white hair I'd recognize anywhere.

Fortunately, he faced the clerk and didn't see me. I knew who it was, but had to be sure. Risking being seen, I crept down another row closer to the front, to get a better view of his face.

My heart thudded in my ears and I held my breath as I poked my head out of the row. Two feet in front of me was Adam Gillman—my stalker.

I gasped and ducked out of the way as he looked my direction. I tiptoed to the back of the store and waited there until he left, a lump in my throat. *What is he doing out of jail? It's only been three years!* I realized I didn't know why he'd been arrested, only that I wished he'd been put away longer than three years.

I stayed rooted to that spot another five minutes before I calmed down enough to make my purchase and leave.

Joe and I weren't spending enough quality time furthering our intimacy and knowledge, with our busy schedules. His demanding career and frequent business trips ensured we scarcely saw each other. Did I say we were off to a great start?

He shared my fears about us not taking time to get to know each other properly, and wrote me a letter a month before our wedding day.

Hi there sweetie! You know, I never really write to you, but I feel like it today!

I've been thinking about you and us, and I want you to know that I'm very happy to take this step with you. I do wish we knew each other better, but that will come. We have waited over a quarter century to form a family and it is almost here. I'm starting to get excited, it's really going to happen.

It will be great in 20 years to look back and reflect—how we met and the way we started. Better yet, let's look forward 20 years. What do you see? Let's promise ourselves to stay close and not get complacent with each other. I don't want to end up like our parents.

Mrs. Joe Spencer, have you thought about it long and hard? Tara Spencer, are you ready to be my one and only? Get ready for a long, forever lasting friend, lover, partner and spouse. I am truly dedicated to you and our relationship. I do have my downfalls, and I'm thankful that you are accepting of them (hopefully). It's tough for me to open all the way up and I appreciate your patience with me. Help me to know you deeper. If it will involve really long stories, that's okay.

I just read all the mail and postcards you sent from NYC, and after reading them a second time, I said, "This girl really loves me." You're so sweet, you treat me nice, take great care of me when I'm sick, and I think you are going to make a fantastic mom. Sometimes I look at you and smile because I'm picturing our future child by your side.

Well, I could write forever, but just know I'm excited, and although our relationship is still in its relevant infancy, it's the closest I've ever felt toward anyone (Mom excluded you know, 'cuz when you're a one-year-old and Mom's holding you, well that's tough to compete with).

I truly Love you,
Joe

In the letter, Joe was referring to the postcards and letters I had sent him while on a business trip in February, two months before our wedding. As a sales representative for a local toy manufacturing company, Hart Toys, I attended the New York Toy Fair to show our new product line to potential vendors. I was gone eight days and missed Joe. Here's some of the mail he was referring to:

Dear Joe,   2/11/96 (postcard)

Live, from <u>New York</u> . . ! Hi Babe! It's Sunday morning and I'm at the Toy building. This place is amazing. Everything is so FAST-PACED. Everyone is in a hurry. I had to cut my demo down to 25 seconds from two minutes! The buyers don't have any time. They just want the facts.

I hated cutting our conversation short last night. I sure wish you were here with me. There's so much to see and do. It's all so bright and glitzy. I miss you! I LOVE YOU MADLY!!
Love, Tara

Dear Joe,   2/11/96

Happy Valentine's Day, my forever Valentine! It's our first Valentine's Day—and we're apart! We'll have to remedy that situation. As soon as I come back, I'm going to shower you with kisses! Then the kisses will get longer, then the kisses will get wetter . . . I want to lay in your arms. I want to sigh and look at you with love-struck eyes. I want to look into your eyes and tell you that I'll be your Valentine and that my heart is yours 'til the day I die. I want to tell you in person that I'll love you forever.

I love and miss you immensely!

Always your Tara

Joe,   2/13/96

I love you so much—it hurts sometimes. I know I tell you all the time, but it's not "just words" to me. I mean it every single time I say it. I feel like I can never say it enough to equal the love I feel inside.

I have never felt this way before. It's such an incredibly freeing feeling to be able to love you so openly and unconditionally. I'm secure enough to know that my love for you won't blow you away. I won't drown you in it, you won't gag on it, and you can't be hurt by it. And I never have to wonder how you feel about me. I feel so loved and good and happy.

In two months, we are going to be joined in a lifetime bond. We'll become husband and wife! Wow! That thought used to scare me, now it feels like the most natural thing in the world. I want to tell everybody. I want to shout it from the

rooftops! I'M GETTING MARRIED!! Because I
found the man of my dreams. Because I'm in love.
Because I've found my soulmate, my forever
friend and lifelong companion. Because it feels
right—as right as breathing. We're breathing in
each other. With each breath I get to know you
even better and love you even more. I love you my
darling. Today and every day is a celebration of
that love. Know that I'm thinking of you and that
you're always in my heart.
Love, Tara (almost/soon-to-be) Spencer

Our wedding day arrived, and I felt I was the luckiest bride in the world. My best friend Julie was my Matron–of–Honor. She flew in from Savannah the day before—at four and a half months pregnant. She wore her pregnancy glow beautifully, didn't complain once, and was the perfect Matron–of–Honor. She took her duties to the bride in stride, kept calm no matter what, and kept me calm as much as possible. I couldn't have asked for a better and truer friend.

We were married in a Lutheran church in Portland that Joe's grandparents belonged to, and then had the reception at a hall we rented a few miles away because the church didn't allow alcohol—we wanted champagne at our reception.

The ceremony was a traditional, straightforward church–type wedding. We had four bridesmaids and four groomsmen, respectively, my ten-year-old sister, Jenny, was the flower girl, and she sprinkled rose petals all the way down the aisle as she walked. Joe and I each wrote our own vows.

It was the white wedding I had dreamed of, and my chosen colors were burgundy and black. Yes, I definitely felt lucky and happy and beautiful, and very much in love. I recall telling someone at the reception that it was the best day of my life. And I suppose up to that point, it was.

Yet, Trey crossed my mind for a second. Part of me wanted him there, as a guest at my wedding, because he was my friend. And another part of me wondered what it would be like if he were the groom, because I still loved him. *No! I must banish these thoughts!*

For our honeymoon, we went on a Caribbean cruise to San Juan, Puerto Rico, St. Thomas, Virgin Islands, and St. Maarten, Netherland Antilles. It was beautiful, romantic, picturesque, and incredibly funny. Funny, you ask? That seems a strange adjective for a honeymoon, right? Well, it was funny because Joe joked constantly. He had me in stitches the whole time. In fact, I seldom saw him in a serious mood. *Night and day from 'intense Trey!'*

The day after we got home from our honeymoon, Joe said he had a surprise—his wedding present for me. We got in the car and he wouldn't tell me where we were going, not even a hint. After about a twenty-mile drive we pulled up in front of a house I didn't recognize. When we knocked on the door, a beautiful sheltie greeted us with her human. *Could this be what I think it is? Dare I hope?*

Joe got me a *real* sheltie puppy! And the dog at the door was our puppy's mama. Our new puppy was a blue–merle, eight-week-old female, and the most precious, adorable puppy I'd ever seen. I instantly fell in love with her. Best wedding present ever! I named her Skye because of her blue–gray coloring, and it suited her.

A month and ten days after getting married, I turned thirty. Joe wrote me a note in my birthday card that encapsulated our whirlwind romance very well.

Dear Tara,

> *First of all, congrats on making the big 30. You look stunning, and even though I flip you crap, 30 is very young. Second, I love you very much and am sorry that your special day falls on a Thursday. It makes it tough to sleep in late together and so on. Lastly, I'm glad we are such good friends, great lovers, and an incredible couple, and I'm glad that your first birthday with me is as husband and wife, as will many more in the future.*
> *I hope this birthday will be memorable as:*
> *A. It's the year you got Skye*
> *B. It's the year you got married*
> *C. It's the year you own a house*
> *D. It's the year you are going to get laid!*
> *Xoxoxoxoxoxoxxxxxxxxxxxoooooxxxoxooxxooxx xoooxxoxoxoxoxoxxooxx!*
> *Love, Joe*

It was also the year I went from the PayLess job, to unemployment, to freelancing, to a sales job. I moved from an apartment, to renting a room from strangers, to my friends' basement, to Joe's condo, to co–owning my own home. I went from single, to first date, to moving in, to engaged, to married—in less than ten months. So yeah, I'd say it was a pretty memorable year. *Damn, what an understatement!*

30   and baby makes three

OUR FIRST YEAR of wedded bliss, the newlywed stage, presented a few obstacles, but we maneuvered through them with poise and grace. And to celebrate our one-year wedding anniversary, we exchanged the traditional gift of paper. Joe's gift to me was this beautiful handwritten love letter.

Dear Tara,

Happy Anniversary, my true love. In keeping with tradition, I am giving you this paper. Paper is a wonderful thing actually. It is used as the ultimate form of communication. That being the case, there are some things I would like to communicate to you on this, our first anniversary of marriage.

First off, let me say that I never thought I would marry such a good person. Your honesty, strong moral character, integrity, and transparency to me are admired. Don't think I don't notice. I'm very aware of your dedication to our marriage and us. I never doubt your loyalty or commitment.

Tara, you are by far the best friend I have ever had. It excites me to think of the many years we have ahead of us. I firmly believe that our marriage is number 1, based on friendship, and that is going to bode well for us.

As I look back over the past 12 months, it probably hasn't been the greatest year for you professionally, in terms of health, or for your family, which is now our family. As I have watched you deal with adversity, it makes me confident of the future. Your ability to cope with all of these obstacles is a true measure of your strength. I consider you a strong woman. You have earned all the respect in the world from me. When I think of you, which is often, it makes me proud to have you as my wife. It also makes me feel very lucky to be your husband.

I am so looking forward to a year filled with love, communication, friendship, health, lots of sex, pregnancy, prosperity, and a whole lot of fun. As long as we have the first three, that is what matters most. I think our second year together will exceed our expectations by far. We have a strong marriage, and as for the rest of our life? Let's just say that all our ducks are in a row. Life is looking good, right now in the present, and in the short–term future as well.

Tara, I want you to know that I am, and always will be dedicated and loyal to you, to our marriage, to our unborn children, and even to most of our pets most of the time. The vows I made to you on this day last year seem easy to fulfill. They don't even come close to describing my love for you and my commitment to our relationship.

I still feel blessed that we found each other. We are a good match. I love to sneak looks at you when you are unaware; I think you catch me sometimes. They say that after you have been married for a while the flame dies down. We can't say that we have been married very long, and the ob/gyn has all but extinguished most of our flame lately, but let me just say that I still find you drop dead gorgeous. You make me as horny as ever, and as you know, I get rock hard around you on a regular basis. You are a beautiful woman, and you are my woman. The chemistry is still very strong for me and if I don't make that known enough, then refer back to this page.

I am still going to take you on a hot air balloon, but for this mere gift of paper, I wanted to write you a letter. It sounds simple, but I want you to have all my love, and at least some of it in writing.

I love you tons,
Joe

And now for those pesky obstacles he referred to…two months after we got married, I left my job with the toy company because it involved too much travel. Since Joe was gone so much with his job too, we barely saw each other, and something had to give. I took an inside sales job with a local lumber company that assured me I wouldn't have to go anywhere. However, there were two problems with this job:

1. I knew nothing about lumber.

2. I was the only female among many testosterone– heavy males, and sexual harassment at the office is putting it nicely. I lasted less than three months at that job and came home in tears most days. It just wasn't worth it, so I turned in my resignation and had to look for work

again. Fortunately, in this case, the third time was the charm, and I got a job as a proposal writer and marketing assistant for an Architect firm in downtown Vancouver.

After I settled into my new job and things were going well, we decided to start trying to have a baby. We tried and tried and tried. Unfortunately, I kept having periods month after month after month, and I wasn't getting pregnant after six months of trying; we opted for fertility testing. It turned out I had a blocked fallopian tube, so my one functioning fallopian tube released an egg every other month, which diminished my chances of getting pregnant by fifty percent.

To make matters worse, my gynecologist discovered I had cervical dysplasia (pre–cancerous cells) and I had to have a LEEP surgery to remove the abnormal tissue from my cervix. After the LEEP, we weren't allowed to have sex for four weeks, so that month was wasted too. Therefore, by the time our one-year anniversary rolled around, I was a bit of an emotional mess, and Joe was my rock. I felt closer to him and more in love with him than ever.

We decided to stop 'trying' so hard to get pregnant and just have fun, and that if it was truly meant to be, it would happen. We went out of town for an extended Fourth of July vacation and visited my relatives in Wichita Falls; a family reunion of sorts. I completely forgot about trying to conceive and actually drank alcohol for the first time in months—two Zimas. The next day I went to a water park with my cousins (who were all twenty or more years younger than me) and went down every slide, and some multiple times. I also sunburned my back and shoulders.

A couple days later I felt headachy and nauseous. I thought I had sun poisoning from the sunburn or was dehydrated, so I didn't pay much attention to it. At the airport, as we were about to fly home, I felt light–headed and thought it was because I got up too fast. As my dad hugged me goodbye, he whispered in my ear, "I bet you're pregnant."

"Nah," I quickly dismissed it, gave him a smile, and boarded the plane with Joe. About a week later, I got dizzy and felt faint at work. Plus, my period was late. On my lunch hour I went to the drug store and bought a home pregnancy test but was too chicken to take it. I left work a couple hours early, went home and took the test.

There it was, staring boldly up at me: **TWO SOLID PINK LINES!** I was so excited I was bursting to tell someone—anyone. I told the only other living creatures in the house with me at the time, my dog and cat. Yep, I told Skye and Foxy we were having a baby. Sadly, Tia had developed liver failure and died a month earlier.

I also called Kaiser Medical and went down to the lab to get the official test, just to be sure. They said the results would be in the next day, but I couldn't wait that long. I called Joe and had to leave a message for him to call me back (he was out of town) and I called my mom. After that, I had so much pent up energy that I mowed the yard.

Funny, this thing called life, isn't it? All those months of trying, and when I finally relaxed and even did 'dangerous' things, like consuming alcohol and sliding down giant slides at water parks, I was actually two weeks pregnant. No wonder my kid likes roller coasters and water parks! Ah, but I'm getting ahead of myself. *Let's see, where were we? Oh yeah*—the next day at work I got the official call from my doctor's nurse that the test was positive and that I was, in fact, pregnant.

I did not take their advice to wait until the end of my first trimester to tell people, and began telling everyone right there and then—even my boss at work. Yep, I was an open book, and there was no doubt in my mind that this was going to be a healthy pregnancy and I was going to have a healthy full–term baby.

By day three of knowing, I felt sick again. I also woke up in a bad mood and realized that I was going through hormonal changes, which meant mood swings and whacked out emotions. *Great.* But then I got a dozen beautiful long–stemmed Ecuadorian red roses delivered at work from Joe. I missed him and hated that I had to tell him about the pregnancy over the phone. He was so sweet and thoughtful and loving. I just wanted him to come home, so I could be in his arms and we could be delighted together about our imminent parenthood.

Overall, I had a relatively normal pregnancy, with the usual morning sickness during the first trimester. As far as pregnancies go, I'd say it was standard textbook stuff. I read everything I could get my hands on, like, *What to Expect When You're Expecting, Baby's First Year,* and half a dozen others. I put headphones on my tummy and played Mozart, made Joe sing to my belly, and all the other crazy stuff first–time parents did then. We even found out the sex of the baby. During the ultrasound, Joe was talking about painting the nursery. He said we were prepping it that weekend.

The technician smiled and said, "Well, you better go with pink." For the record, we opted for a sunny, pale yellow instead. Since we just found out we were having a girl, we no longer had to call her "Baby It," so we decided on a name. This made things much more real for me and I wrote my baby girl her first letter.

Dear Jalina,

We found out you were a girl yesterday and it made me so happy. I can't wait until the day I can look at you and hold you in my arms. I daydream about your first steps, first words, the first time you can truly hug me back. I look forward to the

long mother/daughter talks we'll have and hope you and I can be as close as I am to my own mother. Your grandmother is a very special lady and I hope I can do as well raising you as I feel she did raising me. I hope you can come to me with your problems and that you'll feel as though you can tell me anything. You can. I love you already—and you're still just a tiny fetus in my womb. By the way, your daddy is a very amazing guy and if you don't know it by now, you're very lucky to have him. Some dads don't stick around to help raise their kids. It's sad, but I didn't know my dad very well growing up. I know you and your dad will have a special relationship and I know we'll both love you very, very much. I am looking forward to meeting you in a few months!
I love you,
　　　Mommy

As my stomach grew bigger and bigger, my lower back hurt more and more. The backaches, coupled with the fact that I was at risk for gestational diabetes, forced me to take an early maternity leave. I still had about six weeks left until my due date, and spent much of my time in the nursery, sorting, organizing, putting baby clothes away, and other "nesting" activities. After three weeks of that, I felt and looked like I had swallowed a watermelon, had to pee all the time, and was ready to get the enormous alien out of my body.

As if in answer to my pleas, I had my first contractions twenty-three days before my due date. But it turns out they were just Braxton Hicks contractions, known as false labor. I guess my body needed a rehearsal before the big event. Even though I felt ready to have a baby, I was still relieved she wasn't coming quite that early.

A few days after that, I had the contractions again. This time I was on the phone with my Grandpa and he advised me to call the hospital, just to be safe. I was sure they were Braxton Hicks though, because they were mild and didn't hurt. The nurse at the hospital told me to call back when my contractions were five minutes apart.

It was a Saturday afternoon, and Joe had been out running errands. When he got home, and I told him about the contractions, he immediately started timing them and hoped this was the real thing. Well, he got his wish. The contractions began getting harder and closer together, and they didn't go away when I walked around. We called the hospital again and they told us to come on in. The adrenaline kicked in and I was getting excited too—this was it!

To pass the time while waiting for my contractions to get closer, I French–braided my hair, which was now the length of my back, and Joe wrote a spontaneous poem.

The pain, it hurts so bad
The rain, it makes us sad
Our daughter Jalina, her start is near
If she comes tonight I'll shed a tear

Another surge, my wife endures
This miracle, this child, will soon be hers
The contractions come quick, then they go
They are 10 minutes then 5 minutes apart or so
An hour of this, we'll be on our way
To the big white building where we will stay

It's been 9 long months of added girth
Tonight's the night, the night of birth
Our lives will soon forever alter
As parents our love will never falter

I was admitted to the hospital at 7:15 that evening. When Dr. Hagenrathspiel (we called her Dr. H) examined me, she said I had a small tear in my amniotic sac, causing a slow leak in the fluids; she asked if I had noticed any wetness. I told her I felt wetness Friday while at Home Depot but thought I had just peed my pants a little. She was concerned about the risk of infection, so she decided to break the fore bag and induce labor.

At this point, I was dilated to about one and a half centimeters. When Dr. H broke the waters, a warm river gushed out of me—very surreal experience and caused active labor right away. This was good because I didn't have to be induced with Pitocin.

Within two hours I dilated to four and a half centimeters, and the contractions came hard and fast. I begged for the epidural. The doctor said she was afraid my contractions would stop and wanted to make sure my labor was good and strong before administering the pain–numbing meds I so desired; she told me to wait another hour.

Did I mention what a pain wimp I was? I was not okay with this and was convinced it was a conspiracy. I was afraid they wouldn't give me an epidural at all (because I had heard about a window and feared I was getting past that).

By this time, Joe massaged my back and was being the best coach in the world. He couldn't have been more supportive. We also had a full room, comprising of Dr. H, the nurse, Joe, my mom, and Joe's two sisters, Lynn and Lisa. His mom wanted to be there too, but she was out of town (I wasn't due for three weeks, so she thought she'd be back in time).

After another hour of pain and torture, the good Dr. checked on me and I was still at four and a half. She said I was too tense and needed to relax my body, and that the confusing signals weren't allowing the cervix to open further. *Ya think?*

They FINALLY listened to me and allowed the epidural. Once that was administered, I went from four and a half to nine and a half centimeters in two hours, and the pain was gone. It was wonderful. I was having contractions and not even feeling them.

Just when I thought this delivery thing was going to be a breeze, the doctor told me that I had to do it without the epidural drip. I pushed a couple times with the epidural on, but I couldn't feel my legs, I was completely numbed from the waist down, which made it nearly impossible to push properly. My attempts did nothing.

They turned off the epidural and then had to wait for it to get out of my system and wear off. Suddenly, the pain of the contractions was back in full–force. Apparently, I was having this baby naturally after all. *Sigh.*

"Okay now, you're pushing it out," said coach Joe.

"Use your feet, use your feet. Push!" instructed Dr. H. "Good, there you go."

"Boy, now she's pushin'!" chimed in the nurse.

"It makes a big difference when you can feel it," remarked Dr. H

"Yeah!" replied the nurse.

Then at the same time, the nurse said, "One more big one," while Dr. H said, "Give me some more, give me some more."

"Baby's comin'."

"A little more. Good, good. OK? Come on, come on, come on. Give me a push."

"It's here."

"It's crowning, feel it," Dr. H instructed.

She guided my fingers to the top of the baby's head. I felt my baby! But something was wrong; she was stuck. I couldn't push her out by myself, so the doctor used a vacuum extraction—a plastic thing she put on top of the baby's head with an internal fetal monitor on her scalp. Then she cut the episiotomy and we were ready to push again. Dr. H pulled while I pushed, and the baby's head and face came out.

"Here we go, big breath in—and push!"

"Good job! Good one, good one," Joe finally said.

"Goooood. Great! Now just hang out for a second, I'm going to suction the baby," and Dr. H went to work as we all collectively held our breaths. "Take a look, see?" she said for the camera.

Lisa, who was videotaping the event, said, "Ahhh, she's out."

"A little more…a little bit more for me. A little bit, nice and slow, ease it out."

"Good job!"

"Gasp!" I could hear sniffles, crying, then one final push and she was all the way out. Then I heard *her*—the faint, soft cries of a newborn infant. I also heard sighs of relief all around.

"Ohhhhh Tara! Look what you did!" my mom cried out.

"You made it, you made it," Joe said softly to me, through his tears.

"Hello girlie, hello sweet baby," the nurse cooed, as she placed her on my chest, and I watched Dr. H suction her mouth again. "Well, let's dry her off, she hates the cold. Come on, Daddy, let's go."

She wrapped a blanket around my newborn, but left her on me, as she motioned for Joe to come up and cut the cord.

There was some indiscernible mumbling, then Dr. H said, "No, he doesn't want to, but we'll make him."

Then to Joe, "What I need you to do is just cut right between here."

"Here?" asked Joe.

"Yep."

"Okay," and he cut the cord like a pro.

"There you go. Great."

Then the nurse said, "Let's go see mama. Oh, she's a tiny little tot. She's not very big," as she bundled her up and put her in my arms.

As I gazed down at this tiny miracle of life, I thought three things: *she is very sticky; I'm still in pain;* and *why does Doctor H have her hand inside me?*

I finally found my voice. And my first words? "Why does it still hurt so much?" Yep, told you I was a pain wimp.

It wasn't how it was supposed to be, you know, like in the movies. I wanted to fall in love with my baby and have this profound mother/daughter bonding experience so many new mothers talk about, but all I could focus on was the fact that I was still in a bewildering amount of pain. *Wasn't the hard part over?*

In fact, my mom shared with me later that she was concerned I had postpartum depression because I didn't bond with my baby at first sight, that my reaction was so unexpected. *Fortunately, I wasn't depressed, just temporarily delirious with overwhelming pain, no big deal.*

It turns out the doctor said she had to massage my uterus, she called it manual contraction, to help the placenta detach and expel it more quickly. This procedure actually made delivery of the placenta more painful than delivering my baby. *Go figure.*

Once the placenta was out, Dr. H stitched up the episiotomy, and it was finally over. But Joe didn't mind, because he got to hold baby Jalina for forty-five minutes, while they were busy with me, before they whisked her away for her pediatric exam and put her under the warmer.

I didn't get to hold my baby again until more than two hours later, when I nursed her for the first time. Jalina was born at 6:13 AM, weighed seven pounds two ounces, and was twenty inches long, with a full head of dark–brown hair. Joe and I agreed—she was the most beautiful baby we had ever seen.

31   california dreamin'

THE HOSPITAL STAFF kept us an additional two days. Since Jalina was born about three weeks early, and because my waters had leaked, they wanted to monitor her for infection: a "forty-eight-hour sepsis watch." She was also jaundiced and had to receive light therapy treatments to lower the level of bilirubin in her blood.

Jalina was so dark–skinned from the jaundice that a nurse assumed she was a bi–racial baby and asked me several questions about sickle cell anemia. When I realized why she was asking, I laughed and told her the baby's father was white. When I told Joe and our family about it we all had a good laugh. Of course, we'd also been up all night and were sleep–deprived, so we probably would have laughed at just about anything.

As any parent knows, the sleep–deprivation didn't improve any time soon. But it was a small price to pay for the way my heart swelled with unconditional love and joy every time I held my baby. I had no idea how much that tiny human would forever change my life, and there was no question I felt that bond now.

We decided I would stay home with Jalina, and my boss at work didn't seem surprised when I told her I wouldn't be coming back from maternity leave.

The next few months were a blur of feedings, diaper changes, baths, laundry, visitors, trying to sleep when the baby slept, laundry . . . oh, did I mention laundry? *Man, babies are messy!* I also cut my hair super short, a pixie cut, because I was tired of Jalina constantly pulling it, and it was always a tangled mess. We soon went to Mommy & Me classes and playgroups with friends, and I entered the wide world of MOTHERHOOD and all it entailed. I realized my full–time job had become being Jalina's mommy and I embraced my new job enthusiastically.

Then tragedy struck. When Jalina was ten months old and taking her first steps in the Stride Rite shoe store at the mall, my Uncle Tim's Cessna airplane went down over the Sandia Mountains, near Albuquerque, New Mexico. He was flying home from a golf tournament with two friends when he reported a dual vacuum pump failure. There were no survivors.

I was devastated when I found out. I adored Uncle Tim (who was responsible for my going to college) and didn't know how I could function in a world without him in it. He was only forty-two and left behind a wife and two young children, ages eight and ten, my cousins. My grief was beyond consolation and I truly felt that life wasn't fair.

Joe didn't know how to comfort me and didn't understand the depths of my sorrow. My tears made him uncomfortable. He couldn't fathom how I could be so close to an uncle I only saw a few times a year and failed to realize how important it was to me that he attend the funeral with me. Basically, he just couldn't relate at all. He said he had a mandatory sales meeting in Las Vegas that he couldn't get out of and wouldn't be able to go to the funeral. That news hit me like a slap in the face. I felt unsupported, misunderstood and unloved by my husband. *Trey would know what to say.*

Less than three months later, Joe's company merged with another company and lay–offs were imminent. His position was being restructured and he had to decide if he wanted to stay or look for other employment. Coincidentally, his grandfather was a consultant with a toy company in California that just happened to be hiring sales managers. Joe flew down for an interview.

Life in the Pacific Northwest was wet, but that year it was even wetter and colder than usual, and it had rained every day for more than two months. Therefore, when Joe called from sunny southern California to tell me he got a job offer, what do you think I said? I believe my exact words were, "I'll get the suitcases and start packing!"

His new boss wanted him to start right away, so I stayed in Vancouver with Jalina and the pets, and sold and packed up the house, while he moved in temporarily with his grandparents in Mission Viejo. Our house sold quickly, so we put everything in storage, and fifteen-month-old Jalina and I went to Mission Viejo to join Joe and shop for a house.

I was amazed how fast everything happened. Although, when it came time to say goodbye to our family and friends, I realized we were leaving our support network, our built–in babysitters—our family! We were taking the only grandchild and moving her more than a thousand miles away. Let's just say the grandmas were less than thrilled. Admittedly, I was sad to be leaving my loved ones but also excited to get out of the rain and explore a new area. I looked at this move as a grand adventure.

Even though Joe's grandparents were very happy we moved to California, living with a toddler in their house was not the adventure any of us had in mind. They lived in a nice home with fragile knick–knacks a plenty, most within toddler grasp, and didn't believe in baby–proofing anything. I had to stay on top of Jalina around the clock, and it seemed all she heard was every form of "no" imaginable, and "don't touch." The only time I could relax was when she took a nap or was strapped into a high chair or stroller. On the plus side though, I must have driven all the curiosity out of her, because by the time we got our own place, she didn't get into anything, and we never had to put baby–locks on our cabinets.

Fortunately, Joe and I found a house we liked right away. In fact, it was new construction and still being built, so we got to choose many of the features ourselves. It was my dream home and I was excited to move in. Since we were from the Northwest, we were not familiar with the area or California real estate. We were shocked at home values in Orange County, where his grandparents lived, so we looked further inland and bought much more affordable property in Corona.

32   stepford wives

WE LIVED IN A PLANNED community, in the second phase of a large new development—everything was brand new. Our street was a cul–de–sac with seventeen homes on it. We were the second family to move in, so I made it my mission to welcome each new neighbor with a plate of homemade chocolate chip cookies and a friendly smile. Soon, we were all good friends and enjoyed block parties, pool parties and assorted occasions together. Most of the families had young kids, like we did, so it was the perfect place for Jalina to play in the front yard. There was always a mom outside, and we all took turns watching each other's kids. It was a great street—seemingly safe and idyllic.

Our main concern, regarding our children's safety, was the local wildlife. A month after we moved in, my seven-year-old cat, Foxy, disappeared. I canvassed the neighborhood for him and hung up missing cat posters everywhere. About a week later, someone found the remains of a cat, the prey of a coyote, in the hills behind our house. I hoped it wasn't Foxy, but as time passed, I realized it probably was. He had been a great cat and companion for me, and it was hard to accept that he was gone.

We began hearing reports that the coyotes in the area went after small dogs, cats, and even toddlers. We also had to be vigilant of rattlesnakes, scorpions, black widow spiders, and other animals indigenous to the desert climate.

When my half-sister, Nicole, visited from Seattle, she made an interesting observation. It was a Tuesday night, known in our neighborhood as trash night and as if on cue, as I wheeled my trash containers to the curb, my neighbors did the same. We waved to each other and made polite conversation, then walked back to our respective houses. Nicole, watching all of this incredulously, rolled her eyes and said, "Wow, your street reminds me of *The Stepford Wives*. Doesn't anybody do anything independently around here?"

I laughed good–naturedly and shrugged my shoulders, but inside I didn't find it funny at all. I liked my neighbors and I liked that we took our trashes out at the same time every Tuesday night. I didn't see anything wrong with it. But for some reason, Nicole's comment stayed with me. Over time, my idyllic neighbors lost some of their charm, as life tends to happen, and our perfect street weathered infidelities, alcoholism, divorce, unemployment, loss of loved ones, and other hardships.

Meanwhile, in my own home, Joe felt the pressure of being "the only bread winner" and encouraged me to get a part–time job. Jalina hadn't turned two yet and we didn't want to put her in daycare, so I looked for something I could do from home.

Fortunately, one of my neighbors was in a similar situation, and she had already taken a job. I watched her two kids every day while she worked, and she paid me what she could. It wasn't much, but it helped a lot because Joe saw that I was making a contribution, and I think that meant more to him than how much money I could bring in.

But about six months later, he changed his mind and decided it wasn't enough. He wanted me to be working—outside the home. In July, we saw on the news that there was a teacher shortage in California because they were reducing the student–teacher ratio to twenty to one and had an urgent need to hire more teachers for the 2000–2001 school year.

Although my maternal grandparents had both been teachers, it had never occurred to me to become a teacher myself. But, on the other hand, I adored children, seemed to have a way with them, and enjoyed babysitting; and of course, I loved being a mom.

Plus, all I had to do was pass a test and get an emergency substitute credential—sounded easy enough. Within a few weeks I had the credentials I needed and became a kindergarten through twelfth grades substitute teacher with the local school district—Jalina was barely two and a half years old.

I still refused to put her in daycare, since I wasn't working every day, and traded favors and babysitting with some of the other stay–home moms on my street instead. Leaving Jalina was hard on both of us and I was racked with guilt every morning, dropping off my crying child in someone else's arms. *How did other working moms do it?* It ate me up inside.

That summer, while I worked on becoming a teacher, a neighbor friend invited us to her church. Joe was raised Lutheran, yet didn't attend church when I met him. He said he believed in God and considered himself a Christian. I wasn't raised in a religious home environment at all, but believed something was missing from my life, and felt there was more to life than merely living it. I was open to learning more about it, and Joe and I had gone to a variety of churches a few times in Vancouver, but nothing stuck. I felt uncomfortable and awkward, like religion was being forced on me, and I just couldn't get into it. I remained skeptical and had too many questions to suddenly and blindly have faith in something I knew I could never fully comprehend. Besides, I had no theological background and little knowledge of what was actually written in the bible.

When we went to church with our friends that Sunday morning in July, I expected it to be similar to the other times I had gone in the past. I figured there would be a nice enough message that I might even get something out of, but that ultimately, I would forget about it by the time I finished eating lunch.

But instead, I felt relaxed and comfortable, with a sense of belonging. I felt a soothing blanket of peace envelop me as I opened my mind and my heart to *really listen* and take in the message the Pastor was delivering. I felt a thirst and hunger for more—bought a bible and began reading it from the beginning. The next weekend I prayed to Jesus for salvation and asked Him into my heart.

As if to test my newfound fledgling faith, I had a close call with a "road rage" driver. Remember my car accident at age sixteen? When I sensed I had a guardian angel? I was reminded of that day eighteen years earlier, as I drove south on I-15. In my dark blue 1994 Nissan Altima, and in the center lane, I drove with the flow of traffic, about sixty-five to seventy miles per hour. Suddenly, a driver in a black 1990 Chevy Camaro sped up behind me, so close that I thought he was going to tap my bumper.

Naturally, this scared me; I lightly tapped my brakes and slowed down to let him pass. That only seemed to enrage him, as he quickly moved into the left lane next to me, gave me the finger, then got right in front of me and stomped on his brakes. I moved over to the far right–hand lane and slowed way down, figuring he would just speed away and that would be the end of it.

Instead, he also slowed way down, and then got into the far right–hand lane behind me once more. Again, following me closely. Scared and shaking, I prayed to be saved from this maniac. I immediately veered off at the next exit. He *followed me off the freeway!* By this time, I thought he would follow me until I stopped, at which point he would drag me out of my car and murder me. I was terrified. *"God, I need a miracle, and I need it right now."*

As I proceeded down the off ramp, I saw a police car parked in the dirt, on the left shoulder of the exit ramp. Perhaps he was trying to catch speeders, I didn't know and I didn't care. I immediately swerved to the left and parked right behind him, crying, shaking, and hyperventilating. The driver in the black car passed by us slowly, and then turned right at the stop sign and I never saw him again.

With tears streaming down my face, I told the policeman what had just happened, and also told him that he saved my life and was my guardian angel. He was kind and suggested I take time to clear my head before driving again. He also asked where I was going and if I was going to be okay.

I absolutely believed my prayers were answered that day, and that the policeman just happening to be *at that exit* at that precise moment in time—when I needed him—was no mere coincidence.

33   the end of the world?

I DISCOVERED that I had a knack for teaching and enjoyed subbing at the local schools. The church I attended had a private kinder through twelve school, so I began subbing for them as well. Even though I subbed for all grades, I preferred the lower grades, and was actually intimidated by the high schoolers. I felt they were more disrespectful toward authority than I remembered at that age, and I couldn't relate to them on any level. Perhaps it was because I was "just a sub" and commanded zero respect, but I began to request elementary jobs only, and stayed away from the high schoolers as much as possible.

Late that spring, I learned there was an opening at the private school for a Drama teacher, kinder through eighth grade, for the 2001–2002 school year. I loved Theatre and had minored in it in college, so I was encouraged to apply. Plus, I would get to work with a variety of ages and grades, which I felt was perfect for me. I was super excited and couldn't wait to interview for the position— and the best part? I wouldn't have to deal with high school students at all.

I was given the job that summer, and soon began preparing acting exercises, theatre games, warm–ups, scenes and other curriculum, for what I thought was going to be my dream job—I couldn't wait for the new school year to start. The first week was super fun, and the kids were great. I felt like I had won the "best job" lottery. They even asked me to cast and direct the school play. I had never directed a play before, but I'd been in plays. Besides, how hard could it be, right? I had a great job working with adorable children, ages five through thirteen; what could possibly go wrong?

The unimaginable happened, unspeakable tragedy that affected the entire world, the terrorist attacks of September 11, 2001. My husband was in New York at a Toy Convention, something he goes to in September every year, and he called me at 5:55 that morning (pacific daylight-saving time).

"Hello?" I answered sleepily.

"Turn on the TV," Joe demanded.

"Joe? Why? What's going on?"

"Just do it, turn on the TV."

"But I have to get ready for work soon. Why can't you just tell me?"

"Why can't you just do what I ask without questioning it?" Joe said heavily, then, "Okay, uh, a plane just flew into the World Trade Center! We're being attacked! Now turn on the T—"

"WHAT? Okay, okay!" I hung up the phone in disbelief, then went downstairs to the living room and turned on the TV. Immediately I saw the footage confirming what Joe had just told me. Then I saw the second plane hit the other tower and couldn't take my eyes off the television set, as I sat dazed, trying to make sense out of the nonsensical.

Jalina, now three and a half, came downstairs and asked for breakfast. Suddenly I was slammed back into my reality as I realized I had to get us fed, dressed, ready and out the door in half an hour. I turned off the TV, gave her a big smile, and tried to remain calm.

I listened to the news on the radio while I drove to Jalina's preschool to drop her off for the day. The way they reported and the things they said made it sound like World War III had just begun. *Was this the end of the world?* There was no way I was about to drop off my daughter when I thought the world might come to an end. I turned around and headed to work, with my daughter in tow. After all, I worked at a private Christian school; they'd understand why I had to bring her with me, right?

When I got to work, the other teachers and administrators were talking about it in serious and hushed tones. I wanted to protect Jalina, so I put her in a friend's kindergarten classroom with some paper and crayons. She loved being around the older kids and was happy to be there.

I went to the principal's office and told him I was worried about Joe—that he was there, in New York, and I desperately needed to talk to him. The principal let me use the phone in his office, but the lines were overloaded, and I couldn't get through. I kept redialing only to get a recorded "all circuits are busy, please try your call again later" message. Horrible images raced through my mind as I became frantic and feared the worst.

About two hours later, on my break, I got through the phone lines and Joe answered the phone in his hotel room. His voice was shaky, and he sounded hollow. He told me all the airports were closed and he couldn't get a flight out to come home. He told me he had seen the second plane hit live, with his own eyes. He said he was standing on the sidewalk just a few blocks from the

World Trade Center when it happened. He told me he saw terrible things, things no one should ever have to see. . . .

How I got through that day, remained calm and professional, taught classes, and took care of my daughter, while in anguish and turmoil and afraid for my husband and wanting him home safe with me, was miraculous. I leaned hard on God for strength and support and He gave it to me. Still, that was one of the hardest days of my life, not knowing if I would ever see my husband again.

I woke up the next morning and noticed the world had not come to an end, but I also knew that the events of the day before were, unfortunately, not a bad dream either. Joe was still stuck in New York, and news reports were still flooding in of the horrific terror attacks and climbing death toll. With a heavy sigh, I got ready for work and took Jalina to preschool.

When I got to work, I was immediately called in to the principal's office. He said their high school English teacher had quit suddenly and unexpectedly, and they needed a replacement right away. There had also been numerous substitutes because the teacher had called in sick a lot over the past two weeks. I told him I wasn't qualified to teach high school English. He said, "You have a Journalism degree, right? You're the most qualified staff member we have."

"High school? Me? I don't know…"

"Tara, we need you. We're desperate, there's no one else."

"What about Drama? Who will take my place?"

"Believe it or not, it's a lot easier to find someone who can teach elementary school Drama. You can still teach the eighth grade Drama class and you can still direct the school play."

"When would I start?"

"Tomorrow."

"Oh! Um, uh, I need to think about it?"

"Of course, please pray about it. But we need your answer as soon as possible. Take the morning and get back to me by lunchtime today, okay? And, Tara, I know you'll do the right thing."

Wow. I did not see that coming! The high school addition was new, due to growth and expansion, and that year's senior class would be the school's first graduating class ever, so there was only one class of each grade, which meant I would have **FIVE** separate classes to prep for. I was in over my head and I knew it. Of course, I took the new job assignment—but *high school*? It was my worst nightmare.

I'd heard stories that the seniors caused their last teacher to have a nervous breakdown and that's why she quit. I'd also heard that they couldn't keep a sub because the kids were so unruly. As you can imagine, since I already had a fear of high school students, now I was beyond terrified. It didn't help that I'd seen the movie *Dangerous Minds,* starring Michelle Pfeiffer in 1995 about tough inner–city kids. Nevertheless, as I prepared to meet my impending doom, I took the advice of other teachers who told me to start out stern and mean—they said the kids could smell fear. *What are they? Wild animals?*

As it turned out, they saw through my 'tough guy' façade right away—tyranny was not part of my teaching style, and I loathed yelling at the students. Eventually, by treating my students with respect, I won their respect in return. I stayed with them throughout the school year and we even joked about our dreadful first day together and how I was "oh so intimidating—not!" And the best part? I learned that they weren't so intimidating either, and that I actually like high school students.

34   if my life is so wonderful why do I feel like shit?

I WAS LIVING THE DREAM. My life was perfect. I had it all—a handsome husband, beautiful, healthy little girl, lived in a gorgeous house, and had fabulous friends and neighbors. I even had a 'great' job, went to a 'great' church, and owned a 'great' dog. I had everything I had ever dreamed of. A husband. A family.

Yet I woke up with a knot in my stomach every morning and an overwhelming sadness I couldn't shake. I had no energy and was tired all the time. Sometimes, in the middle of making dinner in the kitchen, I'd just start sobbing uncontrollably, unable to stop. I silently cried myself to sleep nearly every night. I even had irrational thoughts like; *the world would be a better place if I weren't in it.* Sometimes my thoughts were so dark, I scared myself with the depths of my despair. What was wrong with me? Was I losing my mind? Why couldn't I just snap out of it?

I kept my thoughts to myself, put on a 'happy face' and continued my routine of life, even though I felt like a fraud and desperately wanted the demons to go away. I wanted the pain to stop but I didn't know how to make that happen. I couldn't talk to anybody about it, because I didn't know what to say. I didn't understand it myself so how could I possibly explain it to someone else? I did the only thing I could think of, short of giving in to the darkness: I prayed.

That Sunday, as I sat in church with Joe, one of the associate Pastors gave the sermon, as the senior Pastor was out of town or something. I didn't pay attention to the details until I realized the change in sermon affected me. He told the entire congregation about his own personal struggles with depression, yet I felt like I was the only one there. I identified with and related to nearly every word of his story. Soon, the tears were flowing freely.

After church that day I told Joe I thought I had depression. "I related to everything Pastor Rich said. It was like he was talking just to me. I've been so sad, and I don't understand why."

"You're not depressed. Happiness is a choice, Tara. Just choose to flip the switch and be happy. Poof. No more depression," he said, sounding agitated.

"Joe, it's not that easy. Don't you think I've tried? I'm sad all the time, deep in my bones, sad. I can't explain it."

No matter what I said, he couldn't relate or understand anything I tried to tell him; it was so frustrating. I needed to talk to someone who could tell me what to do, someone who'd been there.

That night, I called Pastor Rich at home. Thankfully, he was gracious to me, and didn't seem bothered that I had called him at home. After a candid conversation, in which I opened up about my dark thoughts and feelings for the first time, he advised me to see my physician. He said a doctor would be able to diagnose me properly and help me determine the next steps to take toward getting better.

Just before Thanksgiving that year, I was officially diagnosed with clinical depression. My doctor referred me to a psychiatrist, who then put me on anti–depressant medication. Frankly, I didn't feel thankful at all. I felt like I had a terrible burden to bear, that it was some kind of embarrassing social stigma, and I just wanted to be normal. Sadly, Joe too, was also embarrassed by my diagnosis, and it soon became the family skeleton in the closet not to be spoken of. I had a mental illness that apparently needed to be swept under the rug.

My depression became a source of contention in our marriage and I felt Joe distancing himself from me. We had talked about having more children, and suddenly he was dead set against it and said he wanted a vasectomy.

We argued, we fought, and I cried—a lot. I felt betrayed; I always believed we would have at least two or three kids. I thought we were in agreement about that from day one. He knew how I felt about growing up predominantly an only child. I had two half-sisters by my father, but they had grown up with their own mothers and mine had raised me, so I was not raised with siblings. I was vehemently against raising our daughter as an only child.

When people asked Jalina, at age three and a half, if she had any brothers or sisters, she would say, "No, I'm a *lonely* child." She meant to say, "an only" but it always came out "a lonely" and it was heartbreaking for me.

Since the timing could not possibly be worse, out of the blue, I got a letter from Trey. Our moms still kept in touch, at least with annual Christmas cards, and we had kind of kept tabs on each other over the years. He knew I was married and living in California, and he easily got my address. He was feeling reminiscent and decided to drop me a brief note. Despite my conscience screaming at me to throw the letter away and forget about it, I read it.

Dear Tara,

Howdy! I hope this letter finds you and your family healthy and happy. This is just a quick note to say 'hi' and let you know that you are in my thoughts and prayers.

I'm doing well. I'm up for two different promotions at work and making enough money to pay child support and still have a life.

I thought about you as I attended the Arizona vs. Washington State game last weekend. Dad had canceled out with a stomachache and Rosalie canceled with an earache, so I sat by myself (in 3 seats) and watched your team pummel us. All in all, I found it to be a depressing evening, except for the thought of you celebrating each time they scored.

I trust that all is well for you in family and career. Drop me a line if you are not too busy these days. Take good care of yourself. I'll do the same.

Love,
Trey

I read the letter again and again and finally put it back in the envelope. My hands were trembling. I was suddenly very curious about his life and I had questions I felt needed answers. I called my mom and asked her for Jill's number. She gave it to me but warned me to be careful.

Jill was wonderful, as always. She gave me Trey's number and wished me well. She asked me to give her love to my mom.

As I picked up the phone one more time, to make the call I was eager and yet dreading to make, I thought about

Joe. I felt guilty and almost hung up when a familiar voice answered the ring on the other end. "Hello?"

"Trey? Hi, it's Tara."

"Tara! Hey, what a nice surprise!"

"I got your letter today. What made you write to me after all this time?"

"Well, like I said in the letter, I was at a WSU football game and I thought of you."

"I see. You know I'm married, right?"

"Yeah, of course. I just wrote as a friend. I didn't mean anything by it. Sorry if I upset you. It's just that I still care about you. I will always care about you, and I wanted to reach out and let you know I was thinking of you. I'm curious about you and your life, that's all."

"I know the feeling. It's good to hear your voice, Trey."

"It's good to hear your voice too, Tara."

"Are you still married? Who's Rosalie?"

"Rosalie is my daughter. Remember the baby I'd just had when you called a few years ago? Well, she's eight now. And no, her mother and I are not together anymore."

"Oh, sorry. Your letter said your dad was supposed to go to the game with you?"

"Yeah, he lives down here now. He moved to Phoenix a few years ago to be close to his grandkids."

"Wow, that's great. You must love having him so close."

"I do. We've grown really close since he mo—".

"And your brother? How's Chad?"

"Chad's good. He's married now. Tara, are you okay?"

"Yeah. I'm okay," I lied. "But I have to go. Joe's going to be home soon, and I shouldn't have called you. I really should talk to him about this before we communicate any further. I don't feel right sneaking around behind his back."

"Okay, I understand. I don't want to cause trouble for you or your marriage. I hope to hear from you soon, if it's okay with Joe."

"Yeah, okay. Goodbye Trey."

"Bye, Tara. Take care of yourself."

"You too. Bye."

When Joe got home from work that night, I told him everything. He could always read me anyway, and I seemed to have the inability to lie to him. He was deeply hurt and lashed out, "I knew it! You've always loved him more than me! He's your real true love; he's the one who got away. Are you going to go see him? You're still in love with him, aren't you?"

"No! It's not like that! He was my first love and I'll always care about him because I've known him for so long, but we were so young. What I had with him was a childlike love. What I have with you is real, lasting, grown up love. He was my first love, but you're my forever love!" I shouted back, in between sobs, as he paced angrily in our bedroom.

Relentlessly, he shouted back, "No, you never loved me! You just wanted a baby! You just needed a sperm donor!"

"No! That's not true! How can you even say that? I love you! I've always loved you! You can't—"

"I don't believe you. You called him. If you value our marriage at all you will cease all communication with him!"

"Okay! Of course! I won't call him again; anything you want . . ." I was still sobbing when he walked out the door. Then I heard the front door slam downstairs and the sound of his car as he drove away. *God, what have I done? I'm in serious trouble.*

Just then, Jalina came home from playing outside with the neighbor kids. Looking up at me with her big brown beautiful eyes (her father's eyes) she asked, "Mommy, why are you crying?"

"Mommy doesn't feel good right now, sweetie. But you know what would make me feel better?"

"What?"

"A hug from my favorite girl."

"It's okay, Mommy. I'm here to hug you. It's okay Mommy. You feel better now," she said, as she held me tight and gently patted my back with her tiny, delicate hand, fingers splayed. I knew right then that I had to fix the mess I made.

Whatever confusion and mixed feelings I had about Trey needed to be forgotten, and whatever doubts and resentments I was harboring toward Joe needed to be forgiven. No matter what, at all costs, I desperately needed to save my marriage. If not for me, then for this precious little girl who deserved to grow up with *two* loving parents.

35   faking it

JOE FORGAVE ME, my anti–depressant medication
kicked in, and life seemed to normalize somewhat. I
didn't feel sad or depressed anymore, but then again, I
didn't feel much of anything anymore. I stopped crying,
but I also stopped experiencing great joy as well. My
emotions basically flat–lined somewhere in the middle,
between joy and melancholy—I didn't have highs, but the
lows were gone too, so I learned to cope with it and began
coasting through life on autopilot.

I was true to my word and didn't call Trey again, but I
did write him a brief note:

> *Trey,*
>
> *My marriage and my family need to come
> first right now. I hope you understand. Joe does
> not want us to keep in touch and I need to respect
> my husband's wishes. I hope you're doing well.
> But it's best if we don't communicate at this time.
> Please don't write back.*
>
> *Take care,*
> *Tara*

Even though I was considered mentally and emotionally stable, I was still a mess—physically. It seemed I was sick all the time, catching cold after cold. Colds turned into Bronchitis and Bronchitis turned into lingering coughs that wouldn't go away—it was always something. After numerous doctor visits and some trial and error, we discovered that I had bad allergies, and since my body was constantly 'under attack' from these allergens, my immune system was too low to fight off anything else.

After being tested I found out I was allergic to dogs. Skye, our seven-year-old Sheltie, had slept in our room since day one, and my cough was worse at night. Once we kept her out of our bedroom for about a week, my coughing lessened, and I slept better. Skye started sleeping in the hallway outside our bedroom door, not understanding why she was being punished. It made me feel like I was a bad dog owner. We reduced or eliminated the other allergens as much as possible, and I began to feel much better.

Then the next crisis hit—Joe lost his job. It was spring, Jalina had just turned four, the school year wasn't over yet, and I was still teaching high school English. He was unemployed for an entire week. Yep, just one week, when he got another Sales Manager job, also in toys. But his new job was in Los Angeles and Joe had over a two-hour commute in traffic—each way. The job also required him to travel *even more*, so Jalina and I hardly saw him over the next few months.

We agreed that I would stay with my job the remainder of the school year, and then we would sell the house and move closer to Joe's new job. Fortunately, his company relocated to new offices closer to north Orange County before we bought, so we found a house we liked in Brea. Sadly, Joe felt that because of my allergies, we couldn't take Skye with us. We gave her to our neighbors, who had three boys and adored her; but it was heartbreaking for Jalina and me.

Once we were settled in our new home in Brea, we talked about my career options and decided it would be best for me to go back to school to get my professional teaching credential. I had a year of teaching experience, but it was without the proper credentials, and at a private school. I wouldn't be able to get a public school teaching job without a teaching credential, so it was back to college for me.

Going back to school, grad school, was interesting at my age. Surprisingly, I wasn't the oldest student in the credential program (I was the second oldest) and we joked that we were the curve busters for the rest of the cohort. The first year, I took night classes so I could be home with Jalina during the day. I was also a parent volunteer and room mom in her kindergarten and first grade classrooms, which was a lot of fun.

Since Joe was often away, Jalina and I quickly made friends with the kids and moms at her school, and soon had a routine of our own. In fact, he would be gone for such lengthy business trips, sometimes two months long, that Jalina shied away from him on his return, as if she barely knew him. If he tried to give her a bath, or tuck her in at night, she'd say, "I want Mommy." It was difficult for Joe, and we had to go through an adjustment period every time he came home from a long trip.

Even Joe and I went through a similar adjustment period. With him gone so much, I learned to become self–sufficient and independent, with my own friends, hobbies and interests. Sometimes my friends even teased me that I was a "single mom" because Joe was hardly ever around. At Jalina's school events, people assumed I was either divorced or widowed, because I always showed up alone.

Unfortunately, to say that Joe's extensive traveling was a hardship on our marriage would be an understatement. I started feeling a distance growing between us, and I was at a loss as to what to do about it. I stayed busy while he was gone so I wouldn't miss him so much, so my heart wouldn't hurt. But, in protecting my heart, I was pushing away the one person I wanted most.

36   the damn cat died

IT WAS MID–MARCH 2006, a month before our tenth Anniversary, and Joe dropped the D-word. I was student teaching and going to school full–time, and Jalina was nearing the end of second grade. For me, the timing couldn't have been worse because I was so focused on finishing school. It was a Sunday morning and I was in bed, recovering from a bad ear infection. I had just apologized for being sick, yet again. Instead of forgiving me and assuaging my fears, Joe admitted to being unhappy and said he'd been thinking about divorcing me.

Incredulously, I dismissed his divulgence as temporary insanity and wouldn't hear of entertaining this conversation topic a minute more. I refused to accept that he was willing to give up on us so easily. What he said next stopped me in my tracks.

"You've changed. You are not who I thought I married ten years ago and I'm not in love with you anymore."

I went from shock to anger to indignation in thirty seconds. I had no words. The next few days were a blur and I'm not sure how I made it through the week. Joe and I were polite to each other, made small talk, even slept in the same bed—but it was a big bed. I bought a book, *When Love Dies,* to save my marriage and read it cover to cover, since I wasn't sleeping anyway.

I barely functioned at school that week. I remember sitting in the parking lot on campus, feeling numb and paralyzed. I couldn't get out of the car, and I couldn't drive. I just sat there. Then I pondered what it might be like if Joe actually made good on his threat to leave me. What would I do?

For a brief moment, I fantasized about starting over and running to Trey. It was a six-hour drive to Phoenix. As far as I knew, he was single now. Did I want to take a road trip?

Wow! I have to get a grip! That is the worst thing I could do right now! I immediately berated myself for being so foolish and immature. I was a mess and running away wouldn't fix anything. No, divorce was not an option. I needed to see this through. *I have to save my marriage!*

That weekend Joe and I finally talked, and I brought up commitment, our daughter, and love. Yes, still a hopeless romantic, I believed we could get the love back and I still wanted my happily ever after. I wanted us to grow old together. I wanted us to watch our child grow up and raise a family of her own. I had entered the first stage of grief—denial.

Joe agreed to try to make it work, and two weeks later we went to Las Vegas to celebrate our tenth Anniversary. My mom took care of Jalina for us, so we could have time together, as a couple, to rekindle the romance. Unfortunately, the trip was awkward, but we did the best we could and I appreciated his effort—at least he was trying for me, and that was all I could ask.

A month later, I graduated from the teacher credential program at California State University Fullerton. And four days after that, I turned forty. Or, as my eight-year-old daughter called it, "the F word."

My friend Kirsten and I were in the car, when we overheard Jalina in the back seat, telling her friend, "Oh, my mommy hates the F word. It makes her mad, so don't say it in front of her, okay?"

Shocked, Kirsten and I looked at each other like; *did we just hear that right? What is she talking about?* Treading carefully, Kirsten asked, "Jalina, what word does your mommy hate?"

"Oh! You know, the F word—forty," Jalina stated matter–of–fact, as if Kirsten and I were the children that needed to be taught. This is the same little girl who thought the "S word" stood for stupid.

Anyway, to celebrate my graduation and fortieth birthday, Joe took me to Amsterdam, where we enjoyed a four-day get–away before his business trip to Moscow. Overall, I thought the trip was a success, because it was a step in the right direction to bring Joe and I close again.

When I got home, I got another birthday present, of sorts. Ready? The day after I got back from Amsterdam, I found out I was five weeks pregnant. *Surprise! Happy FORTIETH birthday!*

Of course, I was elated, but also completely baffled. I didn't think I could even get pregnant anymore. Joe and I had tried off and on for years (and also had numerous arguments; he never did get that vasectomy he'd threatened, but he did make it abundantly clear he did not want more children). I'd even been to a fertility specialist and had completely given up the idea.

Yet, here I was, pregnant—a week after turning forty. Jalina would be nine when the baby was born, and I'd be nearly forty-one. To say I had a few doubts would be an understatement. *Is forty too old? People have babies in their forties all the time, don't they?*

As you can imagine, Joe was less than thrilled when I had to tell him over the phone, while he was in Russia. Therefore, this pregnancy was bittersweet. I didn't know whether to laugh or cry. I was also trying to start a brand-new career.

All of these factors weighed heavily on me. To make matters worse, I had severe morning sickness nearly every day for the next two months. It was worse than my first pregnancy, by far.

That summer, Joe received an offer for a job in Portland. Since most of our family resided in that area, and we'd been in California, away from them for more than seven years, we put the house up for sale with every intention of moving back to the Pacific Northwest. I even flew up to attend a job fair for the Evergreen School District in Vancouver, Washington. But the opportunity wasn't as good as Joe initially thought, and he decided to stay with his current company.

Sadly, it was too late because we got an offer on our house right away, and it was already in escrow by the time we decided to stay—we were forced to move. We rented a condo a few miles away, in Fullerton, until we could figure out where we wanted to plant ourselves.

Concurrently, by the time my twelve-week prenatal checkup had arrived, I had fully embraced the pregnancy, had decorated the nursery over and over in my head, and had already bought my daughter a cutesy 'big sister' t-shirt.

I was heading into my second trimester, the morning sickness was dissipating, and I was getting some energy back. I was optimistic and letting myself get excited at the prospect of having a baby in my forties.

Just when I was supposedly 'out of the woods' of the risk of miscarriage—I had one. The doctor said he wasn't able to detect the baby's heartbeat.

By this point I'd already had ultrasounds, seen the fetus moving on the screen, and heard the heartbeat multiple times. I was not prepared for the sudden shock of hearing the words "missed abortion" and "dead fetus" inside my womb. They scheduled me for surgery the next day, and forty hours after being told that my baby had died inside me, I was no longer pregnant.

A week later, my paternal grandfather died. He was eighty-six and suffered from Alzheimer's disease. I flew up to Seattle by myself to attend the funeral, and my dad asked me to write and deliver the eulogy.

The day I got back from burying my grandfather, on a Sunday afternoon, our four-year-old cat, Patrick, suddenly collapsed. His breathing was slow, shallow, and labored. His sides were grotesquely heaving in and out. I hadn't even unpacked my suitcase yet.

Patrick was a voracious eater and a bit on the chubby side. He was affectionately named after the soft, lovable, not too bright starfish on "Sponge Bob Square Pants." The name fit the champagne-colored Burmese aptly and we got him as a kitten when we moved to the Brea house. We got him because Jalina wanted a kitten, and also to assuage the guilt that Joe felt for making us give Skye away.

I had to take Patrick to the animal emergency clinic twenty miles away because our Veterinarian's office was closed Sundays. Jalina insisted on accompanying me, and she held Patrick on her lap in the car.

The Vet at the clinic gave Patrick something to help him breathe easier, and they ran a few tests. They said he had congenital heart failure. They said they could do surgery but there were no guarantees, and the prognosis did not look good.

They told me I had to make the decision to put him down. *Are you kidding me?* He was only four years old! I had to decide this *now*? It wasn't fair.

My beautiful, sweet Jalina looked up at me with her big brown eyes, brimming with tears, and asked, "Mommy, can they save Patrick?" It was more than I could bear. I didn't know what to do so I called Joe, ever the voice of reason.

When I told him how much the surgery would cost to save the cat, and that there was no guarantee it would even, in fact, save him, it was a no-brainer decision for my husband. But I was the one who had to tell our daughter that we had to kill her sweet kitty. *Damn it.*

I hung up the phone, took a deep breath, and told the Vet I'd made my decision.

While they were getting the injections ready, Jalina said her goodbyes to Patrick. Then I told her she had to wait in the lobby and that I would be out in a few minutes. I felt she was too young to witness the euthanasia of her precious cat. As it was, I felt I made the right call because I had a difficult time keeping it together myself, holding his head and stroking his fur while I watched the light go out of his eyes.

That night I cried. Well, that's an understatement— more like broke down and wailed loud heart wrenching sobs that wracked my body as I grieved and mourned the loss of my unborn child, grandfather, and cat. I had held it together for two deaths, been strong for my family, and even spoke at my grandfather's funeral with nearly perfect composure. Why is it that the third thing, a cat of all things, is the one that broke me?

What's that superstition, bad things happen in threes? Yeah, I'd had enough. I was done.

37   dark and stormy

IT WAS AUGUST, we'd just moved into the condo, Jalina was about to start third grade, and I felt myself slipping back into my old depression like a worn, comfortable robe. Every day I had to fight the urge to stay in bed all day. I had to be the grown up and put on a happy face for my daughter. I had to be the parent and take care of her needs. I had to be the wife and—?

This is where I failed. I curled up into a ball and withdrew, afraid of intimacy with my husband because I couldn't bear another pregnancy. I couldn't bear the thought of going through that again, losing another baby. Logically, I knew it made no sense, but I blamed Joe for part of it too. I resented him for so many trivial things that I let it eat away at me, until a chasm opened up between us. Eventually the chasm turned into an abyss, and there was no way back.

But that doesn't mean we didn't try. Joe signed us up for sailing lessons. He thought it would be a great way for us to connect, as a couple. We drove to Newport Beach every Saturday morning for five weeks. Unfortunately, sometimes we'd have a ridiculous argument on the way there, so by the time we got to class and were divided into fours, Joe made sure he wasn't in my boat; *so much for couple bonding time.* It was too bad too; it was a great idea and I enjoyed the lessons. After that, he stopped trying for a while, and instead of doing couple or family activities on the weekends, he took up golf. It got him out of the house and away from me, which became his new goal.

I joined a gym, got a personal trainer, and began the process of losing the weight I'd gained during my three months of pregnancy. I also started substitute teaching and volunteering in Jalina's third grade classroom. In other words, I stopped feeling sorry for myself (wallowing in my depression) and started becoming a productive human being again. Joe could see that I was making an effort and soon we began doing things together as a family again.

By the following school year, I was hired at a middle school in Norwalk, to teach sixth grade. We decided it was time to put down roots and bought a house in Fullerton, near Jalina's school; she had just begun fourth grade and we wanted to keep her in the same school for consistency.

My new job soon proved challenging because the school was on year five of a program improvement plan for not meeting their AYP (Adequate Yearly Progress). As part of the corrective action, they became the only public school in the district to fully implement a mandatory school uniform policy.

Most of the students were labeled "at–risk" and "underachievers," and were treated more like prisoners than children. The majority of my students lived below poverty level, had immigrant families who didn't speak English, and some were even homeless.

Most of the teachers utilized aggressive behavior management techniques, known as a punitive/authoritarian teaching style. In other words, they yelled at their students on a daily basis. They seemed jaded and hard–hearted, and definitely didn't respect or trust the students. At best, it was a strict environment—but a war zone would be a more accurate assessment. Therefore, when I refused to yell at my students, I was deemed "permissive," and my–coworkers were quick to let me know they did not approve. They told me not to try to befriend the students. They told me that my lack of classroom management and discipline only made the students behave worse.

Instead of building positive relationships where students are nurtured to grow and learn, where respect and accountability are modeled and taught, they told me that I had to demand respect. Suffice it to say, I didn't make any friends among my colleagues, and the students were used to an adversarial student–teacher relationship, so they didn't trust me either. It was a heartrending uphill battle, and it took a lot out of me.

It was a rainy evening in January, and I sat at the kitchen counter, lesson planning for work on my laptop, when Joe called via Skype. He was in Hong Kong, his usual business trip every January, and eating breakfast while video chatting (it was seven the next morning in Hong Kong). He immediately asked to talk to Jalina.

"Jalina, come talk to Daddy on the video," I called to our nine-year-old, doing homework in the living room.

"DADDY!" She ran in, hopped up on the barstool, looked into the built-in webcam, and beamed at him.

"Hi Squirt! Whatchya doin'?" I heard him ask her, as I walked down the hall toward the bathroom. As soon as I came back out, I heard Jalina calling me from the kitchen.

"Mommy, Daddy wants to talk to you again!" She kissed the computer, said goodbye, and ran back into the living room.

As I approached the screen all I could think about was how much work I still needed to get done that night and how tired I felt. I was getting over another cold, having trouble with my boss at work, behind in my grading, and feeling stressed out. Joe was going on and on about his trip and meetings in Hong Kong, and I was bored. I didn't have time for this. I was busy and just wanted to hang up. I pretended to be listening, pretended to be interested. Finally, he wrapped up and said, "I love you."

"I love you too," was my conditioned response. We said goodbye and the screen went black, like the blackness I felt in my heart. Suddenly, there was a sick, sinking feeling in the pit of my stomach. I said the words, but I didn't mean them—and I knew I didn't mean them. I felt empty inside. They were just words, words with no meaning behind them. This realization made my heart hurt and I wondered when I had settled into complacency.

38   the abyss

IT WAS THURSDAY NIGHT, March 27, 2008. I was on spring break, my mom was visiting, and a colleague of Joe's was staying with us for a week. The previous Friday, the last day of school before spring break, our principal announced that our school would be closing permanently at the end of the school year in June, and I would be out of a job.

Yet, it was at this precise moment, as I was getting ready for bed that night, that Joe decided to tell me he no longer wanted to be married to me. I realize there's never a *good* time to tell one's spouse you want out of a marriage, but *now*—with a house full of guests, and kicking me when I'm already down? It was too much for me to bear. My life, as I knew it, came to a crashing halt and I was devastated.

A few days later, when our houseguests left, Joe moved out of our bedroom and into the guest room. Seeing the empty dresser drawers and closet space made it too real for me, and I turned into a ball of grief and confusion. I became emotionally raw and found it painfully difficult to do my job. I couldn't talk about it with my co–workers or friends because they trivialized it and no one understood my suffering. In an effort to cheer me up, they said, "It's no big deal; people get divorced all the time." At work, my boss expected me to pull myself together and "get on with it." My friends avoided me and made excuses not to call or hang out. I was expected to pick up the pieces of my shattered life quickly and quietly, and move on.

Are you kidding me? Divorce is like death! It is the death of a relationship and I wasn't allowed to mourn. If Joe had actually died, I would be given time off for bereavement. Instead, I was judged for falling apart. I was expected to carry on as if my life were normal and nothing major had happened. I felt as if my heart were being ripped out of my chest and trampled on, yet I had to put on a 'happy face' so that I wouldn't make others feel uncomfortable to be around me.

I didn't want their pity, I just wanted to be granted the privilege to be sad when I was sad, and not have to put on a phony act. I had never felt so utterly alone and isolated; I closed off and withdrew into a shell of despondency.

I felt I had no one to talk to, and what I really wanted and needed right then was to talk to my best friend. But my best friend wanted nothing to do with me—he wanted to divorce me! The knowledge that I was losing my best friend hit me almost as hard as losing my husband. Coupled with the fact that they were the same person, and I was grief stricken one thousand-fold, gutted, raw.

After the initial shock faded, I began seeking ways to save my marriage, I wasn't ready to just give up, not by a long shot. I turned to the Internet and bought self–help books and an interactive CD program that claimed to work, in lieu of marriage counseling, and that one spouse could do alone. The program purported that I could turn my "obstinate" spouse around and we could have an "excellent marriage and fall back in love again." It sounded good to me, and I was desperate enough to try anything.

Joe told our just turned ten-year-old daughter that he wanted to divorce Mommy—it crushed her. She showed me a letter she wrote to God:

> *Dear God,*
> *I hope Mommy and Daddy always love each other. Why Lord, why doesn't Daddy Love Mommy, why? Please do all that you can to help Daddy know he still loves Mommy. Please!! Prevent them from breaking up. Make them love each other.*
> *Love, Jalina*

I wanted to kill him for doing that to her, for telling her the way he did, and without me. She was too young and didn't understand, and so fragile. A few days later, while cleaning her room, I found song lyrics and drawings of little broken hearts on her desk, which made my heart break all over again.

> *Why don't ya love her?*
> *Why don't ya love her? Why don't ya need her?*
> *Why don't ya eat with her, sleep with her, hang out with her?*
> *What's wrong with her?*
> *Is it because your interests aren't all in common?*
> *Why why why don't ya love her?*
> *You're a fool not to take her hand*
> *Why don't ya love her, why don't ya need her, why why whhhhhyyy?*

I couldn't let this happen. My marriage was worth fighting for and I was ready to fight harder than anything I'd ever fought for before. But Joe was so cold toward me, so logical. He treated the whole matter like it was a business deal. He even found a do–it–yourself website and drafted his own version of a Marital Separation Agreement. He said he was not open to trying at all, and that he had already divorced me in his mind. But then he contradicted himself by saying we might get back together after we divorced.

"I want a divorce because I hate the institution of marriage. I feel forced to be with you—chained. If we get a divorce and then decide to reconcile later, it will be by choice."

"But we did choose! No one forced you to marry me; that was your choice. Since when do you care about the institution and the government? It's not about the piece of paper. We made a covenant between God and us. It is sacred and intimate, and it shows faith. We made a vow, a commitment to give ourselves to each other for a lifetime. Marriage means we share everything; I even share your last name. That took an enormous amount of faith, love and trust. Is it logical to want to share your entire life with one person? Just the fact that you said you wanted to do that, that your intentions were to do that, is huge. Why take that away because you now feel trapped?"

"People change when they get married. They grow complacent and take each other for granted. We changed and grew apart. We're not compatible. Living together by choice is much more romantic. It keeps you on your toes because you have a choice and can leave any time, but you don't, because both people want to be there, not because they have to. They're not tied down or trapped . . . I will not ever get married again."

"That's not a relationship based on love and faith, it's convenience. When the going gets rough, you're out the door. Where's the commitment? You still have a choice. LOVE is a choice! It is an actionable verb and we can choose to love each other again. You are trying to base our relationship on logic and compatibility and conditions. Love is not logical!

"True love is *Un*conditional—loving without conditions! You are my mate and I chose you. We made a vow and formed a bond. That vow is my honor, my word, and I stand by it no matter what. I promised to love you in good times and bad, sickness and health, for as long as I shall live. I chose marriage for life and I meant it. I will love you for the rest of my life. We are one. When you are hurting, I am hurting, because we are connected to each other for life."

By this point, I was emotionally drained, exhausted and crying. I couldn't make him understand. I couldn't make him feel. I couldn't make him love me. I did everything in my power to save my marriage, but the truth was, I had no power. He had already left.

We bought our house at the worst possible time in real estate history—November 2007, the height of the housing bubble. By March, when Joe decided he wanted a divorce, we were upside down and our house was worth two hundred and fifty thousand dollars less than we paid for it. We were stuck living in the same house together, but not together.

He lived in the back of the house and I lived in the front. Jalina spent most of her time with me, and to make it easier for her we told her that we were still married but just had different bedrooms. We told her that Mommy and Daddy loved her very much and that we were still a family. This appeased her and bought us time to figure out the details of filing for divorce and planning to live apart.

Since we realized we had to continue to live together, under the same roof, for an indiscernible amount of time, Joe proposed that we try to make it work. I thought he meant full reconciliation and got my hopes up; but he actually meant as co–parents, roommates, and friends. He wanted to stay married for appearances and for Jalina's sake but wanted us to live separate lives and do our own thing.

One of those things involved him finally getting the vasectomy he had wanted six years earlier. He had the procedure done the day before my birthday, and I drove him home and took care of him while he recovered. Since we were separated, he didn't need my permission anymore. Again, I accused him of not having any feelings.

"Tara, I do have feelings, but I don't want to show them because I don't want to give you false hope," Joe said stoically. "I am hurt and angry, and I question the legitimacy of real change. A very big part of my heart feels so dead to you. For now, let's keep being friends and let things play out. I want you to know there is hope and I do love you. But I need a very slow timeline before putting forth any effort to reconnect."

All I heard was "there is hope and I do love you" and I backed off to allow him the time and space he asked for. I began working on myself, the one thing within my control. He told me, "Fixing yourself is easy. Just read some books, eat healthy, exercise, and get a hobby." And that's exactly what I did.

Soon, it got easier to breathe, and I felt more positive about life and myself. I began focusing on my goals and what I wanted out of life. I forgave Joe completely of all wrong doings over the past thirteen years. I learned to let him go. I began to accept that my marriage might be over. And the most difficult of all, I learned to forgive myself.

39   roller coaster

IT WAS JUNE, and the end of the school year, and my job, were fast approaching. With less than two weeks left, the kids were restless. They knew their school was being closed forever, their futures unknown, and they acted out at every opportunity, resorting to mostly harmless pranks.

This particular June day, I found a live cockroach in the classroom. I asked a willing student to take it outside and set it free. Unfortunately, a group of girls saw it and started screaming, which alerted the rest of the class. Four boys jumped out of their seats and grabbed at the roach. I told them to take it outside as I calmed down the remaining students.

After lunch, the students were working in small groups, on weather stations, for Science class. Two minutes before the bell rang, I found a dead cockroach taped to the whiteboard. I pretended not to notice it. After I dismissed the class, I walked over to the whiteboard, disposed of the roach, and thought that was the end of it.

I could not have been more wrong. I opened the door and stood outside as I greeted my last class of the day, which rotated, so it was a different group of students. To my knowledge, they hadn't had any interactions with roaches that day. I stayed outside until all students were inside, then closed the door and entered the classroom. A few students were out of their seats near my desk, acting like they were looking out the window. I told them there was nothing to see and asked everyone to sit down.

Toward the end of class with about five minutes left, I walked over to my desk while talking to a student, and casually reached back for my water bottle, took off the lid, and took a drink (without looking at it). Something passed through my lips that was NOT water. I physically reacted, gagged, and spit it out—water and roach landed on my desk. *Yes, a student placed a dead cockroach into my water bottle!* The same dead cockroach ended up in my mouth.

"Mrs. Spencer! Are you okay?"

"Oh my God! What happened?"

"Are you choking?" Several students were out of their seats, a flurry of activity, surrounding me, and all talking at once. Then they looked at my desk and one girl screamed. Another yelled for someone to go get paper towels.

I sat down completely stunned, in shock, and speechless. I realized I was shaking and crying, and knew I needed to compose myself. Thirty-eight pairs of eyes were trained on me and I was sitting in my chair sobbing in front of them. For once, the room was completely silent.

I took a few deep breaths and tried to get it together. The voices started up again; they genuinely seemed as surprised and shocked as I was. Who would do this to their teacher?

A couple of girls got some paper towels and wiped the water off my desk. I shakily put the roach back into the bottle as evidence. The teacher next door had heard the commotion and called me. I relayed what happened and she called the assistant principal. The bell signaling the end of the school day rang.

"No one move! Get back in your seats and sit down! You have not been dismissed!" the assistant principal commanded as she walked in the door. She then instructed them to take out a piece of paper and write down anything and everything they knew about the roach incident. She told them to name names, reassuring them that they would be anonymous, and the culprits wouldn't know who ratted them out.

She told everyone to write down something, even if they didn't see anything. When they argued that they didn't see anything and didn't know who did it, or what to write, she said, "Write the words 'I didn't see anything' and sign your name." Then she told everyone to sign their names and said they could leave when she collected their papers.

Based on the eyewitness accounts from the class, Mrs. Garcia quickly narrowed it down to four students. She called each of the four suspects into her office one at a time, until two students confessed—a boy and a girl. They were suspended for one week, then placed with another teacher for the remainder of the school year—the last three days.

As a condition of their penitence, they each had to write an apology letter to me. Both students said they never intended for me to drink the water. They said they thought I would see the roach and throw the water out, and laugh it off as a harmless prank. They said they meant it to be funny, to get laughs out of the class and me. They were filled with remorse. Sadly, I never got to say goodbye to them, and I never saw them again.

Surprisingly, as difficult as my year there had been, when the last day of school arrived, I had mixed feelings about it and realized there were many students and staff I would miss; it was a bittersweet moment. I also learned a lot from my students. They taught me many things. But right now, two come to mind:

1.   Have compassion. I learned to see my students not as they'd been labeled—'troublemakers' and 'delinquents,' but as tender children with feelings, struggling to find their way in a world that didn't seem to care about them. I hoped for the best for each student I had met, even the pranksters—especially the pranksters. I knew there was no malice behind their actions and that it was not personal. They were misunderstood kids starved for attention, doing what they had to do to survive. It worked. They got my attention, and I will always care about them.

2.   Look before you drink! To this day, I have an extreme phobia of cockroaches, and I always guard my water bottle.

Two days after my last day of work, Joe sent Jalina and me to Maple Creek, Michigan for two weeks, to visit Mom and Jack, who had a summer cottage there. We also needed the time apart from each other to heal and accept our impending divorce. While on vacation, I read yet another book to help me make sense of it all. I was still struggling with letting go, yet I knew I had to. I put on a brave face for Jalina and my parents, so I wouldn't ruin their vacation, but I still cried on the inside every day, and thought my heart would never mend.

I talked to Joe on the phone a couple times while we were gone, but the conversations were brief and logistical, or he asked to speak to Jalina. When making plans for the flight home, I told him we would take an airport shuttle or taxi, but he insisted on picking us up at the Los Angeles airport.

At the airport, Joe acted nice and sweet, and even seemed happy to see me. After we got home, and tucked Jalina into bed for the night, he told me he had something to show me, and then gave me a letter. In the letter he said that he wanted to work on our marriage now. It said that he wanted to try. *What? Talk about an emotional roller coaster!*

"I missed you while you were in Michigan," Joe began. "I've been doing a lot of thinking and self-reflection. And I've also been seeking advice from my mom and grandpa. Tara, I really want to try."

"Wow, I don't know what to say." I was happy, but bewildered and untrusting too.

"I was thinking we should start slow, but that it might be a good idea if I slept with you tonight. Just to hold you and cuddle. Maybe the physical proximity will help us to feel some closeness again."

I was moved to tears, and speechless. It was the first time he had wanted to touch me since we separated, over three months prior.

Over the next seven days, we got along great. We had amazing talks, were affectionate, cuddled, and slept in the same bed every night. We agreed not to have sex yet though, as he wanted to take it slow. We had gourmet dinners that we enjoyed cooking together, and even watched a couple of movies while cuddling on the couch.

We also made sure to include Jalina and spent quality family time together, including a bike ride through the trails at Coyote Hills. And guess what? We saw a coyote. It was walking along the trail and we had to ride past it. Jalina was scared, but Joe rode in between the coyote and her, with his foot ready to kick it away if he had to. The coyote ignored us; it didn't seem to fear us. It made for an exciting adventure.

The next day, Joe had to go to Hong Kong for eight days, on a business trip. When he came back, on his thirty-ninth birthday, Jalina and I surprised him with balloons, presents and a decorated house, complete with a large birthday banner, and blackberry cobbler, his favorite. He didn't seem happy or appreciative, and his reaction was lukewarm at best. He blamed it on being tired from the long flight.

After Jalina went to bed, he wasn't warm toward me at all; he completely dropped the act. When I prodded, he admitted it. "I've been faking it. I don't have those in love feelings for you—at all. I was doing nice things for you because the marriage books told me to, not because I felt like it. I'm worried I won't get those feelings back. We still have issues to work through."

"Our issues are too big for us to tackle on our own. We need professional help. Go to marriage counseling with me. Please, I beg you! We can't do this on our own," I pleaded.

This wasn't the first time I'd brought it up, but this time he finally agreed. We went to two sessions with a recommended marriage therapist, and he got angry with the therapist during the second session. He said he was done and would never go back. He said she backed him into a corner and made him defensive. He said that trying to reconcile was a mistake, and he wasn't ready. He asked me to be patient, and wanted to go back to being separated again.

It was August and no schools were hiring for the following school year. In fact, we had entered a Great Recession, and teachers were RIF'd (Reduction in Force) all over southern California. Student enrollment declined due to families moving out of the area, looking for more affordable housing, and walking away from their high mortgages. It was a terrible time to be an out of work school teacher. So, what does an unemployed teacher do? Well, I went back to school to get more credentials to become more marketable, and to get a job that required two teaching credentials. If I had a multiple subject *and* a single subject credential, I could teach kinder through twelfth grades.

Then the next thing hit—*literally*. On September 16th, a kid on a bicycle plowed into my daughter, as she walked in a pedestrian only school zone, and broke her leg. After surgery, Jalina's leg was put in a full cast, up to the top of her thigh, for three months.

She missed three weeks of school and had to pee into a portable female urinal standing up, because she couldn't bend her leg to sit down on the toilet. She had just begun fifth grade and had been so excited about school; now she was stuck at home with me. I homeschooled and took care of her while she convalesced.

I was reminded how fragile life is. I tried again, a Hail Mary attempt at reconciling, for Jalina. That's when I got angry, really angry at Joe. How could he do this to us? How could he break up the family unit? What kind of life would our daughter have? He was subjecting her to the very thing I had been trying to protect her from—a broken home. Divorced parents.

I pleaded with him to change his mind. I was so anti–divorce because of my own scarred childhood that I vowed to myself that I would never do that to my kids.

Yet, here we were. It was too late for us. Joe was done; he said he just couldn't anymore. That took a while to sink in. But when it finally did, I slowly began to feel better about things.

On the first of November, I officially resigned myself to the fact that my marriage was over. That's when I gave up, stopped trying, and accepted it. I had finally really and truly let him go.

At long last, I had reached the acceptance stage of grief. I know in my heart I did the best I could. I made peace with it. We're human. We made a lot of mistakes.

It was time to forgive each other and move on. We were finally at the point where it was easier to be nice to each other. We decided to divorce civilly and amicably. Joe filed for divorce in November and we began the proceedings.

40   it's been twenty years

CALL IT SELF–FULFILLING PROPHECY, hopeless idealism, or just plain curiosity, but after all this time I decided to look up Trey on the Internet. I found his email address easily, almost too easily, and wrote to him. Two days later he replied, and the next thing I knew, we had fallen back into the pen pal relationship we had begun twenty-six years earlier.

Thanks to technology, emailing was much faster than letters through the U.S. Postal system, and we either emailed or called each other daily. Soon, the old memories came in full force. I was overcome with raw emotion and confusion. *Could I really fall back in love with my first love? Was it too soon? I wasn't even divorced yet! What about Jalina? What would Joe think?*

Ironically, Trey was available and unattached, and happy to hear from me. He had four children and a grandchild, and was twice divorced. He lived in Phoenix with his father, and from the sound of things, they enjoyed the bachelor lifestyle. Our lives had taken different paths, and his had been filled with adversity and hardships.

He had been a prison guard for many years, but was now working odd jobs mostly in construction, and it was a lean year. He was estranged from his two ex-wives, and most of his children were too busy with their adult lives to have much contact with their dad. He wasn't close to any of them. My heart went out to him, and we confided in and consoled each other. He was a safe person to vent my feelings to, and writing an email then pushing the send button felt liberating, therapeutic.

I was lonely, insecure, lacked self–confidence, and even had some self–loathing going on. I allowed Joe to convince me that I was unlovable, and I even believed that I was damaged goods and would remain single for the rest of my life.

Trey made me feel good about myself again. He made me feel loved and desired, and helped me pick up the pieces of my shattered life and failed marriage. I don't know how I would have gotten through that difficult time without his support, acceptance, and free therapy. After nearly a month of phone calls and emails, I requested a face–to–face meeting.

From: Tara
Subject: I need to see you . . .
Date: December 4, 2008 7:20 A.M.
To: Trey

You have no idea how many times I have had a recurring daydream of you showing up at my door. When I lived in Wilsonville, in my 20s, everyone I dated I compared to you. No one measured up and I didn't have a relationship for over three years. Part of me was waiting for you. I'm not telling you this to make you feel bad, that's just how I felt. I held everyone at arm's length and kept my heart guarded. Joe was the first person to break through, but even he said I never gave him my whole heart. Perhaps he's right. I didn't get married until a month before my 30th birthday.

I want to know if it's still there—our connection; if you can still read me like no one else ever could. I won't be able to tell over emails. I need to see you in person. I am being very vulnerable right now—I have to see you. No one has to know.

Love, Tara

From: Trey
Subject: Re: I need to see you . . .
Date: December 4, 2008 5:46 P.M.
To: Tara

I don't feel comfortable seeing you without Joe's knowledge and dislike the idea of sneaking around behind his back. It is a violation of my golden rule policy. I know that you want to see me soon, but I honestly feel we will end up regretting it if we move so quickly that we have to hide things from Joe.

It is not lightly that I suggest this. I miss you very much too. But I must also be true to my own sense of personal honor. Besides, I'm not sure you're emotionally ready for this either. You still need time to heal and you have a lot of unresolved anger surrounding Joe and your marriage.
Love, Trey

He was the voice of reason and I didn't want to be reasonable. I felt the need to start my life over—immediately—the sooner the better. I didn't want to take time to heal. I had completely run out of patience and operated from a sense of urgency. I made one last appeal.

> From: Tara
> Subject: Life is too short!
> Date: December 4, 2008 10:35 P.M.
> To: Trey
>
> I have made it clear to Joe that I don't want to be alone. I asked him how he would feel if I started dating and he says he wants me to, that he wants me to be happy. He has been encouraging me to go out with friends and so far, I haven't taken him up on it. He seems to be adapting to his new single life quite well. He has a bachelor friend from work, and they've gone out a few times to sports bars, a Halloween party in Hollywood, and other stuff I'm sure I don't know about. He actually already went on a date with a 24-year-old and brought her here. So no, he has no right to make me feel guilty for anything.
>
> He did tell me that he doesn't want another man in Jalina's life; he said he doesn't want her to have a step–dad. Well, he doesn't get to make that decision. In some ways, he is still very controlling. He cannot tell me whom Jalina is allowed to meet or not meet. I was eleven when my mom met Jack. They've been together over thirty years now.
>
> Our situation is not ideal. We're stuck in this house together. But, healthy or unhealthy, functional or dysfunctional—we are trying to do the best we can

in spite of our circumstances. He says he fully expects me to "have a life," to date and have fun. But he thinks I should wait until Jalina is 18 to get seriously involved with anyone. He told me I should take a cruise with one of my girlfriends—go on a vacation. It's like he's trying to get rid of me. He said he'd watch Jalina while I'm gone too, strange.

When Jalina had her accident, it shocked me to my core. It felt like my heart stopped and I got a huge JOLT of realization about our mortality and how fragile and precious life is. I could have lost her; the accident could have been so much worse.

But her life was spared, and I felt as though I'd been given a new lease on life, one I plan on taking full advantage of! My uncle was killed in a plane crash when he was just 42. He left behind a wife and two children, ages 8 and 10. I am now 42. Right now, I am *OLDER* than my uncle was when he died nine years ago. Am I living life to the fullest? Am I happy? What do I have to show for my time spent on this planet? If I died tomorrow, would I be satisfied with the life I had lived?

Hell no! I want to LIVE. I want to be happy. I realize now that I can't do that with Joe. We clearly took each other for granted and settled into complacency many years ago. I deserve better than that. I want more out of life than that. I'm figuring out what I want and going for it.

What do you think? Are you willing to go down this road with me? To see what there is to see? Maybe this time around the timing is finally right.

Maybe it is now OUR time. I think we owe it to ourselves to find out.
Love, Tara

From: Trey
Subject: Re: Life is too short!
Date: December 4, 2008 11:02 P.M.
To: Tara

Let's talk about it. I'll call you tomorrow.
Good night, sweet dreams.

Love, Trey

From: Tara
Subject: Amazed!
Date: December 5, 2008 10:01 P.M.
To: Trey

Joe gave me 'permission' to contact you! Seriously, we had the best talk we've had in months and he told me he really does care about me and he wants me to be happy. He hopes we can be friends, especially after the divorce, because we'll still be connected to each other through Jalina. It would be a lot easier if it were friendly and civil. He says I'm a good person, just not compatible for him. He says we want different things from life.

I made a joke about online dating or something and he said, "No really, I totally see you getting married and being happy with someone. I know you'll find someone else, or maybe you'll go back to your old boyfriend—the one whose name starts with a T."

I tried to hide my shock and said, "Do you mean Trey?"

Then he said, "The one who dumped you 'cuz he got someone pregnant or something like that."
I said, "Well, when you put it like that, it doesn't sound so good. He was very young—"

He interrupted and said, "Exactly. People change in 20 years. Who knows? Maybe you two would be compatible now. Maybe he's married or maybe he's not. Maybe you two will get back together. He was the love of your life."

I was speechless.

Do you know what this means? This is great news! It means that he's okay with it and won't make things difficult for me. I reminded him that I had been in touch with you before, when we lived in Corona.

He didn't remember at first, but then said, "Oh yeah! Yes, I was threatened that the love of my wife's life was in contact with her. It made me feel very insecure."

I was surprised by his candor.
I'll write more soon.
Love, Tara

From: Trey
Subject: Re: Amazed!
Date: December 5, 2008 10:52 P.M.
To: Tara

Maybe he knows, or at least suspects, that you've already been exploring those thoughts. He seems like a smart man. You wear your heart on your sleeve. I keep having dreams where I'm sitting in his bedroom and he comes in and sits down next to me. Except, I've never met him. So somehow, he looks exactly like me, but I can tell. It's a lot like looking in a mirror, except different. We don't talk or fight or make faces. We just sit there. Makes me feel strange as hell when I wake up.

I'm glad he's going to be "okay" with me. Not that I had planned to seek his approval, but anything that makes you feel more comfortable is good.
I'll write more later.
Love, Trey

From: Tara
Subject: Rough Day
Date: December 6, 2008 10:36 P.M.
To: Trey

Today was a hard day to get through. Joe and I went through our assets and talked about child and spousal support. We talked about custody and divorce terms and he said he wants to be fair. It made it all so real.

There have been many days where the only thing that kept me going, kept getting me out of bed every day was my child—knowing I had to be there for her. I had someone who needed me, depended on me. I've been strong for her. Now I'm being strong for me. There's a difference. Thank you for making me feel alive again—like someone who matters.

Love, Tara

From: Trey
Subject: Re: Rough Day
Date: December 6, 2008 11:42 P.M.
To: Tara

Of course you matter. To a lot of different people. For a lot of reasons. I love you. Always have. Always will.

It's late . . . more tomorrow.

Love, Trey

From: Tara
Subject: Re: Re: Rough Day
Date: December 7, 2008 12:08 A.M.
To: Trey

I miss you like crazy and what I really wish is that you could just hold me and tell me everything is going to be all right. Did you ever see the movie "Waitress?" It's awesome. It's about a waitress in a small-town diner who has a horrible husband (it's a dark comedy). In some ways I identify with her and one of the lines in the movie is, "I hope someday somebody wants to hold you for 20 minutes straight. All they do is wrap you in their arms without an ounce of selfishness to it." Joe never holds me like that. Hasn't for years, maybe not ever. He hates long hugs. His hugs are usually one-arm hugs that are quick and obligatory. Of course, he stopped giving me those too.

I want that. I want to be hugged for real, by somebody who means it.

I should probably end this rambling now, before I embarrass myself.

I love you, Trey. I've loved you since I was 4 and you told your mom you were going to marry me when you grew up. I've loved you since I was 10 and you kissed me in the basement. I've loved you since I was 15 and we made out in the middle of the night at my mom's house while everyone was sleeping. I've loved you since I was 16 and you wrote me those amazing letters.

I've loved you since I was 17 and I visited you in Tucson. You told me Lucy was pregnant and swore me to secrecy. You were so sad. I would have given anything to take your sadness away.

I've loved you since I was 19 and I got your letters while living in Pennsylvania. I dropped everything and booked the first ticket out of NYC to DFW—to move into a dumpy little trailer in Killeen to be with you.

I've loved you since I was 21 and you visited my dorm room at WSU. I've loved you since I was 22 and we spent part of Christmas together on your houseboat.

I never stopped loving you, Trey. What happened to us? Why did our lives keep intersecting only to be pulled apart again and again? Why did everything go wrong, and we couldn't be together? What happens now?
I did it, didn't I? I said too much.
L, T

From: Trey
Subject: Life
Date: December 7, 2008 4:14 P.M.
To: Tara

You don't ever need to be embarrassed about telling me anything. I like the idea that you feel comfortable telling me what's on your mind. In fact, I'm going to give you a big hug for no other reason than that I love you. Of course, I like big hugs too, so my motivation is not entirely selfless like in the movie.

Life happened, and it continues to happen all around us. It used to be that I thought there was something automatic that was supposed to guide us. But I'm done leaving things to fate. Besides, who's to say that us getting together later rather than earlier isn't what our "higher power" had in mind the entire time? Maybe this is just what we needed, just when we needed it.
Love, Trey

From: Tara
Subject: Yay!
Date: December 7, 2008 9:42 P.M.
To: Trey

It was so good to hear your voice! I'm glad you called. I can't believe we're finally going to see each other in less than a week! Yay! I remember when you picked me up at the bus station in Texas. I was sitting on my suitcase as you pulled up in that cab. When I stood up, I tripped over one of my bags and was so embarrassed. You showed me all around the military base, then Freddy took us to his place in his brown Camaro. I sat on your lap and took in the moment. I must have truly 'taken it in' because when I close my eyes, I can still see it vividly. It was hot and humid, Freddy's car didn't have a/c, and I was exhausted from all my traveling—yet I felt safe in your arms, like that's where I belonged.

That car ride from the base to Freddy's house is one of my all-time great memories. Strange, isn't it? That something as simple as a ride in a car was so life affirming. But don't get me started on Brenda! ;)
Know I'll be thinking of you all week, and looking forward to your visit.
L, T

From: Trey
Subject: Re: Yay!
Date: December 7, 2008 10:19 P.M.
To: Tara

Wow. I hadn't thought about Brenda in forever (giant forehead, he he).

I miss you. It may seem stupid to say that when we haven't actually seen each other for so long, but I can't help but think about you when I get stressed out and feel like saying, "fuck it." In truth, I feel ashamed to be at this point in my life and so ill prepared to be there for anybody. I've got to get back in the game if I'm ever going to be the kind of man that is worthy of love. I've got to balance my desire to run to see you with the knowledge that if I can't back it up with some sort of future, then all I'd be doing is giving you another memory, and myself more regret.
Love, Trey

From: Tara
Subject: The future
Date: December 7, 2008 10:32 P.M.
To: Trey

If we are to have a future, it probably won't work too well with you living in Phoenix and me in Fullerton. I am bound to my child and the court is binding me to this state within a reasonable distance of my ex. Therefore, it would put the burden on you to relocate.

Rent in this area is not cheap. Because I'm about to be a single mom, I think we should actually date first before moving in together. Not sure how I'd explain it to my kid if you just moved in! But perhaps we're getting ahead of ourselves. We have plenty of time to talk about these things in person, down the road.

Anyway, know that I love you, and that I am not worried about your ability to get a job or to "get back in the game." I know you will. I have faith in you. I believe in you. You've definitely had your share of bad luck, but your luck is about to change—as is mine.
Be safe. Get here healthy and uninjured, ok?
Love, Tara

From: Trey
Subject: Re: The future
Date: December 7, 2008 11:36 P.M.
To: Tara

Thank you for the words of encouragement. It means the world to me to know that you believe in me. I'm tired of wandering back and forth between rage and despair and I want to believe in myself too. I'm just really looking forward to seeing you again. We can talk about the details of what comes next when I get there.

In an office today, I saw three buttons on a windowsill. Each had one word on it. "Believe," "Dream," and "Dare." I looked at them and thought, "That used to be me. When did I let go of that and how do I get it back?"

Know that I love you too and nothing in the world can stop me from reaching you as quickly as possible. I'm off to take a shower and hit the sack.
Love, Trey

41   t–n–t

A FEW DAYS LATER Trey pulled into my driveway on a motorcycle. I had arranged for Jalina to go home with a friend from school and spend the night. I watched him walk up to the front door, pull off his helmet and grin at me. He still had a full head of thick hair, which was now graying. His face was a little more rugged, with a few crow's-feet and laugh lines, but easily recognizable, and his lean, sinewy muscles had turned into more bulk and mass than I was prepared for.

He was big and strong, and about forty pounds overweight, but it wasn't a deal breaker. "How about a hug?" he winked, as he crossed the threshold into my home.

"Just like old times!" I smiled and gave him a quick, awkward hug. He had a bulky leather coat on and was still carrying his helmet.

"Man, I'm freezing!"

"Come in, come in! Let me close the door. Can I get you a blanket or hot beverage? Or both?"

"Nah, I'll warm up in a bit, thanks."

We stood in the entryway for a few uncomfortable seconds, sizing each other up. The moment was surreal— he was *here,* in my home, and we hadn't seen each other in twenty years.

Shaking myself out of my stupor, I realized I forgot my manners. "Here, let me take your jacket and helmet." He gave me his helmet and I set it down next to the front door. He took off his jacket and I hung it up in the coat closet. "Would you like a tour of the house?"

"Sure."

After a brief tour, we sat down on the couch to talk. But for some reason I was a bundle of nerves. It wasn't remotely the reunion I had pictured in my mind. I needed something to do and offered to cook dinner.

Trey sat at the counter and watched as I busied myself preparing a simple green salad, potatoes, and baked salmon. (Later he confessed that he hated salmon because he'd worked on a fishing boat in Alaska many summers ago. He said he could never look at fish the same way ever again).

Thankfully, I had a bottle of wine to go with dinner. I rarely drank, but I needed something to take the edge off my nerves—it was laughable how nervous I was. We ate dinner at the dining room table and I downed my first glass pretty quick. I soon began to feel more relaxed and comfortable.

"So, why did you ride a motorcycle all the way out here in December? Weren't you cold?" I asked.

"Yeah, I forgot to consider the wind factor. It blew right through me! I've been driving my mom's truck lately, but she needed it, so the bike was my only option."

"Yikes, I feel bad. Maybe we should have rescheduled for when you had the truck?"

"It's all good. I'm here now, so . . . nice place you have here, Tara. Joe must do very well for himself."

"Thanks. He does. He's a VP at a Toy company, and right now he's on another business trip. He's gone a lot."

Just then Trey dropped his napkin. When he leaned over to pick it up, he winced, "Ow. Damn shoulder."

"What did you do? Are you okay?"

"I injured my rotator cuff a couple months back. I'll be fine, it's okay."

"Did you go to a doctor? Isn't there anything you can do for it?"

"Sure there is. But I don't have that kind of cash and I don't have insurance."

"You don't have medical insurance?" I could hear the judgment in my voice, and the look on Trey's face was pained. I quickly asked, "How did you injure your shoulder?"

"It's a funny story, actually. I was beating up on some of your San Diego boys."

"Beating up—?"

"Yeah! Well, not really. You know, through the SCA. Remember, I told you. I'm a knight."

"You actually re-enact these battle scenes? In full armour?"

"Yep."

"Sorry, remind me what SCA stands for again?"

"Society for Creative Anachronism."

The SCA is a national group that is known to re–create pre-seventeenth century battles and scenes from European history. They wear period clothing from the Middle Ages, and their events feature tournaments, royal courts, feasts, dancing, and many battles.

The idea, during one of these events, is to live as much as possible the way they did in that time period. They stay in tents, don't use electricity, make things by hand, etc. Oh, and no cell phones!

Many people also refer to these events as Renaissance Fairs. Trey was heavily involved in the SCA, and often fought in these armoured combat recreations. It was more than a hobby for him, it was a way of life, and he had been a member of the SCA for eighteen years.

After dinner I suggested we get in the hot tub as hydrotherapy for his sore shoulder. I left the hot tub heater on too long without checking it, and when we got in it was way too hot. I turned off the heater and splashed myself repeatedly with the cold water from the pool.

Trey thought that was hilarious, but I was burning up. We were in the hot tub less than ten minutes, when I'd had enough. But we were in there long enough for me to receive my first kiss in twenty years from the man I'd dreamt about off and on since childhood. Things were heating up all around.

We toweled off and went inside. Then we got dressed and played a challenging game of chess—*not*. I took him to bed, what do you think we did? Suffice it to say, it was a memorable milestone—the first time I'd been with anyone other than Joe in sixteen years.

The next morning, I made a light breakfast and we talked about the past, the future, and us—it was nice. We lost track of time and I realized Jalina would be home from school in less than an hour. It was way too soon for them to meet each other, so Trey had to be on his way. We did not make any immediate plans, but promised that somehow, we would see each other again soon.

December went by surprisingly fast. Trey and I emailed and called each other nearly every day since he'd left. But I noticed myself pulling away because I was afraid to get hurt again.

Or, perhaps the thought of rushing into another relationship, when I wasn't even fully divorced yet, scared me. Whatever it was, I think Trey sensed it, because his emails began getting less personal. Maybe he was having second thoughts too? Did he really want to get involved with a freshly divorced, single mom who lived four hundred miles away? Doesn't sound too enticing, does it?

Getting through Christmas that year is one of the hardest things I've ever had to do. We flew up to Portland to spend the holiday with our families. Joe and I agreed not to talk about the divorce, and pretended to be a happy family for everyone so we wouldn't ruin their holidays. But the irony is, everyone in the family already knew about our impending divorce. Who were we pretending for? It was one of those walk-on-eggshells-over-the-elephant-in-the room moments and I couldn't wait to get back home.

I needed to escape from the train wreck of my life, so I impulsively bought a plane ticket to Phoenix. I wanted to spend New Year's Eve with Trey, and I wanted to make a big deal out of it. I insisted on going to a NYE party. I felt deprived because Joe had missed New Year's Eve and Valentine's Day every year since he took his first job in the Toy industry. Those two holidays coincide with the annual Hong Kong and New York Toy Fairs. I was a New Year's and Valentine's widow!

Trey accommodated my wishes the best that he could. He took me to a friend's house party, comprised of SCA members. Everyone was dressed casually, in t-shirts and jeans. It wasn't the elegant black-tie affair I had imagined, but the people were friendly, and the alcohol tasted the same.

At midnight, we were standing by a bonfire in the front yard. Trey kissed me and wrapped his arms around me—and held me. We just stood there for twenty minutes. There it was. I got my twenty-minute hug. Silent tears streamed down my face as I felt his love.

Over the next few months we continued a long-distance romance that consisted mainly of emails, interspersed with phone calls, and an occasional visit. I drove out to Phoenix to celebrate Valentine's Day with him. He was participating in a large SCA event, called Estrella War, and wanted me to see what it was like. It was a huge part of his world and he was eager to share it with me.

I tried to understand why he was so passionate about it, this world of medieval role playing. But I just couldn't relate—to any of it. I didn't understand why guys wanted to recreate battle scenes and pretend to beat each other up. And it wasn't always pretend. People actually got hurt! I started realizing that Trey and I didn't have much in common.

In March I bought him a plane ticket to Long Beach for his birthday. He met Joe and Jalina. It was a surreal moment. My two greatest loves finally met face-to-face. They were polite to each other and exchanged pleasantries, but I rescued a floundering Trey as quickly as I could and took him out to dinner. I could tell he was nervous and out of his element.

Meeting my eleven-year-old daughter was painfully awkward for him. He didn't know how to act around her at all. This was a huge red flag for me as it was obvious that he was not a 'kid friendly' person. I understand that not everyone likes kids, but whatever man I'm with sure better—Jalina and I were a package deal.

In April, I flew him out for another visit and to spend Easter together. Jalina spent the holiday weekend with her dad and his grandparents in Mission Viejo. Trey and I spent a week together, thoroughly getting to know each other again.

Our week was comprised of fun, frivolous activities, like spending a day at Six Flags Magic Mountain (a dream of his). I also gave him the LA/Hollywood tour and we walked up the hill to the Hollywood sign. We even went to the beach.

But we also looked into the logistics of moving him to the area. We went apartment hunting, met with a couple of my friends about possible job leads, and tried to come up with a realistic plan and timeline for what it would take to move Trey from Phoenix to Los Angeles.

One day, while sitting in gridlock on the 10 (Interstate 10 freeway) we had a serious discussion about our circumstances—and our differences.

"Rents are so high here. I don't see how I'm ever going to afford to move out here," Trey sighed. "And the traffic! Man, this sucks. I don't know. It may be a long time. How long are you prepared to wait for me?"

"What do you mean? You sound like you're giving up."

"I'm not giving up, Tara. I'm being realistic. Where am I gonna live? I can't move in with you and Joe! Ha! Can you imagine?"

"That's not funny. You know I'm stuck in that house right now. Besides, even if I had my own place you couldn't move in. I have Jalina to think about now. It's not like when we were nineteen. We can't just move in together. We need time to figure out who we are as a couple, at this age. Ideally, we should live *near* each other so we can actually date and form a foundation of an adult relationship. That's what grown-ups do."

"Oh *really?* Thanks for telling me. I didn't know."

"Trey, I'm sorry. I didn't mean anything by it. I just meant we rushed into everything so fast when we were young. We're not those kids anymore." He turned the radio up and I looked over at him, "Will you please change the station? I don't like that song."

"You don't like any of my music."

"That's not true. But I agree, we do have very different tastes in music."

"We seem to have different tastes in everything. In case you hadn't noticed, Tara, we are *very different*. Opposites attract, right? Hey, at least we have love."

"But is it enough?"

"What are you talking about? Of course it's enough! All you need is love. Love IS enough. If two people love each other, they can get through anything."

42   closure

ON THE WAY HOME from dropping Trey off at the airport I got a sick, sinking feeling in the pit of my stomach. Tears flowed down my face as I drove east on the 91 freeway, and I knew I was kidding myself.

I wanted so desperately to believe him. I wanted to believe that love really was all we needed to make it work. It's true; we were vastly different from each other now—worlds apart. We grew up. We had changed so much from the kids we used to be. We had different tastes in music, food, and fashion; and different views on politics, religion, and parenting. We even had different interests in sports, hobbies, and lifestyle choices—*everything*. We couldn't have been more opposite. In fact, all we truly had in common was our past—and our love for each other.

But Trey wasn't the same man I fell in love with when we were kids. The man I had fallen in love with all those years ago was the one who wrote me all those beautiful love letters. I fell in love with him *through those letters*. And now I realize they were just flowery words on paper.

I had built him up in my mind to be something he wasn't. I had created an ideal, romantic, perfect partner that didn't exist. I kept that dream alive, kept going back to him all those years—simply because he said he loved me.

It was that declaration of love that made me believe all things were possible, we could overcome the odds, and that we were destined to be together forever. Why? Because he adored me, cherished me, loved me unconditionally, and never asked me to change; because he loved me despite my flaws, maybe even in spite of them; and because I was so desperate to be loved. That was very difficult to walk away from.

He was safe. I had poured out my heart and soul to him repeatedly over the years. He saw me weak, vulnerable, and broken. I was the walking wounded. Joe had crushed me. I felt unloved and unlovable and was full of insecurities. Trey made me feel good about myself again.

Yet here I was, driving home with a wet face, needing windshield wipers for my eyes. I knew by now that love wasn't enough. How could we possibly have a realistic future together? There were so many obstacles in our way. We were kidding ourselves to think that we could carry on a long-distance relationship.

Neither one of us was in a position to move near the other any time soon. I had to stay in Fullerton and raise my daughter. He wanted to stay in Phoenix, near his own family. Besides, he hated southern California, and I knew he'd be miserable here.

It was time to get my head out of the clouds and be pragmatic. I knew I had to let him go. I had to break up with him and it made me dread what was to come. I didn't want to hurt him, and I knew this was going to break his heart.

I realized that I had rushed into a relationship with someone familiar, someone with whom I felt safe, and not for the right reasons. I needed time to heal from my divorce. I needed time to figure out how to be independent again, how to be my own person.

I had been a wife and a mother for nearly fourteen years. I didn't know how to be me anymore, and trying to be with Trey was like putting a tiny band–aid on a huge gash. My wounds needed time to heal, and I had to do it alone. I had to learn how to stand on my own two feet and take some time for me. All these years, I had been looking for my self–worth in a man.

I felt I owed it to Trey to tell him in person. But he didn't share that sentiment, and he didn't take it well. He was hurt, angry, defensive, and said cruel and hurtful things to lash out at me. He didn't understand my reasons for ending it and he argued with me to try to get me to change my mind.

We talked in circles and I felt that I just wasn't getting through to him; he wasn't hearing me, and he twisted my words around. This was a little too déjà vu for me, only this time, I was the one ending the relationship. Funny how life happens, isn't it?

In an email three weeks later, he wrote: *"You made me feel like I actually had a chance at happiness with you, then you squashed my hope. This is Trey. I've known you for almost 40 years and loved you longer than any other man on the face of this planet. No one will ever love you like I do. Don't give up on me now."*

Ouch. Those words cut me to the core, and I felt ashamed that I was responsible for hurting him so deeply. I wrote him back and told him that I would always care about him and hoped that we could stay friends. He wrote one final email to tell me it would be his last:

Why would I be friends with someone who could cast me aside so easily? My friends advised me not to get involved with you and I did anyway because I wanted it that bad. I used to feel guilty for making the wrong decision 20 years ago and turning my back on your love. Now I'm not so sure you wouldn't have just quit on that too.

Don't worry. I will not write back again. This is the Last One.
-Trey

Our lives had been intertwined and our paths had crossed, joined, and uncrossed throughout the years. From childhood friends and sweethearts, to teenage pen pals, to young lovers and even being engaged, to first love reunion, I'm finally closing the door on that part of my life. I am able to have the closure I have needed all these years. I know now that Trey and I were not meant to be together forever, and that sometimes life *does* work out the way it is meant to.

I searched, and I found my answer. It may not have been the answer I was looking for, but it was the one I needed. I can honestly say that I have no regrets, because I am not asking the questions "if only" or "what if" anymore. Some people live their whole lives with regrets, wondering what would happen if they saw their first love again, wondering if they missed their chance at happiness, or if the person they were meant to be with slipped away. I'm lucky—I got my second chance.

My first love will always be my first love. Nothing can change that. Sometimes we need to stop living in the past and realize that it was supposed to happen the way it happened after all.

Sometimes we need to have faith that a power greater than ourselves is in control. People enter our lives for a reason, a season, or a lifetime. Trey was not meant to be with me for my lifetime. I know that now, I accept it, and am at peace with it. I will treasure our memories and I am thankful for everything I learned from him, and the love and joy he gave me. I am ready to move on.

epilogue

My story may not have a happily ever after fairy tale ending, because it's real life—and real life doesn't always have a happy ending. This is a life story not a love story.

But don't worry about me. I'm a survivor, remember? I'll love and laugh again, in time. For now, I'm enjoying watching my daughter grow up. She truly is the greatest gift Joe gave me, and for that I will forever be grateful.

I've also started a new career as a glamorous studio teacher to the stars! I get to tutor child actors on TV and movie sets. That way, their schooling continues while they work in the entertainment industry. Look for my name buried in the credits!

Well, as they say in show biz . . . that's a wrap.

A note from the author

Dear Reader,

Thank you for taking the time to read *CLOSURE.* By reading this book, you now own a piece of my heart.

To my beta readers, and editor, Tamara, thank you for your support and encouragement! Without you cheering me on, and believing in me, this book never would have been published.

And to my family, thank you for putting up with me through those long hours I was self-sequestered—writing, editing, revising, and more revising. A writer's life is often a solitary one, but when I stumbled out of my writing cave, bleary eyed, it was great to see your smiling faces.

This story was not an easy one to write, as the emotion and feelings are real, but it would not let me rest until I told it. I feel an obligation to be a voice for those who feel silenced. While this is a story about two kids who fell in love, it is also about life and the struggles that come with living it. I'd love to hear your thoughts, questions, or comments. And if you feel so moved, please consider posting a review, the best gift you could give an author.

Thank you,

Tasche Laine
taschelaine@gmail.com
taschelaine.com
Facebook.com/TascheLaine

The adventure continues . . .

What if your *normal* life turned into a psychological thriller? As Tara starts over, life as she knows it is about to get a whole lot scarier.

Watch for **CHAMELEON** in stores soon.

CPSIA information can be obtained
at www.ICGtesting.com
Printed in the USA
LVHW082036191119
637872LV00013B/1372/P